When the
Finch Rises

When the Finch Rises

JACK RIGGS

BALLANTINE BOOKS • NEW YORK

A Ballantine Book
Published by The Random House Publishing Group
Copyright © 2003 by Jack Riggs

Grateful acknowledgement is made to *The Chattahoochee Review*, *Habersham
Review*, *The Crescent Review*, and *Writing, Making It Real*, where portions of
this novel in very different form first appeared.

www.ballantinebooks.com

Library of Congress Cataloging-in-Publication Data is available from the
publisher upon request.

ISBN 0-345-46794-9

Book design by Julie Schroeder

Manufactured in the United States of America

First Edition: October 2003

1 3 5 7 9 10 8 6 4 2

For my parents,
Tom and Betsy Riggs,
Always there, always believing in their sons

To my wife, Debra,
Your presence in my life is pure joy

And to Madison,
My sweet little girl

When the
Finch Rises

MAN IS BORN INTO TROUBLE,
AS SPARKS FLY UPWARD.

Job 5:7

The day Aunt Iris called Daddy and told him to come home, snow lay thick and deep throughout Ellenton. The weather was still deteriorating, and by dark, the snow that had fallen wispy and free all day long came down in wet clumps, dense as sludge, icing the second after touching the ground. It fell wet and sticky and fast making us all look rather abominable as we traversed yards made remarkably unfamiliar in the dark by the sparkling wintry coat. Palmer Conroy, Lucky Luther, Billy Parker, and Tommy Patterson converged along the alley that ran beside my house, and there we built a fire to warm frozen hands and feet as we battled the frigid night taking breaks from downhill runs that began in front of my house and ended in Palmer Conroy's driveway.

Palmer's sled could carry six down the hill at incredible speed. The only problem was we could not steer the thing at all. Our slim, gangly bodies could not coax the sled to do anything but fly in a straight line, and so we grabbed hold of one another, the cold air whipping tears from our eyes, blurring our world as we raced out of control. On each daring ride, at the last possible moment, somebody would yell, "Jump!" and all would bail out rolling off the sled for lack of nerve to stay on. Our bodies tumbled and slid through snow and slush as the unmanned rocket careened across Third Street and up Palmer's driveway before crashing into the backend of the Conroys' still new 1965 Pontiac Catalina.

Each time the sled drove headlong into the rear of the car, we rolled ourselves up and out of the snow to stand erect, bodies raw and chapped watching the empty collision take place. It was as if we were still waiting for Palmer's father to come blasting out of the house in undershirt and boxer shorts as he'd so often done to laugh at us. But RC Conroy had been dead for almost three years, and so the sled sat immobile in the quiet emptiness, lodged beneath the Catalina until one of us gave in and walked the short distance across the street to retrieve it.

The night my daddy slipped out of the storm, the winter sky broke open momentarily to produce a shower of moonlight catching our attention and drawing our gaze upward. We had studied space in school, knew our planets and could pick out the redness of Mars in the evening sky and Venus in the morning. We knew what NASA stood for, and could imagine the power of a Saturn V rocket blasting an Apollo capsule into the vast emptiness of space. Through that brief patch of clear night, we strained to see astronauts streak across the sky, but our imaginations could not stay aloft for very long. The brilliant flames of the fire in front of us kept pulling them back down to earth. When the sky disappeared behind the storm, snow resumed and a figure appeared out beyond the fire trudging his way along the street curb. It was Daddy coming home.

We watched as he slowly plodded toward us, hands pushing hard against thighs with every step in an effort to wade through nearly a foot of snow. He made his way slipping and sliding across Robbins Street and then pushed the final distance to arrive upright, melted snow freezing quickly to his unshaven face. A blanket of white lay evenly over his hat and well-worn hunting jacket, and though he did not say, I knew he had been outside for a long time, that the walk had brought him a great distance home. He came close to the fire, and there, within the circle, sat down on a concrete block to warm exposed hands and thaw plastic loafers that were cracked in the seams, packed full with snow.

He sipped Jim Beam from a pocket flask, his body steaming heavily like he was on fire. He whistled for us to come around, waved us in close to the flames with his flask. From where I stood, I could see his hands were clawed up, his knuckles scraped until the soft red exposed meat glistened with the wetness of damp blood. Though his eyes were no more than bruised slits, they still could lock a boy down, and he pulled each of us in from the cold without question to talk about things my daddy said were important.

When we were all accounted for, he spread the snow to uncover raw ground and pluck up a short, wide blade of grass, delicately positioning it between his two thumbs. He lifted his torn hands to his face like he was ready to pray, but instead, blew across the paper-thin edge to create a warbling, gobblelike sound of a turkey.

The awkward noise pierced the winter night, echoing off houses down the alleyway filling the air with the sudden sound of anxious mutts pulling hard on chains and clawing up fences. As each warbling echo died and the darkness outside the range of our fire began to settle, Daddy would lift his hands to his lips and break the silence wide open again. Three times he did this. Three times he brought lights on in bedrooms and robe-wrapped bodies out onto front porches.

We all laughed out loud, as drunk on the evening as my daddy was on his Jim Beam. Tommy Patterson rolled around on the ground and started making monkey sounds. Billy Parker stuffed his mouth full with raw snow and then blew it out into the fire, the hiss soft and subtle in the burning coals. Lucky Luther laughed so hard at Billy spitting snow that he peed in his pants and had to go home early. Palmer Conroy asked my daddy for a cigarette, and that stopped us all. We watched as he thought about it and then gave the boy a Camel. Palmer held the nonfiltered cigarette as if it were a natural extension of his hand. He lit the end with a burning twig and then inhaled the aromatic smoke before letting it seep out of his mouth and nose.

Tommy Patterson sat up and stopped acting like a monkey. "Goddamn Palmer, I didn't know you smoked."

Billy Parker said, "My daddy says smoking will stunt your growth."

I said, "Give me one of those," and Tommy Patterson said goddamn again.

Daddy took a long swig rolling the liquor cheek to cheek before spitting into the fire. The sudden blast of alcohol reignited the flames and sent sparks floating through leafless trees. The burst of flame projected Daddy's shadow onto our house and he became bigger than life.

He stood up holding the flask out before him. "All you boys got mouths dirtier than dog shit, so just shut up 'cause

there's something you ought to know about what I just did."
He pointed out into the dark alley toward a field that lay deep
in snow. "I seen the animal when I was your age right out
there by the Parker house. It wasn't there yet, Billy Parker's
house I mean. There was only a field of weeds most of the
time. We played a lot of ball out there. I hit the hell out of
a baseball on that field. I could hit it all the way to Perty
Spears's back porch. Hell, I took out her kitchen window
more than once. Got my hide tanned for that, I'll damn
guarantee you. But I could hit it and so I did. I suffered the
consequences for a talent I just had to use. I was about your
age when I first saw the turkey. I was eleven or twelve years
old. Biggest bird I ever laid eyes on."

Palmer Conroy had moved away when Daddy ignited
the flames and now sat in deep shadows cast like fingers
from the trees rooted on the edge of the fire pit. The ember
from his cigarette pulsed each time he drew his lungs full of
smoke, and I could see Daddy was watching him out the corner of his eye. Palmer flicked ashes, then spit into the snow.
"RC said that turkey story was just bull. He said this ain't no
Wild Kingdom. They ain't no wild nothing roaming around
here."

Palmer had always called his parents by their first names,
something I could never have done and then lived to tell
about it. And even though RC was dead, Palmer talked about
him all the time like he was still alive and walking around.
I looked at him and said, "How do you know about the
turkey?"

Tommy Patterson said, "Everybody knows about the turkey, Raybert. Where you been all your life?"

Everyone at the fire laughed for a moment and tossed
loose snow at me, the cold flakes stinging where they stuck

to chapped skin. I looked over at Daddy embarrassed and he winked at me like it was nothing, like he had been there forever and had not just shown up for the first time in two weeks. I wanted to spit at him for not telling me about the turkey sooner than in this public offering. I wanted to say I could smoke a cigarette, that I had just smoked one from a pack Palmer stole from Nichols Market before we came to build the fire. I wanted to scream that he could go back to wherever it was he had come from, that he shouldn't be there anyway. But of course, I didn't dare.

Palmer made nothing out of any of this. He smoked his cigarette and looked at Daddy, still challenging, making him work harder than I imagine he really wanted to. Daddy paused only long enough to lift his flask to his lips and then turn his gaze toward the boy. "Palmer, God rest your daddy's ghost, but he was just wrong about all that. I seen the turkey and right after I seen it, the next day, Perty Spears was dead on the ground out in back of her house. She had tried to mow her grass in the middle of the afternoon in August heat and her heart give out. Now, Perty Spears wasn't no crazy old coot. She knew better than to do a fool thing like that. They say she saw the turkey and went insane, tried to use the lawnmower to get the old bird. Instead, she had a heart attack and was already cold when they found her." Daddy swigged at his flask and then looked directly at me. "And you know what?"

I shook my head.

He looked beyond the flames into the dark sky, his narrowed eyes roaming, reaching out past our wet bodies. "When old man Vance came to get Perty, the turkey was only fifteen feet away from her. It had flown off as best turkeys can fly when the hearse drove up into the yard. Old man Vance nearly had a heart attack himself when he saw what the bird had done. Perty Spears's eyes had been pecked out. Yes sir, pecked out clean. At the funeral, they kept the casket closed. Wasn't nobody gonna look at her without eyes."

Billy Parker rose up on his knees at that. "My uncle Charlie died last year and his eyes were closed when they buried him. Daddy said they sew 'em shut, so that old woman's could've been gone, and there ain't nobody could have told the difference. Not you, me, not nobody." Billy looked around at all of us like he was proud of what he just said before he settled his eyes back down on Daddy.

"You ever seen a soul without eyes, boy?" Daddy looked right at Billy waiting until he was sure he was scared shitless. The boy shook his head, his mouth a gaping hole like he just had the wind knocked out of him. Daddy said, "Well, I have. I seen it more than once. And you can't fix something like that. It's against nature. Your skin's got nowhere to go except into the holes like in that *Psycho* movie at the drive-in, and ain't nobody gonna look at something like that. It's a natural reflex to close your eyes and not look. Understand what I'm telling you?" Billy Parker shook his head again, but I'm pretty sure he had never seen *Psycho* nor been to the drive-in over in Hickory Point. After that he just slid back from the fire almost like he was trying to hide from the rest of the story.

Daddy widened his gaze to take us all back in, kept going like Billy hadn't interrupted nothing. "That was the first time I ever seen the turkey out there with Perty Spears. Seen it since and whenever it shows up, there's hell to pay. Someone dies or there's disaster, tornadoes or floods, or Finch Creek tops its banks and takes the life of a small child. I've seen the bird at car wrecks where deaths occurred or outside homes where people died in their sleep or by fire or gas line explosions."

We all flinched when Daddy shoved his hand up in the air like a hitchhiker thumbing a ride. "Shooting rockets into that bellyful of stars can bring it out, too. They shouldn't be doing that. Brings bad things out in people. That turkey's been around here tonight. It's a bad sign. It's an omen." Daddy lifted the flask to his mouth and swallowed hard until the liquor was all gone, the last drops licked from the spout by his thick tongue. He returned the blade of grass to his lips, but this time, the results were weak and tedious, the warble broken and full of drunkenness. The neighborhood dogs remained silent and this seemed to depress my daddy. His eyes cut across the fire and caught me looking, waiting for what he would do next, his swollen lips fighting back when he tried to smile. Daddy said, "How's your momma doing?"

I said, "Okay. I guess."

He said, "Is she feeling better?"

"Aunt Iris said she ain't chasing her tail no more."

Daddy laughed at that, spit into the fire again. It was like right then no one else was sitting there but him and me, or else he just didn't care if others knew more about our dirty laundry than the clothes he picked up and delivered to the dry cleaning plant each day. "Well, Iris does have a way with words now, don't she."

I said, "Yes sir, she does, I guess."

Momma had been sick since I could remember, on and off sick that would sneak up on her and like Aunt Iris said, make her chase her tail like a crazy dog. She tried to explain it that way after she had told Daddy to come home. She said, "Your mother's like a dog that chases its tail. When she's quiet and not paying any attention, she doesn't even know the tail is there, but when she's all excited, not thinking straight, she spins around and around going nowhere. When she's spinning like that, there's not much we can do. She's steady for now. I just hope that brother of mine will come home and do what he needs to do."

Daddy was looking at me from across the fire again. I tried to hold his eyes, grab on to what little certainty I could find in his presence there. I said, "Are you home to stay?"

He lowered his gaze for a moment like he was sorry I had to ask such a thing, and then raised his eyes skyward, the moon breaking free of the storm once again. The spray of light took our breath away and distracted Daddy from ever answering my question. He looked around at each boy like he had never drifted away from the turkey story and, in one last attempt to scare us, stood up and kicked snow into the fire pit just as the moon went *Poof!* heavy clouds pouring darkness back down on top of us.

Without the flames, Palmer was no longer in shadow or separated. He stood up and tossed his cigarette into the smoldering pit. "Bullshit." Then he spit and stomped off toward the sled.

Daddy looked after Palmer. "That mouth don't make you a man. I'll box your ears, boy."

Palmer said, "You drunk, that's all. It's why you give me that cigarette. It's why you said all those things. You won't remember any of it tomorrow." He looked over to where we all stood frozen in shock at what he had just said, then he bent down and pushed off, the sled quickly gaining speed, racing out of control toward Third.

Had Daddy really wanted to chase him down, he never had a chance. Jim Beam was working him over real good and

I am not sure he even knew exactly where his legs were by the time Palmer made the intersection. He staggered then, almost fell before righting himself in time to see the boy stay on the sled as it flew across the street. When Palmer slid up into the drive, the sudden raw concrete stopped the sled and sent the boy careening up under the Catalina.

Daddy said, "That boy's got RC rolling over in his grave."

Billy said, "Maybe he saw the turkey and got scared."

"He ain't seen nothing. He ain't seen nothing yet." Then Daddy staggered off into the shrubs alongside our house to take a pee before disappearing inside to wake Momma and make sure Iris was right about her tail.

The turkey story got to Billy, and I had to walk him up the alley to his house. He kept listening into the darkness for that warble, looking for tracks in the snow. He asked me if my daddy really had played baseball in his yard and wondered out loud what it might look like to see a dead person without eyes. I had no answers for him. The night had spun me around and I was dizzy with Palmer Conroy and my Daddy—my life as I knew it at that precise moment.

I had no idea if Momma was well or if my daddy would be home when I woke up. I could not tell Billy Parker for sure if there really was a wild turkey out there in the dark night, but part of me was thinking at the time, if the creature Daddy spoke about was real, then it had crawled somewhere beneath my house waiting for a moment still undefined to rise out and bring despair and destruction unlike I had ever seen.

Later that night, I stood by the window in my room and watched Palmer Conroy's house. I waited until the light in his window disappeared before I turned out my own. Then I stayed put, staring out into the storm. I never considered the fact Daddy was telling lies. He had not even grown up in

Ellenton. He did not arrive until after the war and from that moment on, his existence in our lives was precarious at best. It was late February, 1968, and while snow swept across the yards and streets of Ellenton, my thoughts remained outside, a treacherous storm spinning the world dark and still, more uncertain than ever.

*O*n winter mornings, my small room remained filled with cold shadowed light. During warmer months when heat rose early, such shade kept me cool and sleepy until nearly noon, but in February, the blueness refused to relinquish its hold on the small cramped space that had been built off the side of our house while I'd grown in Momma's belly. The draft from the window alone woke me early, turned my nose red and sent me deep beneath a pile of blankets.

I could hear Momma and Daddy in their bedroom, Momma vowing never to be sick again. Daddy was talking loudly, like he was almost yelling at her for saying such a thing. "Don't you think that's promising too much? Don't you think you just set us up when you say things like that?"

Momma was crying when she said, "That's the best I can offer. That's the best I can do." Then Daddy turned on the radio like he was ignoring her, tuned in a station playing old jazz tunes, music he had loved since the war. He only played the radio behind doors that remained closed and off-limits to me. Still, I could hear them talk over AM static, their voices loud through the thin barrier of plasterboard.

Momma said, "You were gone too long this time. That's no good either."

Daddy said, "Two wrongs don't make it right, I know that, but what can I do? You drive me crazy, woman. On top of everything else, you just drive me crazy when you go off like that. Ain't much choice here, is there?"

Momma said, "Not much if any. But then, it's been that way forever."

Once when Aunt Iris was taking care of Momma, she told me how Daddy came to Ellenton after the war in Europe was over. Aunt Iris was already married to Uncle Clewell when Daddy arrived looking for a start. Clewell had just opened his Cadillac dealership back then, and so Daddy worked in the engine shop. A good flight engineer flying a B-25, he could do anything to a Cadillac engine on the ground. When he married Momma, he was given the dry cleaning plant Grandma Mae had started before the war as a simple wash and fold business, but he never was very good at running it. The dry cleaning plant always seemed to be in need of more than Daddy knew how to give.

Aunt Iris's scavenger hunts through drawers and cabinets while Momma tried to heal herself always unearthed reminders of my parents' life before I was born. It was almost like Iris was looking for clues to tell her where things went wrong, where my parents' life began to crumble into such disrepair. There are pictures of them both. Daddy in full uniform, though he was no longer required to wear it, tall and erect, a man prepared for a war that ended before he got to go. Momma always looked skittish beside him, awkwardly smiling, her lips pinched tightly into a half pucker, half frown.

A year before they met, she had been forced to have her teeth removed because of decay. Awkwardly fitted false teeth seemed to embarrass her, and Aunt Iris thought that might be when everything started, the way Momma could not look at herself without crying, how she had started doing odd sorts of things that became more difficult to explain as normal behavior.

Of course, Daddy carried his own part of the burden, too. From the beginning he had been drunk, using Jim Beam to dull his world. He had not even kissed Momma on their first date, not because he was a gentleman, but because of the pint of bourbon they had consumed during the evening that then tripped him up and sent him tumbling off the front porch and into the azaleas. The knot on his head was so huge that Grandma Mae called the doctor because she thought he might die right there in her front yard. Aunt Iris said it was the first scandal of a scandalous life.

They were married later in the fall on a Saturday evening, the ceremony at the Ellenton Baptist Church. Momma wore white silk chiffon, Daddy his Army Air Corps dress uniform. In a life begun in the warm glow of candles and promises of fidelity, the signs of something less loomed heavy.

Momma came home from the reception at the March Hotel and disappeared into her room screaming profanities because of Daddy's behavior with other ladies in attendance. When he followed her into the house, he was drunk, and when she slammed the bedroom door in his face, he said nothing. Daddy passed out on the other side of the door on his honeymoon night, and the next morning, took the train to Atlanta without his new bride. He stayed by himself at the Winecoff Hotel for three days before Uncle Clewell drove down and brought him back home. It was December 7, 1946.

They left Atlanta, and later that night 119 people were killed when fire gutted the Winecoff. When Daddy returned to the house, Momma was sitting on the porch with Mae and Aunt Iris. She read aloud about the fire in Atlanta, how the majority of the dead had been boys and girls attending YMCA and YWCA meetings held there that weekend.

There was a picture of the wounded hotel on the front page of *The Ellenton Dispatch* with the headline, WHAT COULD BE WORSE? Below that picture was a photo of Pearl Harbor, the *Arizona* sunk with flames boiling on top of the water, the tragic connection between the attack and the fire too obvious to miss. Momma looked up at Daddy, her lips pinched into a tight frown. She said, "You should have stayed one more day." Then she got up and locked herself in the bedroom again.

Uncle Clewell lent Daddy a cot and from that moment on, he stayed in the dimly lit backside of the dry cleaning plant whenever Momma would start chasing her tail and he could no longer live in the same house. He did not, as Momma would accuse him in her darkest moments, "drink with niggers and sleep with whores." He lay there alone and drank heavily, and then he fought with other men, hard and mean-spirited men who beat him up good in the alley behind the plant.

I believe he remained in love with Momma through it all. He just never knew what he was supposed to do when she became ill. For whatever reason, he could not help her nor could he help himself, and so he ran away to the cleaners and was regularly beaten by strangers, who I imagine cared little about his soul.

From beneath the covers in my room, I could hear Momma start crying when Daddy said, "I wish it wasn't like it is. I really mean that."

Momma said, "What's done is done, you know it can't be changed."

Daddy said, "Then I wish I could forget it all, stop living with it like I do."

"I don't know, Ray. That's like asking for heaven on earth and that'll never happen."

"Maybe there's just too much poison in my life, then. Maybe I'm your poison."

"You're not poisoning me, Ray. Those are your wounds, now let me kiss them, let me try and suck the poison out."

Outside the weather was not brightening at all, the sky heavy and dull, ready to deliver more snow. The bleak landscape was in terrible contrast to the heat rising inside my house, and I was disturbed by the images my twelve-year-old mind conjured up as I was forced to listen to bedsprings squeak and feel walls shake pictures crooked; these for the most part, were the only signs I ever knew of Momma and Daddy's love for each other.

I needed to get out, and so I summoned the courage to climb from under my blankets and wrestle with the cold. I dressed warmly leaving flannel pajamas underneath my jeans and pulled on a sweatshirt, that had been thawed and dried in front of radiators overnight. I snuck through the dark hallway to gather tennis shoes and galoshes from the hearth of the fireplace, peed in the sink so I would not have to flush the toilet and finally escaped through the kitchen door, grabbing my sled from the garage so I could race down-hill toward Palmer Conroy.

Palmer was standing in his front yard having built several snowmen and now was chopping off their heads. He was a strange little boy, his body small and thin, with ears protruding out from a head that was too big for his body. His features were delicate, a mixture of pinkish baby skin and sun-bleached shell. He held a flat-edged shovel as if he were throwing a harpoon, aiming with the blade in his left hand and the pole in his right. He would thrust the flat edge into the head of the snowman severing the top ball so it rolled off the backside of its body. Sometimes the head exploded when he struck it, disintegrating into chunks of wet snow. He kicked the chunks to scatter the pieces of the imaginary head until there was no longer an identifiable body part, and then he moved on to build his next victim. He would not roll up a new ball for the headless bodies. Instead, Palmer left them there in a gruesome decapitated state and moved over to create a whole new body for the unforgiving blade of his shovel.

Palmer had not always lived in Ellenton. He had moved there when we were in second grade. I had seen him from a distance when Mrs. Mabry, grim and ashen-faced, brought him to our class and then asked Miss Bonney to step out into the hall. He wore a navy pea coat and baggy Levi's that swallowed him whole. He held a flannel hunting hat in one hand and a book bag in the other giving us all the impression that he wasn't planning to stay very long. Somewhere in the room a girl giggled and then we all laughed at Palmer, but he never looked directly at us, never let us know if he was scared or nervous about standing there in front of us like that.

Just when the room got quiet, Sally Parker sucked air in like she was taking her last breath, and though her words were meant to be whispered at Becky Lugar, they came out as a loud hissing declaration for the entire class to hear. Sally Parker said, "Look at his head!"

In one swift cruel moment, the entire class brought its attention back to the front of the room where Palmer stood motionless. Before us, his head seem to glow. He put his hand over the mark quickly like he had forgotten it was there and now wanted to cover it up. I was close enough to the front that day to see the birthmark gain intensity as Palmer's embarrassment grew, and I suspect if darkness had come to Ellenton at that moment, Palmer's crown could have illuminated an entire room marking his position always.

Maybe such an appearance had been created from an awkward combination of natural events, the late November day, the coldness in the air outside, the fact Miss Bonney had just turned out the lights and asked that we rest our heads on the desks while she read the next chapter from *Robinson Crusoe*. Whatever caused Palmer Conroy to look as he did, to glow, we were mesmerized by this boy. We were held captive by his oddness.

Before we had a chance to do any more damage, Miss Bonney returned from the hallway, her eyes red and wringing her hands nervously in front of her. She looked at Palmer Conroy then touched his shoulders. When she saw the glowing ember on top of his head, her reflexes jerked and she let go of the boy, her hands coming together involuntarily as if she was about to pray. She said, "How unusual. How very odd."

We all remained stunned and silent, immovable as we watched Palmer's birthmark glow even brighter in the dying afternoon light. I think we might have stayed there forever had Palmer not put on his hat. He placed the floppy-eared cap over his pink skull capturing the glow beneath and returning the class to the dull gray moment at hand. Miss Bonney regained her composure and meekly smiled, called Palmer a good little boy and kissed him on the cheek, even though she barely knew him.

Her touch seemed to bring back the grim knowledge she had received in the hallway and a realization of the burden that was before her. In a quivering voice, she said, "Palmer Conroy has come to our school on a very sad day. I am sorry we can't welcome you into our class right now, Palmer, but Mrs. Mabry feels we should all go home and be with those we love." Miss Bonney then wiped the lipstick from Palmer's face with a Kleenex made damp by the touch of her tongue and said, "It is a very dark day, a very dark day, indeed. President Kennedy has been shot and killed in Dallas, so now please go straight home and pray."

Somewhere in the confusion of rubber galoshes and book bags, sweaters and coats, Palmer Conroy disappeared from our classroom, and I took the long way out, walking the dark deep halls saturated with smells of dry heat and freshly oiled floors.

Beyond the doorway, the air was brittle and the ground hard with early frost. I unchained my bike and rode off through air that watered my eyes and burned my chest with each breath I took. The trip home was cold, and though the skies were clear, the air smelled of snow the day Palmer Conroy came into my life.

Now I stood watching as my sled streaked across Third Street to slam into the backend of RC's Catalina, Palmer preparing the next snowman for its unforgiving execution. I did not notice until I came up close that he was not dressed properly for being out in such bitterly cold weather. He only wore a cape and Batman cap that came down over his face with holes cut out for his eyes. He had covered his body with long john underwear and wore a pair of leather ankle boots on his sockless feet. With each step Palmer took, the boots sunk into deep snow, and I could see ice had filled in around the tops and along the zippers on the inside ankle of each boot. His hands were covered with cotton garden gloves already soaked through and freezing stiff.

That morning, Palmer Conroy looked like a clown and a medieval executioner all rolled into one, the combination hilarious, yet unsettling as he sniffled and rubbed his nose across the arm of his long john top then looked at me like he had been expecting my arrival all along. Palmer said, "Hey Raybert."

"Hey Palmer. What ya doin'?"

"Cuttin' off heads. Wanna play?"

Though he stood ridiculously clothed inviting me to participate in the gruesome game of beheading snowmen, I was glad to be in his front yard and not in my house where my parents shook the walls. Palmer held the shovel out offering me a turn at stabbing the throat of his latest snowman, and I didn't hesitate; it looked like fun, so I took the shovel, let Palmer pronounce the sentence and began to whack away.

We rolled four more snowmen and executed each with excruciating detail using techniques devised on the spot or those we remembered from Boris Karloff movies we watched on *Shock Theater*. We split the head down the middle on one revealing pine straw and cones as brain matter. The second Palmer said, "Let's disembowel this asshole," and so we chopped away at the center ball until there was a hole big enough we could stick our heads through. Then Palmer beheaded the poor snowman to the roar of an imaginary crowd.

He came up with the idea of building a guillotine to behead the third. He said, "The French know how to kill, at least in the olden days." He drug his thumb in a slashing motion across his throat while I pulled my sweatshirt up to hide my head and then fell to the ground in writhing agony. We laughed and rolled in snow until our bodies were soaked and we were completely out of breath.

When we could not figure out a way to build the guillotine, Palmer said, "Fuck it," and smashed the snowman's head with the flat side of the shovel.

By the time we built the last snowman, the sky was threatening. Palmer looked at me and said through lips blue and shivering, "I want to give this one a name."

I said, "Okay, who is it?"

Palmer said, "It's Inez's boyfriend. It's Edgar and he needs to be tried for various acts against mankind." Palmer jabbed the shovel into the snow when he said this, his small body driving the blade deep and steady into the frozen ground.

I said, "I didn't know your momma had a boyfriend."

Palmer looked up toward his front door. "I didn't either until last night."

When I followed his gaze, I saw the window curtains in the front room move apart and a pair of unfamiliar eyes look out into the yard where we stood.

"And he's still in there with Inez this morning. Me and RC think that's a crime, don't you?"

I said, "RC would be pissed."

Palmer said, "There's not a jury in the land that would have pity on this guy. He needs his head cut off!" And so we made Edgar the snowman, adding arms and various other body parts that would make the job of executing him even more fun. We took turns chopping, cutting Edgar up until there was nothing left but a patch of dead grass where we had once made the base of the snowman.

By the time Edgar's execution was complete, Palmer looked cold. His face had lost the pinkish coloring from his cheeks and now seemed stiff and ashen. I said, "Palmer, you better get inside and warm up."

Palmer said, "I would if I could." He looked back to the window, the curtain pulled tight. "Momma said I can't come back in until I learn to behave myself."

I said, "What did you do?"

Palmer said, "Momma thinks I'm a fool's fool."

"You ain't no fool, Palmer."

"Guess it's all in how you look at it."

"And what does your momma see?"

Palmer said, "She thinks I wet the bed."

I thought that was funny. Palmer had spent the night at my house a dozen times and never had an accident like that. In fact, I had just seen him smoking a cigarette the night before and telling my daddy to kiss his ass, more or less, so to hear him say he had wet the bed didn't make a whole lot of sense. I said, "Palmer, your momma's got funny ideas," but Palmer said nothing. Instead, he looked over to the Catalina, studying the canvas where snow had gathered along its creases and folds.

RC had bought the car on a whim one morning while walking to work. Passing in front of Thompson Pontiac in July, he had seen the Catalina sitting on the showroom floor fully loaded and ready for the road. Palmer said, "RC told me the car was smiling at him when he walked by and so what could he do? He just had to buy it. Thought it might take us someplace one day."

He was an hour late opening the store because of the note for $3,133 he had to sign and so was nearly fired when old man Robertson saw him pull up in the alley. Palmer said, "RC told me that old fucker kept him on because he knew he couldn't afford that kind of car, and he would lose it before he had a chance to take it for a spin if he fired him. Old man Robertson liked the Catalina so much, they closed the store at lunch and took her for a ride."

Inez was so furious when he pulled up in the driveway she locked him out of the house until nearly ten o'clock that night. She yelled out the window at him, said they didn't need a car, that he could walk to work every day so why on earth had he bought a car, and besides, it was more than they could afford with the kind of jobs he always found. Inez finally let RC come back in, but she yelled and screamed at him all week. Called him a freeloader, a lazy dog, someone she didn't trust any farther than she could spit.

He died less than a month after that while he lay on the love seat.

After the funeral, we were at the grave and Palmer said, "RC just raised up off the couch and said 'What about the car?' like he was talking to someone in front of him, then he fell back down deader than dead. I don't think Inez will ever forgive him for leaving like this. She hates everything that he left her with, and that includes me and Cindy."

I said, "Palmer, your momma doesn't hate you."

But he just shook his head while we stood looking at all the flowers that were piled on top of RC's grave.

Now that Palmer's daddy had been gone for three years, it seemed the boy had always been right: The Catalina sat snow-covered on flattened tires, its battery dead, its sheet metal shrouded with a tarp, while a new man lurked behind curtains drawn so tight that Inez had to keep a lamp lit in the living room all day long.

Palmer shivered in the winter mix, his Batman cape frozen stiff and his cap covered with snow.

Finally he said, "I got to take a piss. You can come inside if you want."

I said, "Sure," and we were off.

Instead of going in through the front door, he led me around back where the yard squared off into a short skirt of grass, barely enough room for a clothesline to stretch out along the back fence and the rusted swings that occupied the middle. A concrete patio pinched the yard even tighter, leaving little room for a camper that sat on cinderblocks behind the carport.

The square aluminum box seemed misplaced, ironically perched to face the car that was supposed to pull it along on family vacations. RC had bought the camper within days of purchasing the Catalina and had the good intentions of fixing it up for trips to the Grand Canyon and the Painted Desert. He taped pictures on the refrigerator of all the places he wanted to take his family, and he promised Palmer then that when the camper was ready, they would take a test run to the beach where he could buy firecrackers and fish off one of the long piers. When RC died, Palmer was working league nights at the YMCA bowling lanes, saving his money for a fishing rod and strands of Blackcats and LadyFingers. Now the camper looked ominously deserted as we walked across the snow-covered patio to check the lock. He inspected the outer shell, looked in the window to see if everything was holding up through the winter storm.

I said, "You ain't got a bathroom in there, do you?"

Palmer said, "No, just looking it over, that's all. Inez won't let me go inside. She give Edgar the key, if you can believe that." He looked at me like he knew I couldn't and then shivered so hard, I thought he was going to pee in his long johns. He patted the camper on its side and then moved quickly back across the yard.

At the base of the cinderblock foundation was an entrance to the crawl space under Palmer's house. He slipped a glove off his hand and with a finger frightfully red, felt for a small grooved-out space between the block and the asbestos siding. There he found a key that unlocked the door, and we slipped in under the house to find warmth and protection from the cold.

The furnace crowded the narrow cavelike space, its jets warming the air around us, creating a musty breeze. He had his comic books, flashlight, and a small folding chair from the patio set up in a corner next to the water heater. Palmer put a finger over his lips to keep me quiet and then brushed up closer until his mouth was at my ear, his breath warm and sweet. When he spoke, his voice was even and calm, and I leaned close wanting to hear every word Palmer had to say.

"When Inez gets the heebie-jeebies, this is where I come. She don't know about it, so she can't find me. Pisses her off. She knows I'm somewhere around here, but she can't figure out where. She's just too stupid to think I'm underneath the house." Palmer smiled and then shut the door.

My eyes found comfort in the absence of light, the darkness edging in from around the crawl space to cover us and keep our whereabouts unknown. When Palmer lit the flashlight, he widened the space outward. He crawled off spreading light farther into the darkness until he came to a small trapdoor that was cut into the floor above. Pipes and venting ducts clung to the framing as he squatted and raised his hands between the beams. With a pocketknife he lifted from a hook, Palmer slipped a dull blade between the edges of the board. The knife slipped effortlessly back and forth until the door loosened and then fell away leaving a black empty square above us.

I said, "Where does that go—" but Palmer only shushed me, putting a finger across my lips, his skin so cold that I shivered.

"Shuuu. It's my room, but you have to be quiet." Then he scanned my body, sizing me up to see if everything fit and was in proper order. He said, "You'll have to strip if you want to fit through there."

For whatever reasons, this command did not bother me. To take off my clothes in a dirty crawl space under the Conroy house seemed as logical a next step as any other I had taken thus far that morning, and so I stripped down to my pajamas while Palmer removed his cape and mask and the stiffly frozen long johns. He was completely naked, the shadowed light revealing dark greenish brown splotches on skin that should have been only soft and pearly white. He grew a small tuft of hair below his waist that drew my attention since I had yet to find anything like that on my body. His birthmark circled the crown of his head. The strange mark I had first seen the day President Kennedy was killed had grown bigger over time and now rose like an ugly scar. It flamed bright red and sent steam into the darkness above us as cold skin thawed in the warmth of the furnace heat.

Even without clothes on, the fit was tight as I watched his fragile body disappear up into the hole. When he did not return immediately, when I could not see him above me, I became scared that Inez and Edgar were waiting in ambush because of what we had done to the snowman. I feared they would gather Palmer up and send him back outside exposed and vulnerable to the snow and cold. This time, he would have nothing to protect him, not even a Batman cape and mask.

I was worried and suddenly wanted to cry out for Palmer's safety. I wanted to break the silence under his house, crack it wide open like my daddy had the night before with his call to the wild turkey. But then Palmer poked his round head through the hole, his birthmark shining back down on me, a star leading the way. Palmer said, "Okay, Kemo sabe. Hi yo Silver, away!"

I smiled and wiped back my tears, then took his hand and shimmied up into the darkness, crawling carefully through a hole that deposited me into Palmer's closet.

efore that day of snowman beheadings, I had never seen a real dead man. It's true that I had been to RC's funeral and viewed his body in a casket. But the corpse seemed only a hollow representation of the man I had known a few days earlier that walked past me upright, whistling the tune from *Bonanza*. What I viewed at the funeral home, or stared at really, was less a dead man and more a presentation of RC's body that no longer lived or breathed life but still carried all the appearances of someone who did.

RC just looked like RC with the exception that his skin was tight around his jaw where in life it had hung loose. If you looked closely, his face was the color of talc and you could see where Billy Stroud, the barber who fixed men for Vance Funeral Home, had applied too much makeup to cover signs of death. He had painted light lipstick across RC's lips and combed his hair in the wrong direction. It's an old cliché, I know, that dead folks in caskets look like they're asleep, but that's pretty much what RC looked like. He appeared to be taking a pretty nap, too pretty I guess, and so I stared at his face for a long time waiting for something to twitch, an eyelid to flutter or his nostril to flare, any sign to me that RC was as much alive as anybody else in that small viewing room. Though I had seen RC's corpse, and later watched as they lowered his casket into the ground, I did not consider that I had seen someone dead. It was too clean and pretty. It was too normal to be death.

When I was safely inside, Palmer reset the trapdoor and made room for the two of us to sit down, clearing out box games, stacking them to one side while I held the flashlight beam steady. He cracked the closet door, checked to make sure the coast was clear and then slipped into his room to put on a fresh pair of Fruit Of The Looms before he snuck out headed for the bathroom to pee.

The house Palmer lived in seemed small, too small for twelve-year-old boys to get away with hiding out or sneaking around rooms while Inez hovered nearby. The walls were thin; they closed in quick, and I could hear the pee hit standing water in the toilet bowl while Inez and Edgar talked in the kitchen at the other end of the short hall. I knew Palmer's momma hated living in this house, that she had expected more from RC, a man with perfect pitch who could tune a piano by ear, but could not keep any other job than the one he held at Robertson's Radio. Palmer said that Inez dreamed of life over in Hickory Point, a big house with a big yard, but RC had ruined everything, even before his death. Palmer said, "It was just a matter of time. He told Inez he'd stick this one out even if it killed him. Guess RC knew what he was talking about." Now that he was gone for good, it was guaranteed Inez would never live anywhere else than in this house on Third Street. The small insurance policy along with the money they still brought in working the bowling leagues at the YMCA was barely enough to keep them off the street.

Palmer was gone for a long time, long enough that I began to worry again until he slipped back into the closet, carrying a paper envelope. It was dirty and bent like someone had carried it around in a back pocket, maybe behind a wallet where it rode against a hip for weeks on end before it was remembered.

He grabbed the flashlight and shone it directly under his chin, sinking his eyes deep into the back of his skull. "You want to see something bad, something real bad?" Then he opened the envelope with great care, slowly like whatever was inside was lethal, something that might crawl out and bite him if he let it out too fast. He pulled out a small picture that could have been taken with a Polaroid or one of those Kodak Instamatics and then crudely developed in a bathroom sink.

The people in the picture were dark and hard to make out, but when Palmer put the photograph under the beam of light, the figure up front took on the undeniable look of death. I was looking into the face of a dead man, a black boy actually, who was hanging from a tree, his neck crooked and broken, arms tied behind him, feet pigeon-toed and limp, just dangling there three feet off the ground. The boy's pants were pulled down to his ankles and his private parts had been lit afire, the skin of his genitals melted and charred. All that was bad enough, but what really made the boy dead to me was his face.

The eyes were half-open slits of empty white and the boy's lips were fat and puffy, drawn back over his teeth like he was right in the middle of a great big grin when they pushed the stepladder out from under him and snapped his neck. There were bruises and cuts all around his eyes and cheeks and on his chest and arms like he had been whipped and beaten. But it was that face, the lack of any life in features already deformed and melting away that struck me as strange and so held my gaze.

The dead boy's appearance was in stark contrast to the white men who stood around the body in the high afternoon light, their faces in full view holding rifles, smoking cigarettes, and smiling big like they stood beside a trophy kill.

Palmer said, "That's Rodney Small hanging there with his pecker on fire." And then I recognized him, knew exactly who the black boy was because his uncle Thurmond had worked for Daddy down at the dry cleaning plant. When I was younger, I had played with Rodney on Saturday mornings while Daddy and Thurmond took laundry in at the dry cleaning plant until around noon. I was just six at the time and Rodney, sixteen, but he seemed more my age on those mornings than someone so much older, a teenager who could drive a car, though Thurmond never let Rodney behind the wheel. He was mildly retarded and his daddy was in the state prison down in Raleigh, so he always stayed with Thurmond and later came to the dry cleaning plant to help out after he had quit school.

Palmer tapped the picture with his finger, said, "See anybody else you know?"

I looked, but it was hard to tell. Though the picture had been taken in broad daylight, it was old and bent, badly exposed. I scanned the faces slowly looking for as much detail as I could see, identifying features that would reveal someone I would have known when the picture was taken.

Palmer said, "Look right there at the tree, that man close enough to pat old Rod on his big black butt."

When I looked again, I saw a man, cigarette dangling from his lips, his eyes squinting because of the smoke. His right arm was extended against the tree with his feet crossed on the ground, Rodney dangling just out of arm's reach on his left. It looked like he could have been the executioner, the man who stood Rodney Small's already dying body on that ladder, steadied him there on the top step, the one manufacturers always warn you not to stand on and then patted him on the back and said, "See ya later alligator," before he kicked the living shit out from beneath his feet.

The man in the picture was my father.

When I first hit Palmer, it was involuntary, something deep inside my bones that said, "Swing!"

Palmer said, "Goddamn!"

When I hit him again, I may have had something to do with the motion of my arm because I sensed that I was aiming, that I was trying to hit Palmer where I might do some real damage.

Palmer said, "Shit Raybert!"

When I hit him in the face, busted his lip, my aim had been purposeful, the strike against Palmer came with full intent and malice.

Palmer screamed, "FUCK! IT'S ONLY A PICTURE!" and that brought Inez exploding into the room.

She was a short wiry woman with a nose that flattened out across her face and made her seem to always look at you cross-eyed. She looked angry when she bolted through the door and stopped dead in the center of the room. Her head snapped around looking for signs of our illegal entry, but she could not find us. Peeking out from the closet, I could see her face. There was something more than anger there, something more dangerous, a life out of control.

Palmer leaned over and whispered close to my ear, "When you can't get at someone who's dead, you tend to take it out on everybody else tenfold." Then he put his fingers up to his bloodied lip, a shadowy motion to stay quiet. I held my breath, tried to feel invisible while my heart raced, terrified by everything that the moment had revealed.

It looked like we were about to get away with our Houdini act, Inez Conroy ready to walk out the door, when Palmer said, "Uh oh, this ought to really piss her off," and then cut a fart the size of Alaska. The sudden explosion ripped through the silence and pinpointed our position, giving Inez a direction in which to renew her attack. She wheeled around taking good aim at the closet, trying to kick Palmer, her bare feet flailing in harmless misses. She yelled at him to get out of the house, but Palmer didn't move. She screamed at Edgar to get his sorry self in there and help, and when he didn't show, she got even madder, reaching into the closet to grab Palmer and jerk him out.

Palmer tried to explain. "I just come in to pee and get warm." But that's all he could get out before Inez slapped him hard, twice, right across the face. While she stung him with the first blow, the second one stunned his body so that his legs gave out and he collapsed back into the closet. Before he fell into my lap, Inez stomped out of the room slamming the door, and we could hear her giving Edgar shit in the living room for not having come when she called.

I lay on the floor of the closet with Palmer's photograph of my daddy and Rodney Small in my hand and felt everything I knew of life and death and love and hate spill out, each torn into a million pieces and littered there on the floor before me. I didn't know who to blame, Palmer for showing me, or Daddy, who I knew at this very moment was taking his fill of Momma, getting what he could before she started chasing her tail again.

When I moved my hand to touch Palmer's head, he flinched, and drew back as best he could in the narrow closet. "Don't hit me again. I didn't mean to hurt you with that picture. It was in Edgar's stuff. It's his picture not mine." He lay in my arms for a minute, his breathing fast and exhausted.

I said, "It ain't your fault, Palmer."

Out in the kitchen Inez was still chewing away on Edgar. We heard her yell, "You're not worth the two legs you walk on if you don't do something about it right now. I done had it with both of you."

I said, "Maybe we ought to get out of here." We looked at the trapdoor and then thought it better to ride out whatever was going to happen for fear Palmer's escape route would be discovered. We hunkered down and listened to Inez criticize and berate Edgar and every other living male who had ever "fallen flat on their faces into her life." She even attacked RC, screaming at him for leaving her with all the shit and getting out when the getting was good. She yelled, "He should have taken those two with him. I can't control them brats. I don't need them messing my life up any more than he already done."

Palmer buried his head into my shoulder while he sucked on his bloodied lip. "See what I mean? She ain't got no use for us anymore, if she ever did."

By then Edgar had heard enough. We felt the floor shake as the La-Z-Boy popped up from where he had been reclined. Inez shut up then. His footsteps were fast and heavy as he came through the small space separating the den from Palmer's bedroom.

Had I not been in the closet that morning, Palmer would have been hit hard. I'm sure later in the day, after I had gone, Palmer was beaten for getting in Inez's way. But when Edgar slammed open the bedroom door that morning and then nearly ripped the closet door from its hinges, it was clear he was not ready for what he found: two boys huddled in the cluttered space of that dark closet. His cold, violent stare ratcheted down instantly to something of surprise. An odd sight no doubt, two boys wearing only underwear and pajamas, clinging to each other for nothing more sinister than protection from what Edgar Doyle had intended to do.

He stared for a long moment, then shook his head, turned away, and said, "Queer bait," under his breath as he left the room. We could hear him cussing Inez down the hall, telling her she should have told him there was another boy back there.

Inez said, "What other boy?"

Palmer thought that was funny. "I guess you're the invisible man, you don't exist. You can go anywhere you want, Raybert, lucky dog."

I felt invisible, I felt naked and I felt nothing in my life was ever going to be the same again, now that I knew my daddy had killed that black boy.

CHAPTER

IV

*H*idden in my chest of drawers was evidence so in-
criminating, so disgusting that for the longest
time when I looked at Daddy, I could not help but feel hate
for the man I could not stop loving. Because of that picture,
I knew he had been there participating, maybe not willingly,
but he was there as the mob hung that boy. And though I
knew he had done nothing to stop it, and perhaps had been
the hangman himself, I wished with all my heart he had
tried anything to save Rodney Small. When I thought about
Rodney's body, mutilated and hung for public viewing, I
wished Daddy had been hanging beside him rather than
standing. I wished he would have been branded and retali-
ated against. At least I could have respected that. As it
stood, after I received the picture from Palmer, I was afraid
of what Daddy was, how far he might go, a man with the
power to call up the devil with a blade of grass.

Momma's behavior was complicated and never made it

easy on anyone. When she got sick it would come to her slowly, not like an upset stomach or a virus of some kind, but quietly and sneaky over time, her behavior seemingly normal until she would do something that was totally ridiculous to anyone who knew better. It was little things like full hot meals for breakfast and lunch when usually we could expect cold cereal and sandwiches that we had to make ourselves. And then she ironed everything, underwear, socks, sheets and pillowcases, even bath towels and washrags. Momma would obsess on people around her, accuse them of being too nosey or somehow in cahoots with Daddy in some obscene or clandestine way.

In March she was ironing everything she could get her hands on and watching Bernie Potter, her neighbor across the street as she began to do her yard cleaning that spring. She had seen Daddy speaking to Bernie one evening when the weather started turning warm. She asked me what was going on out in the yard, said she couldn't watch that woman flirt like that. But when I walked out onto the porch, Daddy was already gone, headed back to the dry cleaning plant where he was still trying to be a good man. Momma started seeing a conspiracy, something about Bernie's body language, the way she held the rake in her hands and stood too close to him when she talked. Momma was chasing her tail, but we just couldn't see it yet.

She was watching too much daytime television while she ironed socks and T-shirts and would not miss Walter Cronkite and the nightly news for anything. She saw an interview with Bobby Kennedy, Cronkite asking him about his run for the presidency, and got real worried about another Kennedy doing that, especially after the assassination of the president just five years earlier. Momma said, "He shouldn't do such a foolish thing. What's he want to do, get shot like his brother?"

Momma started writing to the senator in Washington and Hyannis Port, Cape Cod, trying to convince him he should not be president. *You'll win, no doubt about that. But what then? Do you have a death wish or something? What about all those kids you and Ethel have? Think about them for a change, how about it?* The letters came back every time because she never put a real address on any of them. Sometimes she even forgot to put a stamp on the envelope.

Then Momma got the crazy idea in her head to invite Bobby Kennedy to supper. If he came to eat, she told me after her mind was made up, then she could explain the whole thing to him, how Palmer Conroy had been right that afternoon the president had been shot. I said, "What does Palmer have to do with this?"

Momma looked at me like I was the one who was crazy. "Why everything, Raybert. I am surprised that you didn't know that."

The day the president died, I arrived home and found Momma and Aunt Iris in front of the television, *As The World Turns* preempted while Walter Cronkite read the latest bulletins reporting on the horrible events in Dealy Plaza. Palmer showed up at our front door somehow, though he couldn't have known yet that I lived just up the block. He came in and sat down beside me like I had known him all his life. I had never seen this boy before school that day, yet here he was so close I could feel his breath on my face when he slouched down beside me on the davenport and said, "Hey Raybert, how's it going?"

Palmer smiled through a thawing face, and I could feel

the radiating cold leaving his body as the warmth of our house closed in around him. Small drops of condensation rolled down the edges of exposed ears, and his nose was chapped and runny. Though I felt awkward with Palmer's sudden appearance in my house, there quickly followed a familiarity, smoothed and steadied, a comfortableness justifying his place beside me as well as the quiet and seemingly appropriate question he had just asked. All I could do was reply, "I'm alright, Palmer, better than the president, I'd say."

Aunt Iris said, "Whose idea was it not to put that bubble top on? What a stupid stupid mistake."

Momma said, "He landed at Love Field, isn't that ironic, Love Field."

Palmer said, "He probably never knew what hit him. He probably knew something was wrong when the first bullet hit. The first one probably stung like getting hit with a baseball bat or having a brick thrown at you from up close to smack you good; but after that, I doubt he even cared."

The television station switched Walter Cronkite quickly to Dallas just as Oswald was being transferred to his holding cell. This unshaven defiant young man was denying everything. Standing smaller than those around him, Oswald's face continuously cracked into a sheepish grin. Palmer said, "He doesn't look like an assassin."

Momma said, "He looks like anybody else on the street. How could they have found him so quick?"

I said, "How would you know what an assassin looks like?"

Palmer said, "He would be taller, wouldn't he? He wouldn't wear just a T-shirt. He'd have disguises and decoys to throw them off the trail. He'd escape in a plane that was invisible to radar. Who'd go to a movie after he killed the president, anyway? I don't think he could have done it. No way. He couldn't have done it by himself, not this guy. LEE HARVEY OSWALD DID NOT ACT ALONE!"

The words from Palmer Conroy's mouth seemed to tear through our ears with his sharp, high, squealing voice. His vocal chords tightened, eyes bulged while the birthmark spread like a bruise. Momma said, "My goodness Palmer, where did all that come from?"

Palmer sat on the edge of the couch, his feet dangling inches from the floor. "Sorry about that. But when I get excited or scared, that always happens. The bad news is I can't help it. The good news is it takes a while, but you get used to it."

I said, "Momma, I don't even know this boy. Why is he in our house?"

Momma looked at me like *I* had shot the president from some sixth-story window. She said, "Don't act like your father, and don't be rude. Palmer Conroy is our guest. Besides, he's your best friend."

"But I don't have a best friend, Momma."

She looked at Palmer while she stroked his forehead in the dying afternoon light. "Maybe not before, but you do now."

We all did get used to Palmer's voice, and Momma never forgot his words about Lee Harvey Oswald. It all came rushing back when she saw what Bobby Kennedy was about to do. Those who killed his brother, she had somehow concluded in her spinning head, would get him, too, if she didn't stop this silly notion of his running for the presidency.

When Daddy found out what she was doing, he lost his temper. I know this because I was there when he did it; I heard what he said and then I heard him hit her. They had just come out of the bedroom and were arguing in the kitchen, plates rattling in the cupboards. It was a Sunday, the only time the dry cleaning plant was closed and my parents had to endure each other for an entire day.

I was in the living room watching Ed Sullivan. Two men were spinning plates on tall sticks, dressed in Bavarian knickers and vests and hats with tassels dangling beside their faces. Another man played the accordion while they kept adding sticks and plates, balancing them anywhere they could on their bodies—on knees, foreheads, shoulders, and feet.

I wanted my parents to stop fighting and come into the living room to see this. I wanted them to witness the miracle, the way the men could balance the different plates—each spinning on its own stick, wobbling at times but never falling off. I wanted my family to sit together on the couch and Momma to say, *Why isn't that wonderful! Isn't that spectacular!* Daddy would be right beside me, his hand touching Momma's neck, playing with the silky web of soft hair that fell from the grasp of bobby pins. Daddy would say, *Raybert, I bet you could do that. I bet you could be on the Ed Sullivan Show!*

I wanted to imagine us as I imagined all other families on our block sitting together laughing and enjoying the show. Instead, I lay on the rug with pimento cheese sandwich crusts curled up on a paper plate beside me, my Coke glass sweating a ring into the rug and heard Daddy say, "You can't be writing a man like that. He don't know you from Adam. What makes you think he's even gonna read it, even if he gets the goddamn thing?"

Momma said, "He'll come, I'll make sure of that."

Daddy said, "That's crazy talk, Evelyn. You're out of your mind."

Momma said, "Bobby Kennedy is more of a man than

41

you'll ever be, so why don't you just go on over and fuck Bernie Potter and get it over with."

After that, he hit her just once. The reaction to her words was so fast, I thought for a moment that he must have been right to do it. But the silence following, dead silence like something had just been killed scared me. I closed my eyes and tried to imagine life without her. I was afraid to get up and look into the kitchen, afraid I might see Daddy standing over another lifeless body, a murderer again, just like Rodney Small.

"See the USA in your Chevrolet" filled the room while a shiny new Caprice station wagon driving past Mount Rushmore reilluminated the TV. The station wagon passed Old Faithful, the Grand Canyon, Indian tepees and a dude ranch. The trip was intercut with scenes of the family pulling down seats, loading luggage, and sitting comfortably in the spacious vinyl interior. They were laughing, taking pictures, and singing songs. A girl with pigtails and a boy with a flattop and big ears looked outside the windows. They said, "Gosh! Wow! Gee!" The girl slept easily in the seat while the boy colored a cowboy and horse. The father drove while the mother smiled and seemed to enjoy the passing scenery.

Momma broke the silence in the kitchen reassuring me she was still alive. She said, "That's just what I expected from you."

My daddy said, "I didn't mean to hit you, you know that. I've never done it before—"

"You're a disgusting man."

There was a pause, heavy silence again as a call for Philip Morris dissolved onto the TV screen. I knew he was trying to come up with something more, looking for a way to undo what was done forever. Then the kitchen went dark and Momma walked through the living room without saying a word. She brushed by me, her dress wafting a sweet breeze into my face that I inhaled. Daddy came and stood in the door, and I could see in his eyes that he was sorry. He looked down to his scarred hands and then out to some point beyond the smallness of our living room. I was scared that he would be gone again if he did not come up with something to take away the pain he had just caused.

I said, "Is Bobby Kennedy really coming to dinner?"

Daddy said, "Shut up." Then he disappeared down the hall.

I turned the set off and sat in silence listening as Daddy knocked on the door to their bedroom. I heard him say Honey, Sugar, and Sweetheart, but the door did not open. He said, love of my life, my one and only, my angel from Montgomery. He promised Elvis at a matinee, a better life, said he was sorrier than a dog out in the rain, but he only got silence from her. Then he spoke in a voice so low I think he was trying to keep his pleading at the door for only the two of them to hear. "Name your price. Give me something to work with here."

Momma was crying through the locked door. "Some things can't have a price, Ray. They just can't."

Daddy said, "You don't think I know that?" But Momma didn't answer anymore.

When he came out of the darkened hallway, Daddy looked pitiful. He said, "Go do your homework."

I said, "I don't have none."

"Then make some up."

He got his coat and hat, came back through the living

room on his way out, looked me hard in the eyes. "Take care of Momma, listen to what she says or I'll beat you a new butt."

"Where you going?"

"I got things to do. It's none of your business."

I followed him to the back door and then out onto the porch. It was late March, and though the days were warm, the nights remained cold. The air was still dead, no sounds of returning life stirring in the darkness. He turned to me, the yellow light dying his skin jaundice and said, "I hit your momma tonight."

I said, "I know."

"Problem is you can't take something like that back."

"Not from Momma you can't."

He looked out into the dark night, not trying to look away from me, more like he was trying to see through the blackness, crack the seam and find out what would make the world right again. He said, "Sometimes I think the world gets a flat spot in it, gets out of round just enough to throw the whole thing off. Guess I'm in a corner on this one." He stepped off the porch and then into the alley.

I said, "Does Momma hate you now?"

Daddy said, "I'm the plague."

"Do you hate her?"

"I love her more than life, but she drives me crazy most of the time."

After that he dipped into the shadows, his footsteps crackling the gravel as he disappeared.

I went back into the hall and listened at Momma's door, asked her if I could come in, but she said nothing. I thought this might be the night that she would find enough hurt and sadness and decide to kill herself. No matter if he had meant to hit her or not, the act itself was enough to plunge Momma into the deep depression she always fell into when the spinning stopped. I stood outside the room until I heard her cry. I said, "Momma, can I come in?"

She said, "No, Sweetheart, not tonight. Just call Iris, see if she's busy. Can you do that for me?"

I called Aunt Iris and sat out on the front porch where I could see through the open blinds into her room. Momma knelt at the edge of her bed for the longest time. I do not know if she prayed or just went to sleep that way or maybe was writing Bobby Kennedy another invitation to eat at our house, but I did not take my eyes off her. The weak glow from a small lamp on her dressing table kept the darkness from swallowing her completely, giving me confidence that she would be all right.

I slept restlessly during the next few nights, and sometime later dreamed I was the flattop kid in that Chevrolet commercial. We pulled Palmer in his camper behind us and I rode in the back, watching for Palmer to look out. When he raised the blinds, Palmer saw me and waved, blew me a kiss and mouthed the words *I love you*. Then we were standing along the edge of the Grand Canyon.

Daddy said, *Watch this*. He spit off the side, and we watched the wind sail his saliva deep into the valley below. Palmer cried out *Yippee!* when he did that and Momma took pictures while we all stood along the steep jagged edge of the southern wall trying to match Daddy's distance. Bobby Kennedy hiked up the trail and out of the canyon wearing Daddy's spit on the brim of his Smokey the Bear hat. We all said, *Hey Bobby!* and he smiled, admired us as a family, and then said spitting was illegal. Daddy said, *Hey, hey, hey. Sorry Mister Bobby, sir,* and we all laughed out loud. Momma sang out, *Dinner's at eight, so don't be late!* and then he took out a pad and began writing out tickets for each of us to see *The Ed Sullivan Show*. Through all of this, Palmer and I held hands.

Inside the theater, I was called up from the audience to perform magic tricks that made both of my parents very proud. I pulled a rabbit out of a hat and made doves magically appear from underneath brightly colored handkerchiefs. I found a silver dollar in Palmer's right ear and Palmer said, *How did you do that?*

Daddy said, *You're a chip off the old block!*

Momma said, *You're the apple of my eye.*

Ed Sullivan patted me on the head and called me a *Reeeeally good boy*.

Palmer Conroy kissed me on the lips and said, *Now make us disappear.* But I could not do that. I tried, but everybody just laughed and told my parents we looked funny blinking our eyes shut only to reopen them still standing on the stage where we clung to each other tightly.

In the morning I woke to a noise outside my window, disappointed it had all been a dream, thinking if Palmer ever tried to kiss me, I'd beat the shit out of him. Still the dream had been comforting and I tried to stay asleep and reenter the invisible world that had suddenly left me alone and shivering in my bed.

When I got up, I saw him from the window. Daddy was in the front yard tearing the ground apart while Aunt Iris and Palmer Conroy looked on from the sidewalk. She was still in her robe and curlers standing there shaking her head in disgust, and I could see Palmer straddling his spider bike mouthing words to a question I could not actually hear him ask, but understood him to say, "What does he think he's doing?"

Before them my daddy was rototilling the yard. He had

returned and was breaking up ruts, turning the soil, aerating, renewing the ground for new grass. He was attempting to solve everything by giving Momma a green yard, something I often heard her wish for when Daddy neglected the ground, letting it go to rut and weed. Off the front porch, he had azalea bushes to plant. A new John Coltrane record, *A Love Supreme* sat on the kitchen table along with a torn piece of paper on which Daddy had scrawled the words *Forgive me*.

I was shocked when I picked up the record and looked at John Coltrane for the first time. I had heard his saxophone through the thin plasterboard, the strange and awkward music that hurt my ears, but gave my parents the power to make walls move, but I did not know he was black. The very sight of this record in my house, this black man's palpable presence sent my mind reeling. How could my daddy love the music of John Coltrane and then go out and kill a black boy leaving his body torn and mutilated dangling from a tree?

I dressed and went outside to be with Aunt Iris and Palmer as Daddy made a slow meticulous pass churning up the soil. Aunt Iris looked toward Momma's shaded window and said, "He better not be thinking this is doing any good. Grass won't fix nothing."

I said, "I thought Momma wanted him to fix the yard."

Aunt Iris said, "She did, but he should do it for the right reasons."

Palmer said, "Maybe he is. Maybe this is the right reason."

Aunt Iris looked at the boy like he was crazy. She said, "Sure it is Palmer, and Bobby Kennedy's on his way over to eat breakfast and drink coffee with the family right this minute."

Just then Daddy had to make a turn with the machine.

The tines jumped out into the air and raced across hard ground toward the front porch. Palmer hid behind Aunt Iris waiting for Daddy to get control of the tiller, put it back in a straight line. "Guess your daddy's got his hands full, but he don't seem to know too much about what he's doing."

Aunt Iris smiled at that, pulled him around from behind her and said, "You boys are going to be late for school. You got a lunch?"

Palmer said, "I don't eat lunch."

Aunt Iris said, "Well honey, you will today." She disappeared into the kitchen to get our lunches ready while Palmer and I silently watched the tiller scratching at the unbroken ground. I didn't want to say anything about Inez never sending him to school with a lunch. Since RC died, Palmer had been on free lunch, but I never saw him take one thing from the cafeteria. Instead he chewed gum and drank water. Sometimes, he stole Twinkies from Nichols Market. In the afternoons, he would hang out with Lucky Luther and me, eat saltines covered with peanut butter and drink Coke while we watched reruns of *The Lone Ranger*. Palmer would steal saltines whenever Lucky left the room, hiding each cracker inside a small brown paper bag he carried in his coat pocket.

I said, "Lucky will give you crackers, Palmer, if you ask him."

Palmer said, "I'd rather just take 'em. Besides, he'd give them to me anyway, so what's the difference?"

Aunt Iris came out of the back door with my knapsack and two lunches. When she handed Palmer his sack, he didn't say a word until he had opened it and peered inside. Then he said, "Probably won't eat it, but thanks anyway."

Aunt Iris said, "You eat that lunch; you eat every bit of it so your bones won't break and your teeth won't rot, do you hear me?"

Palmer smiled at Aunt Iris and scrunched up the top of the sack. He gripped his handlebars and said, "I like cheese biscuits and fruit cocktail, guess I'll eat this sometime today."

Aunt Iris looked back out into the yard, her face filling up with worry. She said, "Now get. I don't need no principal calling me on the phone. How would I explain all of this?"

We spun tires against gravel in the alley just as Daddy looked up to see us glide away into the street, a cigarette dangling off a cut lip. He didn't pay us any attention, didn't wave or even act like he had seen us. He just continued to till, struggled to break more ground and dig our family out of the mess.

The hill, like in winter, sent us racing toward the intersection of Robbins Street and Third. Though the response to an out-of-control sled was to bail out and save ourselves, on bikes, we dashed blindly around corners while old mill houses tucked away behind trees and unkept shrubbery blurred in our vision. We created shortcuts that would get us to town sooner than paved road. We crossed yards, took back alleys, and wove through half-empty parking lots, the fastest way to the corner of Hargrave and Main. At the intersection, we didn't even slow down to catch our breath. I was half a block ahead when I noticed Palmer was not with me. I slammed on the brakes and looked back to see him still on Hargrave crossing Main and heading out of town.

I don't think Palmer expected me to follow him. He didn't say he was going to ditch school. Miss Ferguson kept close tabs on our attendance, and I knew my record. I had been warned more than once if I was late again, I would be in for afternoons of slapping erasers, emptying trashcans, and refilling toilet paper dispensers. I should have gone on, so I wouldn't be late to homeroom, but something told me to follow, that wherever Palmer Conroy was going, he would need someone to be there when he arrived. I popped a wheelie turning my bike around and peddled frantically to catch up but was still a good distance behind when he turned off Hargrave into Happy Hill Cemetery. I knew then what he was up to—Palmer needed to talk to RC. He needed to visit his daddy's grave.

He sat on his knees, pulling wild onions and crabgrass that threatened the headstone, straightened plastic flowers in a metal vase while he laughed and pointed toward me like he was telling RC I was nearby. I waved, but Palmer just kept talking, brushing away flies.

Another grave was opened with a vault freshly placed inside, and so I sat in a chair under the funeral tent. The morning was warming quickly, and though it had not rained for over a week, the air was clean and bright like after an early morning downpour.

I looked around to see if Coggin Philpot's truck was still in the cemetery. It was a flatbed with a crane on the back for loading and off-loading cement forms built out at Coggin Philpot's concrete company. It was a truck Daddy drove when he wasn't delivering or picking up clothes.

Daddy just never had much talent for running a dry cleaning plant. He was constantly in need of cash and so he moonlighted driving vaults to cemeteries to make ends meet. I knew if there was a fresh hole in the ground, then Daddy had sunk the vault, and though I had just left him in our yard, I was afraid he would somehow find us, and then make us pay more dearly than slapping erasers after school for our truancy. I searched across the graveyard, my eyes focused at its edges where a narrow road gathered the property in, but all I could see was an old black man pushing a lawnmower around graves, cutting the grass, and tending to each individual plot like it was family.

Palmer stayed beside his daddy's grave for a long time before he leaned down to kiss the headstone and then remount his bike. He peddled over to where I waited, jumped across the opening and took a seat at the end of the row. Palmer said, "Guess RC's getting another neighbor."

I said, "Yeah, guess so."

He looked into the empty grave studying its depth, smelling the musty cool aroma of the freshly dug clay. "RC's in a grave like this, six feet under. You think it's cold in there?"

"My daddy said that it is always 65 degrees underground."

Palmer seemed to like that. "RC's hot-blooded. He always had a fan running in the bedroom. Couldn't sleep without that thing on; summer or winter, he always had it on high. Inez hated him for that, too."

He stared into the hole for a long time and then out toward his daddy's grave. I figured he was thinking about how much he missed RC. They had been so close before he died. I don't know why Inez didn't want Palmer anymore. She never did treat him all that good, but now she treated him so bad, sometimes it hurt to watch. He always got the short end of everything, no matter what he was accused of doing.

After a few minutes, he looked at me and said, "There's something I got to tell you."

"What's that?"

"Well, you know how Inez thinks I wet the bed?"

"Yeah."

"Well, I don't. I just pour water on my sheets at night."

"Why do you do that?"

Palmer looked back toward RC's grave before he spoke. "It pisses Inez off, but RC thinks I should stop it. He thinks I need to grow up and get away from here fast."

"You got someplace to go?"

Palmer grinned then, stretching the birthmark on his head, turning it a deeper red with each word he spoke. "I'm going somewhere RC would appreciate. I'm going to Myrtle Beach." And then he told me the plan, something RC had just suggested, Palmer said, while he spoke with him at the grave.

Right after the trailer had been parked in the backyard, RC read an article advertising the Cherokee Family Campgrounds outside Myrtle Beach. He tore the page from the magazine and gave it to Palmer as a reminder of the vacation he had promised. The picture was hidden under his bedroom in the crawl space after RC's funeral, after Inez went into the kitchen and pulled all the vacation spots off the refrigerator, screaming obscenities at her dead husband for leaving her with their lives in such a mess.

Palmer told me then that he had plans for the camper. "When I get my license I'm gonna hitch that thing up to the Catalina and pull it all the way down to the ocean, park it on the beach, and fire off a few firecrackers for RC. That's what I promised him today. That's what I'm gonna do." Then he jumped into the empty grave and lay in the cold cement vault that sat at the bottom of the hole. "I want to see this from RC's view, as best I can. I want to know what he's going through over there."

While Palmer lay in the open vault, his plans for Myrtle Beach grew in proportion to his imagination until he had made plans to live down there. He would leave Inez and his sister Cindy and live in the Cherokee Family Campgrounds, learn to surf on wild waves and maybe work on a pier or a charter fishing boat. He made mental notes as he made his plans, *he should buy a bathing suit, learn to tie knots,* and try to remember that *you cannot boil the salt out of salt water.* Palmer said, "Too bad I don't live in South Carolina, I could get my permit at fourteen and be driving in two years."

The old black man finally saw us. He yelled and made a feeble attempt to take chase as I leaned over to pull Palmer out of the hole. We pushed off on our bikes and pedaled toward the wall of woods bordering the cemetery, a steep incline dropping us onto trails that snaked through thick foliage, poison ivy, and trees. We escaped along footpaths that our bike tires easily fit into, maneuvered the secluded passageways until they brought us out into a small park along Finch Creek.

The whole area was a floodplain Ellenton Mills cleared some years before and then constructed horseshoe pits, swings, a twirl-a-round, and picnic tables. Each spring you could count on the Finch flooding, harshly thrashing the area until drier weather allowed the mill's maintenance men to drive in and repair the damage.

Palmer stopped in the middle of the sloppy ground. He looked up into limbs crisscrossing the sky, their leaves still thin and fragile. He said, "This is where they hung that boy. This is where Rodney Small died back then."

We walked our bikes through the park hunting for where they hung him, Palmer pretending to be my daddy as he leaned against different trees, a cigarette dangling out of his mouth.

There had always been stories told about Rodney Small's

lynching, and I even remembered the day Thurmond left the cleaners and never came back to work. Daddy said he had found another job in Hickory Point, but now I wondered if he had been scared off or maybe gone into hiding thinking he might be next. I wondered, too, about Rodney and what he must have thought when those men brought him to this place. The park had not yet been built, the land so desolate and remote that he had hung there until he started to swell and stink.

Palmer said, "You don't get accused of showing your pecker to a white girl and just go on like it was any other day. Not back then, and I doubt he could get away with it today either. It don't matter that men are going to walk on the moon real soon. People like Edgar and your daddy are still around to make sure some things don't change."

The hanging never made the paper, but everybody knew what he was supposed to have done. No one searching for Rodney thought he'd be alive when he finally showed up. An old black man who lived off Grove Road smelled the first smell and knew what his nose had found. It took a search party another day, but Rodney wasn't going anywhere. He was waiting right where he had died three days earlier. He was so simple in his mind that I am sure he never understood until it was too late what was about to happen. He probably thought Daddy was his friend when he did whatever he did to get him down there.

I stood straddling my bike wondering why my daddy would have participated in something like that against a boy so young and kind, why he would let his picture be taken—proof of his part in the murder recorded and developed and now held in my possession, but Palmer said, "It's ancient history. I wouldn't worry too much about it, if I was you."

At that moment the sun seemed to blink in the sky a million times, the light strobing against our eyes drawing our heads to a space suddenly filled with the flight of birds. It was that moment in spring, rare and as much a myth as that of the turkey wandering around Ellenton, that blue finches, so richly colored they appeared to be black, returned to Finch Creek to nest there among the trees and thickets that would soon grow full along its banks.

The birds filled our eyes and ears with the noise of their return, the sheer numbers blotting out the sky, stunning us. Thousands upon thousands it seemed would light in the trees momentarily, their high-pitched song so loud and full that we covered our ears. Before they could all settle, a dozen or more would shoot out into the air, catch a breeze lifting up and be gone. The rest followed en masse to shatter the light, explode back into the sky to circle through the high noon sun before dropping back down into leaf and vine to wait for the next renegade birds to start the frantic pattern all over again.

Palmer said, "I heard about this, but I never seen it."

I said, "Me neither. It's the finches returning to Finch Creek."

Palmer looked at me like I was an idiot when I said that. "No shit Sherlock. I thought maybe it was the Turtles or the Beatles or maybe the Rolling Stones."

I said, "Shut up, Palmer."

Palmer said, "They gonna shit all over us, if we don't get out of here."

I said, "No they won't. Look! They're flying out over the fields then flying back in here to land. They're just letting us watch."

Palmer said, "They know we won't hurt them."

I said, "Not a feather, no way."

"They know their secret's safe with us."

I said, "I imagine others can see them, Palmer. After all, they're flying up in the air."

Palmer said, "I doubt that. Everybody is at work or in school. We're the lucky ones, Raybert. We were right here when they came home."

I said, "I can't believe my eyes."

"RC says it's been happening since the Indians were here."

"Why do you think they do it?"

Palmer said, "They know where they're going, like we know where we're going when I get my license."

It was the first time Palmer had said anything about me going to Myrtle Beach, and though he didn't say it outright, he smiled and winked like he knew I understood his point. I hadn't even thought about it until he said it and then Myrtle Beach started sounding pretty good to me, too, a plan hatched and ready, somewhere to go. I smiled and nodded, then looked up to see the birds shoot out of the trees.

Palmer said, "I think this whole show might be Rodney Small thanking us for just coming out here and looking around. Maybe he's saying don't worry about me anymore."

I wanted to believe Palmer, but I had my doubts about all of that. The picture he had given me kept everything alive and burning in my mind. Now each frantic swarm of birds was followed by a pause that grew greater until most seemed to tire of the game. By the time we left the park only a few still flew out from their perches. Most had filled the trees, the limbs full of shimmering motion and song. I followed Palmer home, careful to remain invisible to those who might report us cutting school. We snuck back into the

crawl space to eat our lunches and read about the Cherokee
Family Campgrounds. I pushed Rodney Small and what my
daddy had done as far away as I could ever keep them and
tried to focus on Palmer and the plans he had revealed at
RC's grave.

Palmer's advertisement had pictures of the campsites
with tents unfurled and trailers settled in. There was a beach
at sunset and a beautiful girl stretched out on golden sand.
Behind her, palm trees swayed in the ocean breeze. It all
looked fake to me, but Palmer said, "It's paradise, and I owe
it to RC to go." He smiled and then went back to scribbling
notes in the margins reminding him of things he would want
to bring along. *Tan don't burn get a Coppertone tan. Remember to
bring candles in case of a hurricane. Save fish heads so you can hunt
for crabs. It's a* family *campground, so Raybert's got to come, too.*

Every now and then, Palmer would stop and hold his
hand up for me to be quiet and we would listen for the
sound of the finches rising into the air. We heard nothing
more that day nor did we hear or view that black sea of birds
during the rest of spring. The finches were there, no doubt.
We saw them all over town, but they had settled down, no
longer needing to perform the chaotic race that we had witnessed. They were nesting quietly now all along the banks
of Finch Creek while Palmer Conroy continued to plan our
getaway.

*B*y the time I left Palmer's crawl space, school was out
for the day and Daddy had only tilled half the yard.
There were blisters where the dirt had lodged down in his
gloves and socks to rub his fingers and toes raw. He drank
water from the garden spigot, said, "This is more than I figured on."

Momma was out of her room by then, sitting in the
front porch swing with Aunt Iris. She gave Daddy the evil
eye when he said what he said and then issued her challenge,
"Quit then. You're good at that."

But he never wavered. He said, "I'll get it done. Besides,
I'd look like a fool if I quit now."

Momma said, "Hum, I won't touch that." And then she
smiled at Aunt Iris, laughed a little under her breath.

They sat out on the front porch into the early evening.
Momma never once mentioned having dinner with anyone.
She smoked cigarettes, kept her eyes on Daddy, waiting si-
lently for him to fail. Still, he stayed in the dirt churning and

cutting. His labor turned our lawn into dark rich loam that smelled musty and sweet, the furrows crooked and broken from his inability to keep the tines firmly in the ground. I watched him finish from my bedroom window, his silhouette digging the ground back and forth, back and forth, the puttering Briggs and Stratton pulling him along. He ran out of gas twice, lost the tines off the axle a half-dozen times, and ran over one of his new azaleas when the tines once again pulled out of the ground. He tilled until dark, for twelve hours, and had to finish by duct-taping a flashlight to the front of the rototiller so he could see the ground before him.

Once the yard was finished, Daddy limped into the house to fix a Jim Beam and ginger ale. The ground was soft now, dark and loamy, furrowed and aerated. It smelled rich and made our small house seem more important, bigger when the land was all fluffed up.

Momma said, "If it rains, it'll all be mud."

Daddy said, "By May you'll be ankle deep in green grass."

Momma took a deep drag off her cigarette, exhaling toward the street. "This I got to see."

A few days later, I was coming out of school and saw the van from the dry cleaning plant parked out front, Daddy waiting patiently inside. He was reading brochures on grass seed and fertilizers and looking at the charts that gave exact schedules on when to perform each task. The van was empty of laundry and dry cleaning, and so I loaded my bike through the back door. Daddy said, "Get a move on. We got important things to do." Then we headed uptown.

He stayed quiet while he drove, working things out in his head—figuring about the grass, what all he would need to buy and how much it would take to give Momma a lush green sea outside her window. I sat up in my seat looking at some of the brochures. He smiled and said, "Pretty interesting stuff, huh?"

I said, "Yeah, grass is cool."

Daddy thought about that for a minute and then smiled again. He looked both ways before turning onto Main, and then he said, "Yeah, cool. Grass is definitely cool."

As we pulled in the parking lot of Grubb Feed and Seed Daddy became nervous, looked out of place. He said, "Stay close. I don't want you making a fool of yourself in here."

I said, "You see a fool, you give him a dollar."

Daddy said, "Shut up and do as I say."

We climbed the stairs along the loading dock, wandering aimlessly through the store looking for the bags of seed and fertilizer. Grubb's was where you bought anything that had to do with farms, hardware, or a yard. There were still enough small family farms around Ellenton and Hickory Point to keep him in business. It was a place to gather, a private covey of those who had retired off the land, who sat around waiting for people like my daddy to come in and get lost. I could feel their silent judgment, the way they ended conversations whenever we passed too close to where they sat.

He paid them little mind, his head buried in his brochures. He scribbled notes on the back of one, found a piece of cardboard and sketched out our yard. Daddy tried to figure square footage to determine how much of everything he would need, but he had not thought about our yard in those terms before and so became frustrated with the task, wadding up the sketch, cursing it as he shoved the swatch of cardboard deep into his hip pocket. Around us were bales of hay and fertilizer, hoes, rakes, and broadcast spreaders, yet I began to feel that even though we were surrounded by the very tools and supplies he would need to finish off his yard, Daddy seemed cut loose, lost along the aisles, unable to see what was in front of him.

I slipped away, embarrassed at how out of place he looked walking around in his plastic shoes. I began to despise him for what he was trying to do with his yard. I found myself more comfortable on my own than standing alongside him as he tried to determine what he would need to make his grass grow. I looked at tools, lumber, and tractor parts, ran my hand through bins of nails and along spools of rope and chain. The store was full of rich, thick smells of earth and metal and oiled tools. I stood on concrete mix and piles of roofing shingles. All these things had purpose and reason, and I knew the voices that floated through the cavernous warehouse understood their usefulness and at any given moment could have condemned Daddy for his futile attempt to be more than he was.

He whistled me up, and I found him talking to Grubb when I finally scuffed my way back toward the front of the store. He popped me on the back of my head and said, "What'd I tell you?" Then he turned his attention back to Grubb, not wanting an answer, content he had embarrassed me in front of the men who sat around us.

Grubb Yarborough was short with a stomach laid out over his belt as if at any moment it might topple him to the floor. He smoked a cigar and talked out of the side of his mouth, had dirt caked under his fingernails and white hair sprouting out from where his shirt spread open around his neck. He wheezed when he talked, but his words were firm and sure. Grubb knew everything about the merchandise he sold. He was an expert not because he sold it, but because at some point in his life he had used every tool, every machine, and every piece of hardware in that store.

While he talked, Daddy scribbled furiously. He would glance up every now and then, nod in agreement, slice his eyes toward me to keep me planted. When he was finished, Grubb's store clerks helped stack bags of seed, lime, and fertilizer in the back of the van. Grubb rented him a broadcast spreader and landscaping rake. Daddy paid what he owed, and then we hauled the supplies away in silence, the receipt in his pocket proof to himself that he was trying.

For the next few days, he studied the yard. Daddy would sit on the front porch and look out onto the fine dark loam he had tilled as if he were waiting for something to be revealed to him. He would walk into the middle of the front yard and stand silently for long periods of time just looking around. He'd squat on his haunches and rub the dirt in his fingers, dig little holes and uncover nuts the squirrels had buried the night before. He smelled the dirt. He even tasted some, put a pinch right on his tongue then paused as if he were checking the spiciness of white gravy or spaghetti sauce.

When he decided how he would proceed, it did not take long to plant the new grass. Daddy laid out six forty-pound bags of lime, broadcast starter fertilizer, and finished off with a blend of fescue Grubb had sworn would take root in shade as well as sunlight. The green-coated seed was cool to the touch, light and fragile. When I held a handful, I could feel the potential life, could sense in each sliver the miracle of germination. Back and forth he moved with the spreader, attempting even distribution. He talked to himself, coaxed the chemicals into the soil, bid each seed of grass good luck and

Godspeed. He chanted as he strawed the loose dirt, "Grow grass grow. Grow grass grow."

Aunt Iris called Uncle Clewell to come get her because Momma had evened out. Maybe it was the combination of the slap and the peculiar behavior Daddy exhibited with the yard that helped Momma stop chasing her tail. Whatever it was that caused her to regain a sense of balance, Momma's appearance seemed normal again. Bobby Kennedy and his run for the presidency was no longer cluttering her mind. Her behavior gave us all a small glimmer of hope that maybe this time Daddy really did know what he was doing.

When she left, Iris kissed him on his dirt-covered cheek and said, "Way to go big brother." Uncle Clewell tooted the horn and waved as he slowly pulled his Cadillac DeVille away from the curb, the convertible top automatically lifting off the windshield to disappear behind the backseat. I watched Uncle Clewell vanish from my view wishing I were tucked away in the backseat going home to live in Hickory Point.

I had been to Aunt Iris's before, a house that rose two stories high and then stretched out through long halls and enough hard angles and shadowed recesses to get lost in and never be found. When I visited, I pretended I no longer lived in Ellenton, that my parents were dead and Iris and Clewell were raising me to have an exciting life of driving Cadillacs and living in houses with room to grow. When I was in one of the bedrooms, no wall shook and no voices were heard on the other side. It felt safe and quiet, dreamlike. I wanted to be in Uncle Clewell's Cadillac when it disappeared around the corner because I was scared to be left alone with my parents. Though they appeared to be doing well together living in close quarters, I wanted to be as far away as possible from Robbins Street when they eventually would collide and Daddy's grass refuse to grow.

In the days that followed, instead of losing grip, Momma started watching Daddy in the yard. At first, it was from a distance, peeking out a window or the front door to follow his progress. When he kept going, kept coaxing his grass to grow, she moved out onto the front porch swing. There she smoked her cigarettes but kept the ashtray lifted in her right hand ready for a fast exit if he came too close or tried to sense where he stood in her eyes. She watched him water the yard, evenly soaking the seed and dissolving the fertilizer and lime into the ground. She told him where to plant the azaleas, pointing to the spot with the lit end of her cigarette and complaining when he didn't get it exactly right on the first try. Before her eyes, Daddy brought our yard to life, or at least into the expectancy of life.

When he was finished, he stood before Momma in the twilight, the closest she had allowed him all week. The damp earth smelled rich, a musty aroma of wheat straw invading our senses to make our heads light. Daddy took a deep breath, drunk on the aroma and said, "How about a hug for your farm boy."

Momma said, "You need a bath."

"How about you scrubbing me then."

Momma looked at me and smiled. "Ray . . . the boy."

I said, "You see a boy, you give him a dollar."

Momma smiled at me again.

Daddy said, "I'll give you a dollar to clean up this mess, to wrap up the hose and get Grubb's tools ready to take back."

Momma said, "That's not getting you any closer, Ray Williams."

"Come June, these azaleas will look like a million bucks."

She stood up and put her hand on the doorknob. "It's not that easy, Ray."

Daddy looked at me and winked. "I'll give you five to do my dirty work, to clean up this mess." He turned and winked again, and I took the rake out of his hand. I thought Momma would run inside and lock the door to keep Daddy away. I thought she would hate me for siding with him, for helping with his scheme, but instead, her eyes softened and she let go of the door handle to stub out her cigarette. She looked at Daddy and then laughed, almost a girlish giggle. "You're a good boy, Raybert, for helping your daddy like that," and then they disappeared inside the house.

For the next few weeks, my parents were in love again. Every afternoon Daddy would come home from the dry cleaners to water his yard. Momma would sit on the front porch and read the newspaper to him while he got down on hands and knees looking for signs of life, short green needles breaking the soil to prove he was a good man. People, neighbors we hardly ever spoke to, actually stopped to admire Daddy's work, to say they were proud he was doing so much to his lawn. My parents held hands and took long walks in our neighborhood. They laughed and joked, talked of adding on or maybe moving over toward Hickory Point to get away from the gossipy smallness of a mill town like Ellenton. Momma found Daddy's old dog tags and wore them around her neck on a chain. John Coltrane played into the deep hours of each night until the grooves began to pop and crack with constant wear. I got little sleep but woke up rested each morning because I heard my parents in the kitchen talking in quiet voices, normal and sane while they made their plans.

Palmer Conroy spent the night with me on weekends and

we made plans, too, our great escape to Myrtle Beach. We made more lists of things we would do when we arrived. *Go buy surfboards, have our ears pierced, get fake IDs to buy beer.* We were ecstatic about the possibility that was still four years away but nonetheless closer with each day we struggled through.

The fact I was in trouble with Miss Ferguson at school and had to slap erasers for the next month made little difference to me. To have witnessed the return of the finches the morning Palmer visited RC's grave was worth the loss of my afternoons during that last month of school. Palmer helped out by sneaking in to empty trashcans and change toilet paper. He liked going into the girls' bathroom and pulling Kotex out of the dispensers. The thick cotton pads were a mystery to us as we examined them, tested their ability to stick to walls after being soaked through with water. Palmer stuffed one in his pants and pretended he was having his period. He said, "When Cindy wears these things, she's a real bitch. Now I can see why."

Later when we came home, we watched Daddy pamper his soil, Momma applauding the discovery of each small blade of grass that peeked through the surface. She was radiant and it seemed like she could go on like this forever.

With the excitement of Daddy's new yard, Momma failed to notice things, occurrences in her body that normally she would have been acutely aware of. When she laughed too hard, she wet her pants. When she watched Daddy move hoses in his yard, she cried and said, "He's the man of my dreams," but then threw a mixing bowl at him that shattered against the wall when he didn't take off his muddy shoes before coming through the kitchen door. When she did notice she had stopped having her period, Momma became scared a disease had entered her body, and now just as everything was shaping up, she was going to die and miss it all. She forgot her doctor's appointment and then remembered it the next day, panicked and hysterical. Dr. Redmond saw her promptly, working her in instead of taking lunch. He pronounced her healthy with a strong heart and good blood. Everything about her was "Fine and working well." He also informed her that she was pregnant.

In all the John Coltrane melodies floating through their bedroom, there had been one record that Momma felt sure was playing as Daddy's own squirming, fighting part of the human puzzle journeyed through her body traversing tubes and folds to find her egg, the two to become one and then the beginning of life. The album's title seemed to say it all, *Love Supreme*. That's what it was after all, wasn't it? Love Supreme?

I forgot about Rodney Small, or at least I didn't think about him as much. He was at a safe distance, a disturbance easily kept at the bottom of my chest of drawers. Palmer's momma even eased up for a time, letting him pull the tarp off the Catalina and sit behind the wheel. One day Edgar popped the hood and said, "Bet this thing runs like a bat out of hell."

Palmer smiled at me while Edgar's head was stuck deep into the engine compartment. He said, "Edgar's gonna get this thing running again." Then he leaned over and whispered, "Maybe I was wrong about this guy. Maybe he's all right after all."

I remember this time in my life as one of great joy and love, where Momma was no longer sick and Daddy was brave and strong. It also gave me hope that miracles were possible, Momma would certainly be well from then on, and my daddy's yard would be covered with grass in no time, a thick green carpet with roots so deep I would never see dirt in our yard again.

The summer was coming and at that moment in time, it was all too good.

VII

*A*s temperatures climbed quickly that spring, Daddy's lawn continued to amaze us, fogging memories of the dark dead winter. A warm, hazy veil descended upon our neighborhood. Dogwood trees bloomed. Forsythia and jonquils gave way to roses and gardenias. Trees closed in around us, filling the cracks and seams of our neighborhood sky. Young azaleas Daddy had planted were dotted now with pink and white blossoms, fragile and vulnerable without their flowering mass.

Each day Momma stood in our front yard looking across the street to Bernie Potter's azaleas. She was the same age as Momma but had no kids. She seemed to care for her flowers like they were her babies, always on her hands and knees, coaxing and feeding, floating in a sea of pollinated air. Momma stood in the middle of our struggling yard, direct sunlight forcing her to shade her eyes as she marveled at the plants taken for dead too often in faithless conversations months earlier with Aunt Iris. She spoke across the street, waved a hand and said, "I don't know how on earth you do that Bernie. I don't believe what I see."

Bernie smiled and waved back. "I just let them grow Evelyn, that's all they need." She pointed with a small trowel toward Momma, waved the blade as if to spread good luck. "You have a good start over there. Ray has done some good work in that yard."

Momma agreed, her head nodding when she added, "He's done good work in more than the yard." She raised her shirt to just below her breast and showed Bernie Potter her soft white belly. "I'm gonna have my second."

Bernie said, "You're gonna have a baby? Well my goodness, Evelyn. Why you have been busy." Then her head quickly disappeared back into the explosion of color as she continued doing that which Momma struggled forever to understand—coaxing life and enjoying the beauty that surrounded her.

Though Momma was trying hard to keep focused on good things, there were new signs she was not well. Minor at first, her acts seemed more eccentric than sick, but with each instance there came more worry that she was not getting any better at all, that in fact, she was starting to chase her tail again.

At times Momma would step across the street and back Bernie against bushes while she rubbed her belly and asked questions about the delicate plants Daddy had put into the ground. She'd fire off questions and discuss possibilities while chain-smoking Virginia Slims, tapping her ashes into a gloved hand.

She started worrying out loud about a second child, how

it would change the house, what it might do to me. At dinner one evening, I said, "I've always wanted a brother or sister. I don't care which one I get." But Momma just sat there picking at her food, her face pale and drawn like she had made some kind of mistake.

"They say the second is always more special. Doesn't that scare you that you won't be special anymore?"

I said, "No."

Momma said, "Well it should," and then she left the table without finishing her meal.

Later that night she looked out across the street while Bernie was watering her azaleas. She said, "What's that woman up to now?"

Daddy said, "What woman?"

Momma threw an accusing finger out like she was throwing a dart, "*That* woman," and then she marched straight across the street to confront Bernie. She accused her of flirting with Daddy, making obscene gestures at him that Momma mimicked, embarrassing Bernie in front of anyone who was out for an evening walk or sitting on a front porch swing. She said, "What I got is more than you could ever imagine, so stop dreaming sister." Then she stomped back across the street leaving Bernie standing in her yard, mouth agape, incredulous at what had just happened.

Daddy said, "You can't just go do something like that, Evelyn!"

Momma said, "I just did. She had it coming and she knows it."

A few days later, she found a picture of Liz Taylor in *Life* magazine, the movie star stretched out across a page wearing some kind of sexy outfit that Momma decided she just had to have. She ripped the page out and carried it like a devotional, saying, "I hope it will be worth it, having this baby. I like my flat stomach. I think I look sexy, don't you?"

Daddy said, "What in the world does that have to do with the baby?"

Momma snapped back, "Everything," and then she walked out of the house and disappeared in the Buick. She drove all the way over to Winston Salem to fill the backseat full of clothes that she bought on credit. Momma came home around suppertime and stayed up all night mixing and matching outfits until she had what she hunted and thought she looked just like Liz Taylor.

Daddy said, "I ain't paying for all of this shit."

But Momma just pinched her lips into a smile. She said, "You already did, lover boy."

Daddy left after that and once again, Aunt Iris came over to stay and clean up the mess. She told Momma she looked ridiculous in the outfit, called it her crazy clothes. Momma wore Capri pants, a pushup bra, and a sleeveless silk blouse tied in a knot so her soft powder-white skin showed below her bra. She left the blouse loose from the third button up and wore plastic slipper shoes with small rhinestones glued in shooting star patterns across the toes. The shoes flip-flapped loudly, the *pop* of each bare sole slapping skin against plastic to explode like a firecracker going off as she walked across the room. Once she had it on, Momma would not take it off. She started looking in the mirror measuring her stomach and wearing a girdle to keep it from pouching out.

Aunt Iris said, "That can't be good for the baby."

Momma said, "What baby?"

Aunt Iris said, "Don't say such a thing."

She wore the crazy clothes at home and out to places like the Winn Dixie, where she judged her reflection in front of large plate glass windows filled with signs that read, *Star-Kist Tuna 4 for $1.00* and *Boneless Round Roast .79 cents a pound!* Once she even picked me up from school wearing the outfit. I was embarrassed the way she stood outside the Buick posing like some kind of Kewpie doll. Her behavior had slipped so gradually that I couldn't see the whole picture—subtle changes that alone meant nothing, but when poured together in Momma's head and mixed up, meant everything. I was just angry because she was making me look foolish having to ride around with her like that.

Palmer couldn't see Momma chasing her tail either and he loved riding around with her all dressed up and going nowhere. He told her she was prettier than any girl in the sixth grade. Momma smiled at that and said, "Sounds pretty good to me," then kissed Palmer on the forehead, his birthmark burning hot on top of his skull. All Aunt Iris could do was shake her head and say, "Watch out! There she blows!" as things went from bad to worse. The night of the spring concert at my school was when we all came to realize Momma was out of control. Things just got bad that night.

I had been preparing for the show since Easter, missed PE for weeks so I could go to the auditorium and practice my Johnny Appleseed song. I rehearsed in my room at night; learned the lyrics and the simple moves that were given to me by Miss Ferguson. I was embarrassed by how awkward I felt and didn't want anyone to see me.

Palmer cut PE to watch one of the rehearsals and thought I would make a great movie star when I grew up, all sun-tanned and healthy, he said, from living at Myrtle Beach. "One day, you'll leave me to go live on Hollywood and Vine and then I'll only see you on the silver screen."

I said, "Shut up, Palmer. It's just a silly old song." But mostly I was scared I would mess up, and so I practiced and practiced being Johnny Appleseed, skipping around as I pretended to throw imaginary seeds all across the stage.

Aunt Iris drove me to school that evening because Momma was taking too long to get ready, unable to get her lipstick or eyelashes or something just right on her face. She chain-smoked and smelled of Daddy's Jim Beam, and kept saying, "Got to get this right or none of us will go anywhere."

Aunt Iris slipped me out the door and into the Buick while Momma sat in front of the mirror. She let me out by the auditorium and when I asked, "Will Momma be here tonight?" she just smiled and said, "She wants to look perfect for you, that's all. Don't worry. Your Momma will be here, even if I have to bring her myself, I promise." It was a promise I wish Aunt Iris had broken because of the way Momma finally made her entrance.

While she tried to look just perfect for the concert, Momma had turned on the radio to listen to the music of the WBYU request hour. The announcer interrupted in the middle of a song to report that Martin Luther King had been killed on the balcony of the Lorraine Motel in Memphis, a sniper having again taken a life. She had gone into the front room to turn on the television; she wanted to see Walter Cronkite to hear what he had to say about it all, but instead found Bobby Kennedy on top of a platform telling a crowd of angry blacks that he, too, had been victimized.

Bobby Kennedy spoke softly when he reminded the mob there that his brother had been shot down by an assassin's bullet. He asked that they remember his brother as he was remembering Martin Luther King at that moment.

Indianapolis remained calm while the rest of the cities around the country burned and went crazy. It was all Momma needed to see, Robert Kennedy on top of that platform so alone and vulnerable while delivering his message. She could see the assassin's bullet flashing through the darkness, coming out of nowhere to take Bobby down, and so by the time Momma left for the spring concert, she was unable to see straight and understand where it was she was going. Momma drove herself, came very late, flip-flapping down the aisle while Mrs. Terrell's fourth grade class was in the middle of singing "Climb Every Mountain."

It hurt to see her there, how she purposely called attention to herself. Though there were aisle seats vacant in the back, Momma came straight down to the front where the whole auditorium watched her push across people already watching the program to sit in a seat that was broken. The crash drew everyone's attention, the collective gasp enough to stop the show momentarily until the fourth grade accompanist could find her place again in the music. A student usher tried to help after that, her flashlight cutting across the darkened auditorium, pointing out a vacant seat a row behind. But Momma just waved her off and remained squatting on the floor where the wooden seat had given out under her.

At intermission, I watched from the stage curtain as she flip-flapped up to the front door of the auditorium to confront Mr. Cannon, the assistant principal. She could not understand why the concert was still going on when the country was in crisis again, Bobby Kennedy in more danger now and next in line to go. When she confronted him about the danger she felt all around her, he had smiled and tried to be reassuring, but in her spinning head, Momma had seen more.

She said she had felt Mr. Cannon's eyes all over her, that she knew what he wanted. Momma stood right there in front of everybody who was in the lobby buying a Coke or smoking a cigarette and said, "Bobby Kennedy could die tomorrow and all you're interested in is a piece of my ass." Then she slapped his face, called him a son of a bitch and told him to keep his eyes to himself. She flip-flapped back down the aisle, grabbing me off my mark where I stood waiting for the curtain to rise. We left the auditorium before intermission was over, before I could be Johnnie Appleseed. On the way home, Momma almost ran the car into a ditch twice and couldn't stop crying over what she thought had just happened.

Aunt Iris was on the front porch when we got home, and when Momma saw her she just broke down. She was put to bed, the Liz Taylor clothes packed away, everything that might remind Momma of that night hidden out in the garage. Dr. Redmond came by to make sure the baby was all right, then he gave her something to help her sleep. When the house was finally quiet, Aunt Iris coaxed me from my room asking that I sing my song. She said, "You worked too hard on it not to let it out in the air."

Though I was humiliated by what Momma had done, I stood in the kitchen while Aunt Iris gently rocked to the rhythm of the words. "The Lord is good to me/and so I thank the Lord/for giving me/the things I need/the sun and the rain and the apple seed/the Lord is good to me." Aunt

Iris hugged me hard when I finished, my face stained with tears. She said, "Don't forget that Raybert, don't forget the Lord. Despite what you think, you still got a good life; you still got good family."

I said, "Is Momma gonna lose the baby?"

Aunt Iris said, "No, but she better watch out. We all better watch out."

Afterward, I started looking at Momma; I watched her every move wondering what it was Aunt Iris was looking for. All I could see was Momma struggling to be pregnant. It would be much later when I would find out just how dangerous she was to herself, and how far she would go in proving this to everyone. Martin Luther King was buried that week, his casket carried in a simple wagon pulled by two mules as it wound through the streets of Atlanta, but Momma never saw any of it. Aunt Iris kept the television unplugged and stopped the newspaper delivery until she was sure the events that had turned Momma all around disappeared from the front page.

She never apologized about the concert; it was like nothing had ever happened. At school Miss Ferguson gave me my gift for participating in the show, even though I had not sung a note that night in the auditorium. It was an Apollo space pen, a marker that went into space with the astronauts who circled the moon. Miss Ferguson said, "It writes upside down and never runs out of ink. You can keep a diary this summer, if you want, and maybe one day, you will be an astronaut, too."

I liked thinking about being on the moon, flying in the Apollo capsule deep into space as far as I could go. I said I would write every day, bought a brand new Mead Composition, its inside covers filled with useful information, conversion tables of lengths, capacities and weights, multiplication tables and miscellaneous measures of diameters and atmospheric pressures, (information I imagined anyone who worked for NASA would need to know). I would memorize it all while I took time out each day to write in my new diary.

But when school was out for the summer, the pen got stuffed into my book bag and then lost somewhere on my way home. I looked for it, backtracking twice the path I had taken, but it was gone and so I gave up the search. I figured I could keep a diary with any old pen, but when I sat down and looked at an empty page from my notebook, I could think of nothing to write. And when I tried to memorize conversions of weights and linear measures to metric units, imagining myself as an Apollo astronaut, it felt too much like I was back in school, and so I gave up, stashing the book away in my closet for the summer.

Everything seemed to smooth out for a while after that. Momma even started looking for names for the baby in the Bible and classic novels she had read in school. When she found one she liked, she jotted it down in a loose-leaf notebook. She gathered only four and then stopped, satisfied she had found what she was looking for. It would be Jonah or Ahab for a boy because she thought whales were beautiful creatures, strong and mysterious. Beside these she drew a childish picture of a whale as it swallowed Jonah, a stick figure of Captain Ahab throwing a harpoon with a balloon caption that read, *Watch out!* If it were a girl, she would be named Hester or Abigail, Momma said, because they were both beautiful and found strength from their own suffering. She colored in a scarlet letter under both names, an *A* and *H*, and then scribbled a Bible verse, *Upon me alone, be the guilt.* When Aunt Iris read this she said, "Guilt for what?"

Momma said, "Everything," and then she took the book and put it away in her room, hiding it from the rest of us, like what she had inside needed to be protected, kept hidden and safe if the baby inside her was to have any chance at all.

CHAPTER

VIII

The day after school was out, Palmer spent the night and we stayed up late watching *Shock Theater*. It was a swamp monster flick, the *Creature from the Black Lagoon*. We watched into the small hours of the morning as the creature terrorized a remote Amazon River, the beautiful leading lady always making the wrong turn and ending up in the creature's arms. I said, "You'd think she would learn after the first time she ran into that slimy thing."

Palmer said, "I think she likes it. I think it makes her feel good about herself."

The television came to life with Speedy Alka-Seltzer and Wham-O hatching Instant Fish. Palmer moved closer to the screen when the commercial for the fish appeared. He touched the glowing tube with his thin fingers, static electricity crackling against his skin. "Are those things real?"

I said, "They look real to me. They look like real live fish in a bowl."

Palmer said, "I want to get me some of those."

I knew Briggs Hobby Shop had the Wham-O fish, and I knew Palmer had become a pro at five-finger discounts. He probably would have ended up stealing enough for both of us if I'd have told him about Briggs Hobby, but before I got the words out, Evel Knievel flashed across the screen, and for the next sixty seconds soared over cars, fiery bales of hay, and shooting fountains. The jumps were intercut with spectacular crashes, Evel's body a limp rag doll tumbling out of control down ramps, across parking lots, and into retaining fences. The music was Johnny Cash singing "I Walk the Line" and the voice-over promised that the next jump would make history.

Palmer and I sat glued to the tube, leaning in on elbows to get a better look at Evel Knievel while the announcer told us what was coming. With twenty Greyhound buses side by side, a two hundred-foot leap would be attempted by the motorcycle daredevil in the Houston Astrodome, televised around the world. Palmer said, "Would you look at that. If he jumps all those buses, they ought to give him 'Man of the Year.' "

I didn't care one way or the other about any kind of an award; the jump was enough for me. It would be monumental, a technical marvel, something much greater than writing upside down with a space pen. From that moment on, I could think of nothing better than to be Evel Knievel taking off, flying like a bird inside a building that the announcer had called "the eighth wonder of the world." It was something that swept me clear of my family and for a time held my imagination.

I plastered my walls with pictures from newspapers and magazines, posters that had Evel's autograph, a signature and some sort of motto or saying beneath: EVEL KNIEVEL,

FLYING HIGH! EVEL KNIEVEL, JUMPIN JACK FLASH! EVEL KNIEVEL, WHOLE LOTTA SHAKIN GOIN ON! I took baseball cards and clothespinned them to my bike frame so they would pop against the spokes of my wheels. I roared up and down my neighborhood jumping curbs and leaving skid marks as my calling card. I started practicing my autograph in the Mead Composition I had bought at the end of school, my new signature: *Evel Knievel Williams.*

Palmer stole a pair of aviator sunglasses from the Rexall, wore garden gloves and his leather ankle boots when we pedaled around town. He five-fingered handlebar tassels (and Wham-O Instant Fish) from Briggs Hobby Shop. The red, white, and blue strips of fluttering plastic snapped in the breeze whenever we went downhill, and when Daddy asked me where I got such things, I lied, feeling just as risky as Evel Knievel flying through the air.

One Saturday, Palmer and I rode over to Hickory Point while Daddy delivered laundry. He dropped us off uptown and we spent the morning sitting on minibikes that leaned on kickstands along the front of Delbert Green's Sporting Goods. We ran down to the newspaper and put in an application for a route, tried to figure out how many Fridays we'd have to collect weekly subscriptions to afford one of the Briggs and Stratton powered machines.

Palmer said, "We ought to just steal one before you spend that kind of money."

In the sky above us, clouds built until distant thunderheads rolled every afternoon. At night, the air was sticky, the dark sky filling with heat lightning that we pretended came from Evel's motorcycle blasting across the Astrodome's perfect air. There was a storm brewing that we could not see. It filled itself up each morning turning the afternoon sky above Ellenton dark and threatening only to fade in the evening hours, the heat locked to the ground while everyone left fans running all night in opened windows. Palmer and I watched the lightning shows from pallets we had fashioned on my front porch from blankets and pillows. We lay naked except for our underwear, camping out while we sought relief from the heat. Palmer said, "Evel's gonna make that jump, you mark my word. He's going over the top on this one. *Hi yo Silver, away!*"

I said, "Uncle Clewell says the Astrodome's like no other place in the world. Wish we could be there to see it live. It's going to be spectacular."

Lucky Luther and Tommy Patterson built a makeshift ramp at the dead end by the high school. They put things in its path, stacked logs, cinder blocks, lounge chairs, old scooters and broken wagons. They spread the junk out as much as twenty feet past its end. The asphalt was marked on the other side of the junk with a chalked in bull's-eye for a landing point. We rode our bikes up the ramp, slamming on brakes a split second before committing to go over, calling our meager attempts "test runs," and boasting about how we could easily make the jump. We wore football gear for protection, shoulder pads and helmets. Cleated shoes gripped the pedals. Every boy there acted as if he was ready to commit to air and put his fate in the hands of the luck Evel Knievel called upon with varying degrees of success, but no one in a right mind said anything about going all the way.

I wanted to do it, I really did. I felt good about the world I lived in, my family safe and well. Since that crazy night at the spring concert, Momma had been even. Daddy was home to stay, he said, talking about franchising the dry cleaners while he coaxed his yard to grow. Each day, Momma met him on the front porch at noon with tomato sandwiches and homemade sweet pickles she had just canned from the first batch of fresh cucumbers raised in the backyard garden. She had TV trays set up by the porch swing and they ate together, sipping sweet tea while Daddy watched the sprinkler swish back and forth across fragile blades of young grass still struggling to find the way out of soft dirt.

One evening Daddy came home and swooped down on Momma, taking her in his left arm while the right reached around to pull the apron from her waist. He announced that I was old enough to fix my own dinner and that he was taking Momma out for barbecue and a drive-in movie. Momma loved Elvis Presley and they stayed through two screenings of *Viva Las Vegas*, Daddy slipping the car out of one parking space and into another between showings, so they wouldn't have to pay for the double feature. That night as I waited for them to return, I munched on pimento cheese sandwiches and drank Coca-Cola. I believed miracles were possible, that Evel Knievel would make his jump, my momma would no longer be sick, and I would have a new brother or sister soon.

These gathering thoughts of how good my life could be hung in the thickening summer haze altering my view. The ramp suddenly seemed smaller, less of a threat than when in brilliant sunlight and clear air. A surprising wind swept down the street and hit me flush in the face, pushing me the final distance I needed to go. I looked at my bike wanting it to be capable of midair miracles and then turned to Palmer and said, "I'll jump it." I threw my leg over the banana seat and pedaled back to the chalk mark we had set down as the take-off point. Every boy there, surprised by my declaration, encircled the ramp to wait as judge and jury to see if I would actually do it.

Billy Parker yelled out, "Ball crackin', if you miss the mark."

Tommy Patterson said, "You better have the speed or you'll have the need." He grabbed his crotch and hit the ground moaning until I thought Lucky Luther might pee in his pants again.

Billy Parker said, "Shit, Tommy. You a monkey man, you a fucking monkey man."

I aligned my wheel with the ramp a block away, snapped on my helmet and adjusted myself, pulling my goods up to settle them flat against the banana seat.

Lucky Luther screamed, "Holy shit!" and Billy Parker covered his eyes. Palmer said, "Got a cup for your pecker?"

I shook my head no. He said, "Been nice knowing you then."

Lucky Luther screamed, "Holy shit!" again, and I put foot to pedal pushing hard down toward the ground. With all my weight I stood on the pedal of my spider bike, but it did not move. Some invisible law of nature, a law unknown to Evel Knievel, glued my tires to the asphalt. I was scared. Lucky screamed again, but this time his voice was weak and airless, and I could feel in his loss of excitement strong doubt that I would be coming his way anytime soon.

Tommy Patterson said, "I ain't waiting around for Ray-bert to do nothing."

Palmer yelled, "No guts, no glory."

Billy Parker's laugh started to grate on me, his voice obnoxious when he said, "Come on Weevil Knievel, let her rip."

Above us all a sickening green blotted the sky, shadowing the landscape as the storm that had been threatening each afternoon finally reached its critical mass. The first drops pelted me while I held my bike in that fragile balance at the top of the run. The next came accompanied by a concussion of thunder that rattled my teeth and sent us all scattering for cover.

A wet wind soaked through the armor we wore while legs pumped pedals furiously toward home. Palmer and I split off from the rest of the boys in front of the dry cleaning plant, and when we passed the YMCA, a transformer exploded like a bomb, a ball of fire hissing out into the air. Palmer said, "You want to stop?"

I said, "No, keep going," then I looked above me for a funnel cloud. All around, tall trees bent back and forth, sweeping across the angry sky as streetlights were tricked into thinking it was night and flickered on.

At the corner of Robbins Street and Third, the skies ripped open and the air filled with a river of water. I said good-bye to Palmer and watched as he ran through the carport to check on his trailer. Edgar was rushing around the Catalina closing doors, getting ready to throw the tarp back over a car that now stood on four fully inflated whitewall tires.

Pedaling on against the storm, I could see Daddy was home standing in his yard looking to the sky. As the rivulets ran between strands of straw, he shook his head. "It's a goddamn shame what's going to happen here." Then he shook his head again.

Momma looked outside the door and yelled at both of us to come in. Daddy said, "You go on, boy. I'm gonna stay out here for a while." I looked back to the door where Momma stood. She motioned me in with her cigarette, dropping ashes that missed her cupped hand. Her face was drawn and pale, lifeless in the doorway.

When the storm hit full and angry, anchoring itself over Ellenton, Daddy did not budge. He stayed out in that thick fat slab of wind, hail, and rain as the storm pounded him. And it seemed then if someone would've wanted to place a bet against a man drowning standing up, Daddy was ready to take his money. The front screens slapped hard in the wind and thresholds leaked. From inside, Momma and I watched his silhouette become obscured and then reappear in a blinding storm that cracked our house and shook it good. He stayed put for a long while, watched the yard he had tried to grow for Momma drift away—first the straw, topsoil, and seed, and finally any blade of grass that had found a fragile hold in the ground. It rained for three days until the skies were exhausted, the earth saturated and spongy; then it stopped.

I awoke on the fourth to air crystal blue and cool. It tricked my sense momentarily into believing that I was waking on the other side of summer and would have to get dressed and go back to school. I buried my head below covers until I heard voices outside my window. Momma was talking to Daddy about the storm, how the rain had beaten everything down, crushed all that had been planted—not by a single drop of rain, but by the constant pounding, the "endless fucking pounding of a million fucking water bombs." Momma's voice trailed off as she walked away from my window, "It's all shit now, just shit."

We forgot about Evel Knievel's jump as rising waters started to wreak havoc outside the floodplains that spread along Finch Creek. It came up quick after the rains stopped because of the saturated ground, and by the fifth day, the radio reported one-lane bridges out and missing trailers that sat in the flood's path.

Though all of those who lived in my neighborhood were safe, we all knew someone who was threatened by the storm. Palmer and I knew Lucky Luther was one of those who sat in line of sight of Finch Creek. We had been to his trailer house many times and walked easily the distance across a small field to play in ankle-deep waters. We caught crawfish and salamanders scampering away from overturned rocks and played in the giant tunnel pipes that opened up along the red clay banks. The tunnels were Ellenton Mills' attempt to take the water away, to alter its natural flow and push the Finch into an accommodating attitude toward the town. But these forced diversions only seemed to make matters worse just outside of Ellenton.

Once the waters were released from the navigating pipes, the creek would swell rapidly and send all its swollen force against those less fortunate who lived on the low ground below the town limits. Lucky lived along the lowest of the bottom land, and I knew from looking at the wreckage that the storm had wreaked in my own front yard, the Luthers would be displaced again to live most of the summer in a church-sponsored apartment while his trailer was cleaned out or replaced.

In our front yard, Daddy busied himself with reclaiming what had been destroyed. Moss and toadstools were already taking over; anthills appeared overnight. He started tracking a mole that tunneled in a chaotic path, crossing and recrossing until I could not walk to the curb without sinking into the ground. To me, it all seemed helplessly lost. Momma tried to encourage, but the storm had taken something out of her, put her on edge again. There seemed little for her to do except sit in silence, physically drained, and watch the

struggle, first from the porch and then from the picture window, and then, not at all.

In my room, I could block all of this from my sight by
simply walking backward from the window frame until I
changed the perspective with which I viewed the world outside. I kept Daddy out of the frame, the noises of his fa-
tigued attempt to recover the yard fuzzy and distant while
Palmer's house became my primary focus, Edgar Doyle busy
working on the Catalina.

I watched as he released the handbrake and steered RC's
car quietly down into the street until it came to rest over a
storm drain. He set the brake and then walked back up with
lumbering footsteps, his gait slowed like a great weight was
pushing him down.

In the carport he looked through boxes he had yet to
move into the house, the same boxes from which Palmer
had produced the picture of my daddy at Rodney Small's
lynching. I wondered what other horrors might be hidden in
all the wadded up newspaper, if there might be more evidence of his guilt in all the objects Edgar dug out for quick
inspection.

I turned away from the window and went to my chest
of drawers, digging deep behind socks and underwear until
my fingers felt the dull bent edges of the photograph. The
picture emerged into the full light of my room, its vision of
death as real and as certain as it had been each time I studied
the fuzzy images for reasons Daddy would have been beside
Rodney Small that day. I explored the faces of a blurry crowd,
and like a flickering film, my imagination lit up. There, in
full view, Rodney Small swung from the limb of that tree,
Daddy's hand perched and ready to push the boy like a pen-
dulum on a grandfather clock. Though I did not want him to

be that kind of monster, I only had to hear his voice or see him reading the afternoon paper in our den, a Jim Beam and water balanced on his knee, and the silver screen would come alive. It scared me to think of Daddy that way. It scared me more to think that my blood could boil just as hot.

I leaned hard on my bed studying the photograph, alternating my focus between the world of that small picture and the world outside my window. I watched Edgar look back over his shoulder and say something to Palmer. Whatever it was, Palmer seemed to disagree, scuffing his shoes against the driveway, moving at a slower pace than Edgar intended to tolerate.

Edgar's body was thick and his knees stiff. He wore overalls and a wool-lined denim jacket as if he still expected the air to be cool. For a big man who seemed weighted down, he was all over Palmer in a single breath. They struggled, their movements awkward and unbalanced, feet tangled up in a dance gone wrong until Palmer somehow found his footing.

The sudden stability of his small feet holding firm to the coarse driveway jolted Edgar. He lost his balance on the incline, stumbled to one knee before letting go to catch his fall. Palmer crawled free from Edgar's grasp then clawed his way up into his front yard where only a few months earlier we had whacked off Edgar's head. He stood up, shot the finger at Edgar, then got the shit out of there, his short legs spinning like a cartoon whirlwind as he disappeared behind the house.

Edgar stopped short of giving chase. Instead he made his way up the driveway to forage again through boxes strewn around the carport. He walked back down to the street holding a pair of pliers and ratchet set, and then around to the front of the Catalina, where with great effort, he lowered himself to the ground.

The scene made me anxious. I wanted to hurry as fast as I could to be with Palmer, and so I dressed in cutoff jeans and a T-shirt, sliding my tennis shoes on without socks. I was free now that school was out and wanted nothing more than to get away from Daddy, duck his eye so he would not see me and then force me to go to work. I put Rodney Small back into the bottom of my drawer and then climbed out of my window when Daddy passed around the front corner of the house.

Edgar watched from the ground beneath the Catalina as I glided silently down the hill. I hit my brakes in the driveway, coasting into the carport to stop just short of the boxes full of Edgar Doyle's world. Palmer was juggling five quarts of oil in his arms when he came bounding through the door letting the screen slam hard with a *pop*. The cans nearly covered his face as he struggled to keep all five in his small grasp. When he saw me, he smiled, tossed a loose can up into the air and said, "Hey Raybert. Catch that?"

I caught the oil like a sure-gloved Willie Mays and said, "What ya doing?"

"Edgar said, 'Go get me that oil in the kitchen, son.' " Palmer's words slurred out of his mouth, sassing Edgar's orders. "What a shithead. I told him, I said, 'I ain't your son.' Never will be if I can help it."

Then as we headed down the driveway, Palmer's voice changed. His tone became serious like he had found reason to do what he had been told. Palmer said, "It's for the Catalina, so I figured RC would want me to do what I got to do to take care of the car. You know, for down the road."

He smiled after that, like our trip to Myrtle Beach was a done deal.

At the curb, Edgar was coming out from under the car. He moved quickly toward us, towering, blocking our path, the lines in his face cut with anger. He made a quick move and suddenly, I could no longer see Palmer, his small body obscured completely when Edgar cut in between and separated us. I heard him say, "How many times I told you about slamming the door?"

Palmer said, "A million," his matter-of-fact voice muffled and distant from having to travel through such bulk.

There was a pause then, and I could only see Edgar's back, the seat of his overalls soiled from sliding up under the Catalina. On one sleeve of his coat, burnt oil dripped down onto his hand. Edgar said, "Don't be such an asshole; you're being an asshole."

Palmer said, "Takes one to know—" But as if Edgar had anticipated Palmer's remark, he grabbed the boy by his arm before his words found air and whapped him a good one across the face. Edgar said something about getting manners and not putting up with any shit. He said, "Shoot me the finger again and they'll have to visit you in the cemetery with your daddy; do you understand me, boy?"

By then they had backed around to where I could see both of their faces, Palmer's red with an oil mark down along his jaw. When he popped him again, Palmer's feet jerked off the ground. He backpedaled and dropped the cans of oil in a clatter. Edgar looked at his feet, the cans rolling toward the curb and then under the car. "You little shit." He drew his hand back, cocking it twice to make Palmer flinch like a scared dog, and then he spun around to look at me. "And stop fucking around in that closet. You two look like queers in there."

The rage with which Edgar had punished vanished then, and he again became attentive only to the Catalina. He gathered the cans of oil from the street, lined them up on the fender of the car to slice open each thin metal top and pour the fresh lubricant into the engine. Palmer cleaned his wounded face with an oil rag, and we sulked around the curb waiting, picking out small pieces of colored glass from along the gutter. "Treasures," Palmer whispered as Edgar put in the last quart of oil.

He pulled the dipstick to check the level, and then he topped off everything else, the antifreeze, transmission, and brake fluid. He walked around the car surveying its body, kicking tires like it was still sitting on a car lot. He buffed the finish with the clean arm of his jacket and then smiled at us like we had been his good little helpers. Edgar said, "Goddamn, she's good as new. Let's take her for a spin."

At first I didn't want to go. I looked back toward my house thinking maybe my parents would be standing at the curb waving me home so I would have a good excuse to not get in the car. But from that distance, each of them seemed unaware the other existed. Momma swept along the front sidewalk steps while Daddy wrestled with a lawn hose, straightening it out to remove the tangled knots and kinks so he could water the dirt. Though they were in the yard together, they moved like strangers around each other.

Edgar looked at me and said, "Don't worry about your daddy. He won't care, even if he says he does." He slapped both of us on the back of the head with the palm of his hand and said, "Get in, and let's ride out to the quarry."

We could have left right then, could have run away,

jumped on our bikes and ridden out to check on Lucky Luther and his trailer. We could have ridden out to the Evel Knievel jump, done anything other than stay while Edgar put away his tools and then walked back down to the Catalina.

Palmer's face broke out into a reluctant smile as he tried to warm up to the idea of a road trip, the side of his cheek stained red where Edgar had struck him. He said, "It's a test drive for bigger things to come."

Edgar said, "You got that right, now jump in faggots."

Palmer grabbed hold of the latch and swung the door open. "I ain't no faggot."

Edgar said, "You could have fooled me. Now get in."

Palmer climbed in to ride shotgun. He leaned over the front seat to watch as I slid into the back. Edgar adjusted the front seat to fit his thick body behind the steering wheel and then pumped the gas pedal as he turned over the ignition. The starter caught and then let go. It sputtered and spit turning flywheel and pumping piston over and over, rocking our bodies gently as the engine brought the car to life.

Because the Catalina had sat for so long, the engine took time to work itself up to running. It coughed and missed spark, blew black smoke from the exhaust pipe. Edgar cussed when it didn't respond immediately. He slammed his hand down against the steering wheel. "Goddamn niggers, can't build cars worth shit."

The engine finally took hold and Edgar floored the accelerator winding it out, blowing clear the built-up carbon and dust and death. He punished the car for not responding to his first request to go and made sure the engine learned its lesson, racing and revving the accelerator until the whole car vibrated with an anxious need to find a gear and take off.

Alone in the back, I felt sealed in, surrounded by the

smells of a new car, the air metallic, cool, and sweet. I thought to myself, *This must have been the way the car smelled the day RC died. He must have smelled this very smell.* Before I knew what was coming out of my mouth, I said, "RC's got a fine car. That's for sure."

Edgar sliced a look at me through the rearview mirror and then with a cocked arm caught Palmer above his shoulder to elbow him down into the seat. He said, "Both of you faggots just shut up and ride." He put the car in reverse to back off the storm drain and then turned it around, readying the Catalina for its drive out of town, a test drive, as Palmer and I imagined, for better things to come.

CHAPTER
IX

*M*omma was at the curb when Edgar rolled up and lowered his window. She looked into the backseat, a smile crimped on her face like she was pleased to see us. I hoped she would say get out and stay, but Edgar did most of the talking. He said something about "A breath of fresh air on such a fine day." And Momma agreed. She leaned in too far, too close to Edgar I thought when she said, "A drive might do us all some good. Wish I could jump in and come along for the ride." She looked over her shoulder as Daddy came around the corner hauling a wheelbarrow full of fresh azaleas. He glanced at the car, his eyes catching me looking out at him, but he did not stop.

Edgar said, "That'd piss old Ray off pretty good, if you did that." And then they laughed a little, Momma acting more like a schoolgirl than someone holding a growing child in her belly. Edgar said, "We won't get you in that kind of trouble. We'll take care of Raybert. Won't let him get hurt."

Palmer turned around in the front seat and winked at me

97

when Edgar said this. Then he leaned over Edgar's lap and looked out the window. Palmer said, "He's a big boy, Mrs. Williams, but I'll keep an eye if that makes you feel better."

Momma's face broke into the prettiest smile then, like she wasn't afraid anymore of showing her teeth. Her skin was soft with perspiration and the first touches of early summer sun. Small beads of sweat glistened above her lip as she brushed away loose strands of hair with the backside of a gloved hand. She leaned closer to the window so she could see Palmer's face full and said, "Why Palmer Conroy, you are a blessing in disguise. If you're with my boy, then I know you two will be all right." She blew a kiss into the car, one I hoped wasn't meant for Edgar though he laughed and threw his head back as Momma's lips puckered and touched her glove.

Edgar accelerated the Catalina, pulling away from the curb as Daddy stood at the edge of the yard, his arms crossed against his chest looking at Momma, waiting for her attention, her next orders on how and where to place the azaleas. Edgar's eyes darted into the rearview mirror and caught my gaze. He said, "No doubt about it Raybert, your Momma's got what it takes. Evelyn's a fine piece of snatch." He threw his head back again laughing out loud, his words violating Momma and sending forth a sudden fearful jolt that rattled every joint of my body.

I had never heard anyone say such a thing about Momma before and knowing she was pregnant made the comment even worse. I wanted to tell Edgar that he was full of shit. I wanted to say, *Edgar you are so full of shit your eyes are brown!* but there was something that kept me quiet, the notion that this man did things to my momma when Daddy disappeared.

Sometimes, when Momma was ill, she would get in the car and go searching for Daddy. I was her copilot, always.

We drove along through a land of junkyards and abandoned houses, past trailer parks and small dark shanties where bootleggers waited for those who didn't want to make the trip across the river to a wet county. We drove down dirt roads I never could have found in the daylight much less the pitch black Momma navigated through.

We watched from the distance of these roads and alley-ways as men gathered around bonfires and in shadows be-hind abandoned storefronts. The men drank heavy and then slugged away at one another, the power in their fists and arms provoking, intending to do great harm to those who came within their reach.

We would drive until Momma was tired and distant and then return home. She would make a call on the phone, sending me to bed while she still was dialing the number. By the time Aunt Iris arrived to look after me, Momma would be gone, just like Daddy, without a trace. Though it never lasted very long, Momma disappeared a good enough time for anything to happen. That day in the Catalina I wanted to tell Edgar that he was so full of shit that his breath stank, but I couldn't get past the image that had suddenly lodged in my mind of Momma sneaking off to meet Edgar so he could get him some of that "fine piece of snatch."

Edgar never slowed the car down. He ran the stop sign at the top of the hill as he pushed the cigarette lighter and fumbled around through half-filled pockets of his coat for a crushed pack of Winstons. Edgar said, "Ya'll roll those windows down. Let's get some air in here."

Palmer cranked the handle of his window until the glass disappeared into the panel of the passenger door. He looked into the dark felt-covered crack where the recessed glass rested, his round head half in half out of the window. He raised his eyes, studied his reflection in the side-view mirror until a light seemed to go off. Then he pulled himself back into the car, leaned over the seat, smiling, his body bent in half at the waist to balance across the space that separated us. Palmer said, "I wish my momma was like that. I wish we had the same momma. Then I would look like you. I would be beautiful, too."

Even though the car was full of wind, the blustery kind that fills your ears and whips the hair on top of your head, Edgar heard Palmer's remarks and became angry again. Grabbing a handful of his shirt, he jerked the boy back over the seat, pulled him down so hard that the back of Palmer's head smacked against the dashboard. He tumbled onto the floor of the Catalina, stunned and silent.

Edgar said, "You stay there until you think you can stop acting like queer bait." Then his eyes darted across the rearview mirror glaring at me.

I remained frozen low in the backseat and let the wind fill my head. I tried not to look at Edgar or think about the possibility that Momma had been with him in ways she had been with Daddy. The sound of jazz forced its way into my head and nearly made me sick while I sat in the backseat thinking that the noises the music failed to cover might have been coming from Edgar as he filled the void and had his way with Momma.

I closed my eyes and let the wind become waves crashing at Myrtle Beach. I let the motion of the Catalina rock and sway its way toward the quarry. I imagined Palmer driving, not Edgar Doyle. I thought, *This is the way it will be when we leave this place.* I breathed deeply hoping a hint of salted air would find its way into my mouth, that brackish taste that could stay on your tongue for days after a trip to the beach. I wanted that taste in my mouth permanently. I wanted it always as a reminder of why, once Palmer and I were living in RC's trailer, I would never want to come home again.

On the way to the quarry, we veered off Highway 52 and onto a winding two-lane blacktop leading us out into the opposite direction from the quarry. I knew the road because it was the same one Momma had traveled at night when I was her copilot. Momma called it colored town, but it was no town at all, really. It was what the county welfare projects called Sparkstown—"Spookstown," Edgar said, when he turned into the entrance.

The road into the complex of small, whitewashed cinder block houses wound around in a looping circle, breaking off like fingers into six cul-de-sacs. Each finger stretched out to hold eight duplex apartments cramped together with only a clothesline separating them. The streets were filled with black kids, boys and girls congregating, straddling bikes, jumping rope or hanging off the curbs. There was water in some of the buildings, the Finch running high behind the projects, already taking claim to the low land the homes sat on.

"Spooks," Edgar said again, and then shook his head.

Palmer said, "Coons," from on the floorboard and Edgar let him climb back up onto the seat.

Palmer looked back at me and smiled. "They seem to be enjoying themselves, even when their houses are gonna flood."

Edgar said, "Spooks is spooks. They're used to it." Then he laughed, a great explosion that seemed forced, just to emphasize the point. He got quiet the farther back into the projects we drove, stopped looking around, kept the Catalina moving forward, heading to a house deep into the last dead-end finger. He reached over, pushing Palmer against the seat as he opened the glove box and pulled out a silver .38-caliber pistol. The glint off the gun caught both Palmer and me by surprise, and we sat frozen as Edgar jammed the pistol between his legs on the seat. He looked in the rearview mirror, glanced at me, and then over to Palmer. "Spooks is spooks. Ya'll just shut up."

The apartments along this cul-de-sac were in bad shape. One unit had been burned, its contents floating in ankle-deep water. Beside that, two apartments had missing doors, gaping mouths that opened into pitch-blackness even though the sun was high and no longer cast shadows on the ground.

Edgar pulled alongside the curb where a car was set up on cinder blocks and black men lingered around the only door that seemed to open into a dry apartment. He bought a six-pack of Schlitz from a bootlegger, the deed carried out by a young boy who waded out to the Catalina to take Edgar's cash (twice what he would've paid in a liquor store across the river). He returned with six icy wet cans in a brown paper bag, never looked in the car, just delivered the beer and waded back, his eyes always lowered to the rising waters around his ankles. Edgar raised his chin to acknowledge the men, but no one on the porch seemed to even notice he was there. They just talked among themselves, glancing back into the darkened doorway and then to the boy as he returned to the porch.

Edgar backed the Catalina out of the cul-de-sac, keeping his eyes studying the men who ignored him. When we were a safe distance away, he turned the car around and let it pick up speed, waited until we were moving good before he broke the silence, his words low and under his breath so only Palmer and I could hear, "They let their lives float away, but they keep the goddamn beer cold. Ain't that just like a spook." He shook his head, stashed the .38 back into the glove box. We all stayed quiet until the Catalina cleared the projects, then Edgar gunned the engine leaving rubber as the tires spun dry.

The beer stayed on the floorboard between Edgar's feet until the Catalina was again on the highway. There he drove the speed limit while lifting the bag onto the front seat to stuff his hand inside and count his purchase. He put a cold sixteen-ounce can between his legs and pulled the pop-top, the foam spray shooting up onto the dash.

Edgar said, "Shit, goddamn," and then grabbed the chamois cloth to mop off the metal dashboard. He glanced back through the rearview mirror and said, "Ya'll ever have beer before?"

The question turned Palmer in his seat, his eyes deep set in a glowing skull. His little body was just big enough to allow his head to rest on the top of the seat as he sat on his knees facing me in the back. He said, "You don't have to do it if you don't want. I sometimes just take a sip or two. It's only three-two beer, so it's mostly water. Just be careful if you drink some, you still got to go home, you know. Remember for your momma's sake." I nodded at Palmer and watched Edgar's eyes slice through the mirror again as he raised a can to his lips, the foam bubbling out and over into his mouth.

At the quarry, we spread out on flat rocks that lay beneath towering thirty-foot granite walls and dangled our feet in the icy cold water that had first only bled from the rocks when they cut the stone but then suddenly rushed in, filling a twenty-five foot basin and closing the quarry for good. Edgar took off his shirt, revealing a body branded just below his neck and midarms, a perpetual T-shirt of chalky white skin stretching out against the granite slab to bathe in warm sun. He brought the pistol along, laid it on the shirt beside him, the silver barrel glistening in the afternoon light, hot and dangerous.

Palmer and I sat together dipping our feet into the icy water taking turns sipping from a can of beer. He could turn the can up and swallow a whole mouthful while the bitter liquid gagged my throat and forced me to swallow smaller portions hard, hoping it would not come right back up. The beer made us spit and gave us the courage to cuss in front of Edgar. Palmer said shit and fuck out loud. He said goddamn and motherfucker. I said cocksucker and Edgar told us we were faggots again and then opened another beer.

Palmer gathered up the pop-top rings and put them on his fingers. The sharp silvery edges made a lethal weapon wrapped around his fingers like that. He said, "Remember this if you ever get into a fight. Edgar said he seen a man cut the shit out of someone once with these things, didn't you Edgar?"

Edgar leaned back, his large white body spreading out to catch the rays of a sun finally bright and warm against our skin. He said, "Get that shit off your fingers."

When he got a little drunk, he picked up rocks and launched them like bombs into the quarry, sending water splashing back where we sat along our little beach. Palmer found one twice his weight and struggled to throw it into the water near Edgar. Such strength in his arms and legs surprised me. Palmer was small, his features odd and delicate, but he was developing a build far beyond what I would ever carry, low to the ground, a muscular mass that seemed as natural to him as my weediness did to me.

When Palmer's stone hit the water and soaked Edgar, he said, "You little shit," and then picked up a handful of gravel to sling at us as we scattered to find shelter and return fire. We ended up in the quarry water, the cold sharply burning our skin while alcohol buzzed our heads. Edgar drank four beers. Palmer and I shared one, the last one submerged under rocks to keep it cold.

The afternoon took hold, the sun cutting a sharp edge down the eastern wall of the quarry as Edgar stretched back out and talked about his son Ronnie, who was over in Vietnam. I had seen Ronnie Doyle around town before he left for the war, but knew very little about him. He drove a BelAir Sport Coupe, and from time to time came by Third Street to visit Edgar before he and Palmer left to work the YMCA bowling lanes, setting pins and spitting into the holes of bowling balls before sending them back down the rack.

Sometimes Palmer stole magazines and small things like chewing gum and Tootsie Rolls from the Rexall Drug where Erlene Hobbs worked, and when I was with him, we'd hang out across the street and watch Ronnie drive into town to pick her up after work, the BelAir exploding onto Main Street, its mufflers popping like cherry bombs, rattling windows along the storefronts.

When Edgar talked about his son, his eyes lit up, catching hold of the soft color of the quarry water. He seemed a different man from the one who might so easily take advantage of Momma and then laugh out loud about it. It scared me that he could seem good and evil at the same time, but Edgar did that to me, just like my daddy.

Palmer said, "He shouldn't have to go over there to a place like that. I can't even find it on a map. What good is a place that isn't on a map?"

Edgar said, "Don't talk about something you don't know nothing about. It's there all right 'cause that's where Ronnie is, no doubt about it." Edgar downed the rest of his beer and tossed the can like a hand grenade far out into the quarry. He grabbed the pistol and took aim, shooting off three rounds before finally hitting the can.

The shots were like explosions bouncing off the quarry walls and going on forever in my head. Fire blazed from the barrel and Edgar's arm snapped back with the recoil each time he pulled the trigger. Though he was a big man, the gun seemed to size him down a notch, its power obvious to me as I watched him struggle with control.

A cloud of spent gunpowder filled the small beach, and I strained to hear Palmer's dampened voice when he said, "Damn, that's a gun all right. Better watch out with that thing, Edgar."

But he just ignored Palmer, watching the can fill slowly with water. When it disappeared from the surface, he looked back at us and winked, his voice still distant. "He'll be okay, boys. Ronnie's got hand and eye coordination, and my old drill sergeant told me once that hand and eye coordination is what you need to survive in war. He's got that, so I ain't worried. I ain't worried at all."

The year before Edgar moved into Palmer's house, Ronnie Doyle escorted Erlene in the Christmas parade. They were making a debut of sorts, Miss Ellenton Mills being driven by none other than Ronnie Doyle. I had just put Palmer on my shoulders and then slid him onto the top of a mailbox so he could see above the crowd. Behind his head rose the March Hotel where all the street front rooms were open for spectators to gather if you wanted to pay the three dollars for the treetop view. When I looked up, I was surprised to see Momma and Aunt Iris up there. Aunt Iris had been living with us since Thanksgiving and Momma had seemed too frail that morning to show up at any parade.

Still, when I glanced up, there they were, their feet dangling out of a window right above us. I caught Momma's eye and she laughed out loud, blew me a kiss and mouthed the words *I love you*. She pointed to Palmer, asking me with a twirl of her finger to spin the boy around, point him in her direction. When Palmer saw her, his moonlike face exploded into the biggest grin, and he stood up on the mailbox seemingly floating above the crowd and waved.

He yelled up to Momma, his voice exploding again into that shrill girlish pitch, "YOU LOOK LOVELY ENOUGH TO BE RIDING IN THIS PARADE, MRS. WILLIAMS. YOU REALLY DO!" Momma blew him a kiss, too, his small arm reaching out, acting as if he caught the gesture midflight and then stuffed it deep into his pocket. After that, someone hit him in the head with a cup of ice, the impact nearly knocking him off the top of the mailbox. I caught him halfway off and pushed him back up until he straddled and balanced his small body again.

Palmer smiled, ice still clinging to his wool hat and said, "You're momma is like no other. I love her as much as I love you."

I said, "Palmer, shut up," because I didn't want someone hearing him say such a thing in public.

Palmer turned back to watch a Boy Scout troop marching in spit-shined formation, their uniforms tightly creased with neckerchiefs perfectly rolled and knotted at the ends. He applauded this group of boys as they passed, then he bent over and spoke softly, like what he had to say was only for me to hear. "I stole the scout book from Belk's so I can practice being one. I want to do a good turn daily. Look what I can already do." He put three fingers together, the index, middle and ring fingers of his right hand, clasped thumb down on top of pinky to snap the salute. Just then Ronnie Doyle's 1960 BelAir Sport Coupe exploded into the chilly air.

Everyone else who drove a car in the parade was behind the wheel of a convertible on loan from either Uncle Clewell's Cadillac or Chappell's Ford dealerships over in Hickory Point. All the girls sat coatless on top of the backseats and waved at the crowds, never seeming to lose their composure against the cold wind and mist that fell on rosy cheeks. But Erlene sat on the hood of Ronnie's sport coupe and when he revved up that three-fifty, the whole town turned and watched as Ronnie Doyle brought his girl to town. He sat behind the wheel, easing out the clutch just until the gears would bite to send the car smoothly down the street. Perched like an ornament on Ronnie Doyle's hot rod, Erlene Hobbs floated toward us. They simply stole the show.

Palmer stood up again on top of the mailbox and put his hands over his ears whenever Ronnie revved the engine. We watched as the car glided by and then Palmer came down from his perch with a leap to the sidewalk. "We got to follow this guy, he's gonna be famous someday."

We pushed our way up the sidewalk, followed Ronnie Doyle along Main until he turned onto Fifth Street and disappeared into the Winn Dixie parking lot. There the Christmas parade came apart, floats dismantled and crepe paper bunting discarded in the dumpster behind the Winn Dixie.

Santa arrived just as it started to sleet. He jumped off his sleigh and into a red two-door Corvair still dressed in his beard and elf hat, a cigarette dangling on his lip as he sped off using back streets for his getaway. Ronnie Doyle revved the three-fifty while Erlene slid off the hood and ran to get inside. She scooted up next to the shadowy figure, and then they disappeared, leaving burnt rubber on a wet road, heading out toward the old quarry. We were in awe of Ronnie Doyle and the way he drove Erlene Hobbs into town, and from that moment on, he became indestructible.

That day at the quarry, I'm not sure we were worried about Edgar's boy either. But Palmer had other concerns. He looked at the gun lying next to Edgar, his birthmark starting to glow on his head, "But he's got a baby to think about, not to mention that he needs to marry Erlene. He should be right back here working to support his family."

Edgar said, "You talking like your momma now, and I told her to shut up."

Palmer said, "Well—"

"I said, you don't know what you're talking about." Then he took his hand off the gun and put his arms behind his head to lean back and close his eyes.

I picked up a flat rock and slung it sidearm out across the water toward where Edgar had shot the can, watched it skip five times before disappearing below the surface. I said, "Here Palmer, throw this rock," but he just ignored me.

Palmer said, "Ronnie explained the whole thing to me, how Erlene missed her period and started throwing up in the mornings on the way to her job at the Rexall. He did the deed in the backseat, right out here. Probably right over there, where you parked RC's Catalina."

Edgar cracked open one eye and raised his head in his hands.

Palmer said, "Erlene just smiled and said 'I love you Ronnie Doyle.' Then Ronnie said she closed her eyes like she was waiting for him to do the deed. That's what Ronnie told me before he left, that day he come over to give you the keys to the BelAir. I think they make a great couple, don't you?"

Edgar sat up then, a beer can dangling between an index finger and thumb. He reached beside him and grabbed the gun, cocked the hammer and pointed it at Palmer.

"Goddamn, Edgar."

He wagged the barrel of the gun at the boy, narrowing his eye like he might be taking aim. "I don't know that the baby is even his, but they won't let me have nothing to do with that, and I won't let you. You understand me?"

The reflection from the quarry was gone. Left instead were black holes that set above Edgar's unshaven jaw, deep sockets opening into nothingness, a threat that Palmer should back off or else. When the boy looked away, when he came over beside me and slung a rock sidearm into the quarry, Edgar pulled the trigger and again blew apart the quiet. The bullet sucked below the surface of the quarry out in front of us and Palmer screamed in that strange voice, "GODDAMN, EDGAR, THAT AIN'T FUNNY!"

Edgar put the gun beside him and then lay back down. He said, "Now you boys go suck each other's dicks like you do in that closet. I'm gonna take a nap."

We left him in the quarry but not before Palmer took one last long look at the pistol. He took steps like he was thinking about swiping the gun, maybe doing to Edgar what he had threatened to do to us when he pulled the trigger that second time. Unbelievably, the bullet had zipped between the two of us, split down the middle, chest high with enough power to push me backpeddling on my heels until I fell at the water's edge. Before he got close enough to snatch anything, Palmer did an about-face and ran out of the quarry leaving me alone with Edgar while he took his nap.

I was scared looking at Edgar Doyle that day, afraid he might pop an eye open and see me staring, have second thoughts about what he had just done, then grab the gun and finish me off once and for all. My legs, still weak and shaking, lifted me without my knowing it, and I found myself running quickly up to where the Catalina sat alongside the road with Palmer already behind the steering wheel.

I got in the backseat and leaned over, my face close enough that I could have kissed him on the cheek. I whispered, "Palmer, Edgar don't want you talking about Ronnie Doyle no more."

Palmer said, "I don't give a shit what he wants. He ain't RC."

I said, "It's just, I think you ought to be careful what you say, that's all. That's all I'm saying, be careful. Don't lie too much about things. He's got that gun."

We sat in the Catalina for a long time staring out to a road that ran empty and straight, nothing along the way but stubble fields and scattered gum trees. It seemed Palmer just wanted to leave, wanted to go to Myrtle Beach right from the quarry and never return to Ellenton or anyplace where he would have to live with his family. He never said anything to me about leaving that day. I just figured it was on his mind because he sat there holding on to the steering wheel and looking out to the road, his birthmark about to burn right off the top of his skull. We had to wait for Edgar because he had the keys. We waited for him to wake up and finish off his last beer and then we went home.

While the Catalina was backed into the carport, I went

inside to call Momma and tell her I wanted to spend the night. She seemed distant and tired and said that Bo Wilkins had called on Daddy to join a group of men who were needed to help rescue someone caught in the rising waters of Finch Creek. I asked if she wanted me home, but she just said, "Is Palmer looking forward to your visit?"

I said, "I guess so."

"Then don't disappoint your little friend. Palmer Conroy is an angel." She hung up the phone without saying good-bye.

Outside, the late afternoon sun raced against us. It was a shadow sun, hovering low on the horizon, creating lengthy shadows three to four times our real height. It made us giants with arms stretching across the street, legs that reached out past Third.

With half a beer still buzzing our brains, Palmer said, "Look," and stuck his shadowed arm out over the road, timing perfectly the arrival of a UPS truck into the intersection. It ran over his arm, clipped the shadow in two as Palmer pulled the real thing through the sleeve of his T-shirt. He let out a yell, fell to the ground and rolled around in the grass. Palmer said, "One armed man, one armed man," and then he sat up on his knees. "*The Fugitive,* a Quinn Martin Production." He yelled again in mock agony, his good arm feeling across to where the shadow had been disconnected. When he had writhed in pain long enough, sensed my disinterest growing, he stood up and said, "Now watch this," and from his shadow, longer still from the sun's trek downward, imbalanced and deformed, another arm appeared, slowly, magically.

I watched his shadow grow out of nowhere and believed for a moment I was witnessing a miracle. When the shadow was near full extension, Palmer put a finger from the other hand in his mouth and pulled against his cheek, popping the air, a round full *pop!* that seemed to propel the shadow to its greatest length, complete and renewed.

By now the sun singed the tops of houses, washed Robbins Street orange, deep and rich. Palmer was translucent in the late afternoon light, his birthmark a fiery halo on top of his skull. In a willingness I only had when I was with my best friend, I imagined him as the angel Momma believed him to be. I waited, holding my breath to see the sky above us, blue and tinted with nightfall, open, and Palmer, angelic and on fire, ascend into heaven. He began to flap his shadow wings and call out, "Caw! Caw! Caw!" He ran around the yard moving his arms smoothly, rubberized so that the shadow appeared to be fluid, flawless, and capable of flight. I closed my eyes and prayed, whispering under my breath, "Fly Palmer fly. Fly Palmer fly!" When I opened my eyes, tears flowed down my cheeks. Palmer saw me crying, stopped in mid-flight, and lowered his wings to his sides. Palmer said, "You're drunk." Then the sun went *Poosh!* and fell behind the houses, turning the air blue, the light flat. I wiped my face, embarrassed and afraid Palmer would laugh out loud. Instead, he sat beside me and put a hand on my shoulder. Palmer said, "Don't cry over spilt milk."

I said, "I thought you'd fly. I thought you were an angel."

Palmer laughed at that. "My momma says I'm the devil in disguise."

"Your momma's wrong, Palmer."

"She says I ain't got a snowball's chance in hell."

"Your momma's crazy, Palmer."

"She says when they gave out brains, I thought they said rains and ran for cover."

I said, "Your momma talks funny."

"She wanted me to be a girl, wanted to name me Pamela."

I said, "I like you the way you are."

"Well sometimes I think I am a girl. I take my pecker and put it between my legs and look at myself in the mirror."

"That's disgusting."

"I just wonder sometimes, that's all."

I said, "Momma thinks you're an angel in disguise."

"Then can I be her son, too?"

I said, "I think that would be okay with her. I think she would like that a lot."

Then Palmer put his arm around me, "We dodged a bullet today, Kemo sabe."

I said, "That's the last time I want to ever go anywhere with Edgar."

Palmer said, "No shit, Sherlock."

As we lay sprawled on the sidewalk, the heat making our backs sweat, Palmer did something unexpected. He rolled over on his stomach leaned against me and kissed my cheek. It wasn't a spectacular kiss, just a peck, a dry smack on my salty skin. Palmer said, "No matter what happened today, you're safe now."

I said, "You do that again and you won't be." Still, the touch of Palmer's lips stayed on my cheek long after I wiped the spot with the back of my hand.

That night we stayed in the crawl space until Edgar and Inez went to bed. When the house was dark, Inez and Edgar sound asleep, Cindy snuck out to meet Johnny Troutman. Palmer said, "Come on," and we left to sneak around the back and watch.

Cindy Conroy was beautiful. She was dark and disturbing. She was sixteen, a hippie and slacker who cut sixth period to get high on Friday afternoons. When she saw Palmer and me following, she stopped in the middle of the yard, mouthed the word "idiots," then shot us the bird as she ran for the intersection.

We stayed where we were and watched as Johnny Troutman dissolved out of shadows, stood silently beside his Barracuda waiting for Cindy to sprint across. Under the soft light of the streetlamp, he kissed her, pulling her body close with hands molded to her ass. We could hear Cindy giggle when he did that, and then he opened the car door and they both disappeared inside.

The engine shattered the quiet as it roared to life. Johnny cut a donut in the intersection a block away, and then double-clutched out of second and third when he straightened the Barracuda out. We listened to the explosion of power and peeling rubber fade into the distance heading for destinations we could barely imagine, though now we were helped along greatly knowing Erlene Hobbs and Ronnie Doyle had done the dirty deed at the quarry.

Palmer said, "That Barracuda runs like a bat out of hell."

I said, "You got that right."

He said, "I'd like to see Ronnie Doyle teach Johnny a thing or two."

I said, "Two bats out of hell, I reckon."

"Hell, yeah. But if RC knew what Cindy was doing, he'd wear her a new ass."

I said, "I like the one she's got."

He said, "So does Johnny Troutman." And then Palmer turned around. He looked back over his shoulder just to make sure we were alone, like what he would say next needed to be kept low to the ground. Palmer said, "Think the Catalina will make it to Myrtle Beach?"

Without hesitation, I said, "No doubt about it," because that night I really believed it would.

Palmer repeated my words, "No doubt about it," though I wondered if he was as sure of his own idea as I was.

He led me back under his house and into the crawl space. We stripped to our underwear, pried open the trapdoor and climbed back through the narrow hole into his closet. Palmer went to the bathroom then to fill a glass with water. He came back and poured it onto his bed. He said, "This will piss RC off, but it'll piss off Inez even more."

I said, "Palmer, you beat all I've ever seen."

Palmer smiled at that, his head glowing in the dark. "I'm an angel in disguise, and don't you forget it."

We moved back into the closet as a small exhale of musty air pushed up through the trapdoor and chilled our bodies. In that darkness, the space between us became too great and so we scrunched up together, the reluctance I always carried for Palmer's embrace suddenly gone. Why on earth it disappeared on that night, I would never be able to say. Maybe it was because I just wanted to feel safe, to believe Palmer Conroy really was the angel Momma wanted him to be. I remember praying while Palmer held on tight that we could stay this close and be safe forever. Maybe that's what it was all about after all, this boy Palmer Conroy. That night I had nothing else to pray for, nothing else at all.

CHAPTER

X

I stayed with Palmer throughout the morning watching cartoons and waiting for Cindy to come out of her bedroom. We heard her sneak back in before dawn, Johnny Troutman's Barracuda popping and idling as he eased into the intersection, and I lay in the closet thinking about her getting ready for bed, her naked body in her window or maybe her shadowy figure walking across the hall to the bathroom to brush her teeth. Palmer had stolen nudie magazines from the Rexall Drug, and so I imagined as well Cindy standing in front of a mirror in only stockings and ridiculously high heels, her hands raised above her head to fix a ribbon in her hair—Cindy Conroy, butt naked and glistening in the moonlight.

I got up in the softening darkness and tiptoed out to the bathroom, hoping I might catch a glimpse of what I wanted to see, but Cindy never showed. I stood over the toilet until Palmer came through the door whispering that he was worried I'd fallen in. He told me not to flush because it might wake up Edgar and Inez and then we would both get in trouble. He took my hand and led me back to the closet. I left standing pee in the toilet and Cindy in her room where my imagination wandered sliding underneath the dark crack at the bottom of her door to look at what I imagined Cindy had already shown Johnny Troutman.

Later that morning, it was time for me to go home. The Conroys' phone had rung for what seemed like an hour until Inez finally answered it. She came back into Palmer's room holding a bottle of Lysol in one hand and a toilet brush in the other to tell me I had been summoned home. She looked at Palmer and said, "Raybert's got to go and you got to clean that toilet. If you're not gonna flush it, you can learn to clean it." I looked at Palmer knowing he was getting in trouble because I had peed and not flushed, but he just pushed me through the door and said, "I didn't do that. I peed in bed last night. It was Cindy. She's a pig. You make the pig do it."

When Inez saw Palmer's wet sheets, she exploded and we ran as fast as our feet would carry us outside. From the front yard we could hear Inez through open windows screaming at the top of her lungs, beating on Cindy's door to get her up. We stood awash in light so flat, it erased all shadow and left the houses and trees and cars parked along the curbing exposed and featureless, a two-dimensional flatness that I felt if I reached out and touched would be nothing more than a photograph, not my life as I was living it. I asked Palmer if he wanted to come home with me, but he said no.

I said, "But you can't go back in there."

"I don't want to go back in there. I'll be all right."

"Cindy is gonna be pissed."

"She can't do nothing. She's got bigger fish frying than

that. Besides, she knows I'll tell Edgar about Johnny and then her ass will be grass. She'll leave me alone."

We looked up the street and saw Uncle Clewell's DeVille sitting along the curb. Palmer said, "Looks like you got company. Better get going."

I said, "Yeah, guess so," though at the moment I wanted to stay with Palmer and be an accomplice to whatever it was he had planned. I could not see what, if any good at all, Uncle Clewell's car carried with it, sitting at the curb in front of my house with the engine turned off. It was a bad sign; it always was.

Sweat trickled down the small of my back as I pedaled up into the alley. In the backyard, I could see clothes scattered on top of the straw, so oddly out of place, they appeared to hover above the ground, impossible to miss. What lay there belonged to Daddy, a couple of T-shirts, a pair of pants, underwear, and socks. I found boxes inside the garage that were overflowing, full of Daddy's things. I walked onto the back stoop careful not to be heard as I stood listening to Uncle Clewell and Aunt Iris talk.

Uncle Clewell said, "Do you think she knows what's going on?"

Aunt Iris said, "She knows. She told me what she did, but Ray doesn't know yet, and nobody knows where he is. He hasn't shown up at the cleaners yet."

"You want me to go in there—"

"No, that will just make it worse. You stay here. I'll need you when Dr. Redmond calls, so just wait."

Uncle Clewell put his coffee cup down and walked out. I waited until I heard the front screen slap shut, knew he was on the porch, then I stepped into the small cramped space where brightness dimmed into a dreary light. Aunt Iris looked up from the table when I came inside. She smiled, her face lifting momentarily before it was dragged back down by the weight of the moment.

I stood by the door watching her scribble notes on a piece of paper and sip coffee from a cup she set on the table without a saucer. I said, "Is Momma all right?"

"She's having some trouble with the baby, but she's all right."

"Is Daddy here?"

"No. He's not."

"Did he leave again?"

Aunt Iris nodded and then stopped writing. "Did you have fun with Palmer?"

"Yes ma'am, it was okay."

"Good, that's good you had fun."

I said, "Did he leave because of the baby?"

"No, that's not it at all, honey."

"Then can I see Momma?"

Aunt Iris sighed deeply like what I was asking might be impossible. "She needs to rest now, maybe later." She forced a smile across her face, looked up at me after sipping her coffee. "Why don't you go sit on the front porch with Clewell and see if your daddy comes home? Dr. Redmond is supposed to call us back real soon and I don't want to miss him. Your momma will probably have to go to the hospital."

Momma's miscarriage had started shortly after Daddy came back from the rescue at the Finch. I heard Aunt Iris tell Uncle Clewell about how Daddy had come back home, broken down and exhausted, to find all his clothes thrown into boxes and sitting at the kitchen door. Something was said about Bernie Potter, and then Daddy left without saying a

120

word. Momma just watched him go. She never said *stay* or
don't come back; she just stood there throwing his clothes out
the back door until he was gone and then she carried the
boxes out into the garage. That's when she had cramped real
hard, once, a cramp that doubled her over to the floor and
then nothing but a silence that she told Aunt Iris was felt so
deep inside her, she knew then the baby was dead. She said
she could feel it leaving her body, that little soul rising right
out of her, leaving her shivering there on the tile floor. She
called Iris and tried not to move, tried to hold still so her
baby could leave peacefully, but then she cramped again
and, before she could crawl to the bathroom, soiled her
panties with blood.

On the front porch, Uncle Clewell read through the afternoon paper, his eyes never looking up except whenever he
would glance down the street to search for Daddy's familiar
shape. He read until he could no longer stand the heat, then
he fanned himself with a cardboard fan kept close by on the
floor beside the swing. While he pushed the hot air around
his face, Uncle Clewell looked over at me like he had just
remembered something important. "Don't you have a birthday coming up soon?"

I said, "Yes sir, next month."

"You asked for anything yet?"

"No sir, but I know what I want."

"And what's that?"

I looked out toward Palmer's. The curtains were drawn
tight, the tarp pulled snug around the Catalina. There was
no life to be found in the house or around the yard. I said, "I
want one of them GI Joes."

Uncle Clewell said, "A GI what?"

"A GI Joe."

He pushed the fan harder around his face. "Won't you be thirteen, this time?"

"Yes sir."

"Well your daddy won't get you a baby doll, you know that."

I said, "He ain't a doll. He's an army soldier. He's got a rifle, a knapsack, a helmet, and wears army fatigues. That don't sound like no baby doll to me. He's even got dog tags. Billy Parker's got one with a footlocker full of stuff from two branches of the military. We floated one down the Finch a couple of weeks ago in an Air Force life raft. Ain't no doll that does that kind of stuff."

Uncle Clewell looked at me like I had convinced him of something, then he said, "Well he won't get you no GI Joe either. You better start working on your momma if that's what you want."

"She's sick right now, so I can't."

Clewell said, "No you can't right now, you're right about that. But don't wait too long, your birthday will be here before you know it."

The phone rang and Uncle Clewell stopped fanning himself, his attention drawn inside while Aunt Iris talked to Dr. Redmond, her voice low and full of concern. When she finished with the call, he stood up to go inside. "Get ready, Raybert. We got to take your momma to the hospital."

I said, "Is she all right?"

Uncle Clewell said, "She's gonna be all right, but the baby ain't gonna make it. Your momma's having a miscarriage. I'm sorry about that, son."

It was the first time I had ever heard the word miscarriage, and it brought to mind the image of Momma on a stagecoach that was broken, a wagon wheel fallen off and the passenger carriage crashed and tilted over in the desert. Beyond the stranded stagecoach, on a high mesa, Indians were watching, ready to pounce down with bows and arrows and spears and knives to take scalps. I'd seen a western on Sunday afternoon TV, John Wayne in black-and-white, playing Ringo the Kid. He rode along on a stagecoach carrying a pregnant woman. She was on her way into Indian country to be with her husband who was fighting Geronimo and his warriors. She delivered the baby when a drunken doctor sobered up enough to do his duty. That baby in the movie lived.

I whispered the word, "Miscarriage," my lips sticking together from dried skin making it difficult for me to form the word, get it out into the hot air. Then I thought of Daddy and how he left Momma alone, allowed this miscarriage to happen. I wondered if he was drunk somewhere, unable to come to her rescue. I hated him more now, accused him silently of killing again, guilty of a miscarriage, as he had been guilty of letting Rodney Small swing from that tree.

When Momma came out of her bedroom, she was so weak that Uncle Clewell had to carry her to the car. She looked across her shoulder and tried to smile as they swept past, moving down the front porch steps toward the open door of the DeVille. Her hand, draped across his shoulder, pointed to me and I heard her ask Clewell to stop for a moment, her breath pushed in order to get the words out and into Clewell's ear.

He swung Momma around and looked back at me standing motionless on the steps. "Come on over here son, your momma wants to tell you something."

Momma's head lay on Clewell's shoulder, her eyes narrowed down to small slits so I could hardly tell she was alive.

Her mouth cracked along the edges into a slight smile, and I raced down the steps afraid that if the smile let go, then Momma would, too. When I came to her side, she lifted her head and leaned over as best she could, her arm tight around Clewell's neck so she wouldn't lose her grip and fall. "Were you good at Palmer's?"

"Yes ma'am, I was."

"Did you have fun?"

"Yes ma'am."

She stopped then, her eyes opening wide as she reached out to touch my face. Uncle Clewell said, "We got to go Evelyn; Dr. Redmond's waiting."

Momma ran her fingers down my cheek, rubbed out a dirt spot on my chin. "You need a bath."

I said, "I know. I'll take one tonight."

She said, "I guess Ahab won't come home this time, or Hester. Did you like those names or did you want Abigail and Jonah?"

I said, "Jonah would be fun if he was my brother, but that's all right. I don't need him now. I got Palmer."

Momma's eyes brightened when I said that. She smiled and lay her head back down on Clewell's shoulder. "You remember that when Clewell comes back from the hospital to talk to you. You remember Palmer, okay?"

I said, "Yes ma'am," but I was surprised I had even said it. I wasn't thinking about him at all when the words just flew out of my mouth, *I got Palmer.*

Momma closed her eyes then, "You're still my special boy. You don't have to worry about that being taken away."

I tried to tell her I didn't worry about things like that, but Uncle Clewell had already put her in the backseat and shut the door.

Aunt Iris leaned across the seat to give me orders. "You eat a pimento cheese sandwich and drink some milk for lunch. Don't get into anything because Clewell will be back after we get your momma to the hospital."

I stepped back from the curb and watched Uncle Clewell make a U-turn in front of our house, the Cadillac's bulk too much for such a maneuver in our narrow street. Uncle Clewell had to bump up on the curb across from our house to make the turn and this brought Bernie Potter up and out from her azalea beds. Her hair was tied in a bandana and she stood smoking a cigarette watching the hurried action in front of her. As Uncle Clewell accelerated, Aunt Iris leaned out her window and said, "You eat your lunch and stay out of trouble, you hear?"

I said, "Yes ma'am, I will," and then they were gone. Uncle Clewell, just like Edgar had done the day before, paid no attention to the stop sign at the top of the hill.

I stayed at the curb for a moment watching the corner, half expecting Clewell to come back and half hoping I would see Daddy appear, now that Momma was no longer around. Neither of these things happened. I stood until Bernie Potter spoke quietly from across the street. She said, "Was it the baby?"

I said, "Yes ma'am, she's gonna lose it."

"She's having a miscarriage?"

"Yes ma'am. That's what Uncle Clewell said."

Bernie lifted a hand to adjust her bandana. "You want me to fix you lunch, honey? I got fresh tomatoes and sweet pickles."

"Aunt Iris told me to wait for Uncle Clewell. He'll be back soon."

"Well, I'm real sorry about Evelyn, but I'm sure she will

be all right. The doctors will take good care of her, get her fixed up in no time. You're her pride and joy, growing up so fast. I know both your parents are proud of you."

I smiled. "Yes ma'am." Then Bernie turned and disappeared back down into her azalea beds.

I stayed on the porch forgetting to eat until my stomach ached and burned. When a late shower moved in, I went to the kitchen and fixed pimento cheese sandwiches, just like Aunt Iris told me to do. I sat at the kitchen table while the rain plopped and slapped in puddles out beyond the small back porch. I felt afraid my house might stay like this forever, Momma and Daddy both gone and Uncle Clewell having forgotten to come back for me.

Palmer and I had escape plans and I was more ready than ever to go, but there was more time to come and the rain seemed to wash away any other prospects. I knew one thing for certain, I would not have an Ahab or Jonah or Hester or even Abigail as a baby brother or sister. The names Momma had scribbled in her notebook and then kept safely hidden away would never be used. They would remain only words to be looked at or read, unattached to anything that lived and breathed in this world. I would only have Palmer Conroy, and at that moment in time sitting at the kitchen table, he seemed like enough for me. So I ate and waited for the storm to pass, for someone to return home to give me some news.

CHAPTER XI

*A*fter a while, the rain eased up and then disappeared completely, leaving in its place a boiling sun to steam the streets and rooftops. I felt uncomfortable at the kitchen table, a sweltering feeling that made me want nothing more than to strip naked and lie on the cool tile floor. It was only the unknown, who might show up or when, that kept me clothed and waiting for what was next to come.

When I heard the front screen slam, I jumped up from my seat thinking it was Uncle Clewell until I suddenly came face to face with my daddy in the hallway. The narrow passage caught us both off guard, and as I stood staring at his dark figure, I could see that he had been fighting again.

He had a large gash below his right eye that was patched, the lid nearly swollen shut. Dry blood caked around his nose, and his left ear was taped up, but it wasn't until I followed him outside that I could see the top third was gone.

We stood on the front porch, Daddy sizing me up as he spoke. "What're you doing here?"

"Momma's at the hospital and—"

"I know about that, what're you doing here by yourself like this?"

"Aunt Iris told me to wait here. I thought you were Uncle Clewell."

Daddy stopped then. "Wait here." He went back inside into the hallway and called the hospital, talked to Uncle Clewell in a low and quiet voice. He asked about Momma and then listened for a long time before he spoke again telling Uncle Clewell he was glad he had been there to take care of her. Daddy said he was at home, that we were together. "I got him here and everything's fine. I'll tell him what he needs to know and then bring him on out."

When he hung up the phone, I heard him in the kitchen, "Goddamit." I looked through the screen door and saw Daddy coming back through the hall. His ear dripped blood onto the floor as he went into his bedroom and then came back out again, looked around like he had just lost something out of his pocket. Daddy said, "She moved me out. Where'd she put the goddamn boxes?"

I said, "Some of it's in the backyard. The rest of it's in the garage."

Daddy disappeared out the back door, and when he returned, wore a clean T-shirt, the blood from his ear already staining the sleeve. He slipped into the bathroom, grabbed a wet washrag to cradle his wound and stop the bleeding.

I said, "Did you get bit by a dog?"

Daddy laughed a little at that. "Might as well been a dog, I guess."

"Can I see?"

"Ain't nothing to see. Now come on, we got things to do. Then I'm gonna take you to Clewell's for a few days while your momma gets better."

"Is Momma all right?"

Daddy turned his back and started down the steps, "She will be; now come on."

Coggin Philpot's truck was idling at the curb waiting for us when we left the house. Daddy didn't say nothing, just sat behind the wheel, concentrating on shifting gears, the truck lurching slowly down the street, carrying the weight of a cement vault strapped on the flatbed behind the cab. The truck's girth swallowed the narrow road, branches on low hanging trees swatting at the crane. The air was hot like a furnace had been lit and was blowing right through the window as the truck turned out of town and headed in the opposite direction from the cemetery.

I said, "This ain't the way to Happy Hill."

Daddy said, "We ain't delivering. I got to take the truck back and get the Buick."

The truck smoked out of the exhaust pipe and over-heated, telling Daddy to ease up when the HOT light flickered on. He let it coast on hills, revved the engine as it idled so more water could course through the block. He looked over at me when we were a good ways out of town, when we were coasting a hill. Daddy said, "Look out over there," his chewed up ear gesturing back out beyond his window.

From the road, I could see a long red scar snaking its way against the green landscape. I could see where trees had been cut and the ground leveled. A new road was taking shape right down to the Finch Creek overpass where it was to empty back into the Interstate. Daddy said, "Fifty-two's gonna by-pass this part of the county, take the rest of the world right past Ellenton. When they finish that road, we're deader than we already are." He grabbed the gearshift to find second and begin a long climb up from where the hill had just bottomed out. "They're creating a no-man's-land out here, already relocated twelve families surveyed into the right-of-way. The state moved two homes and tore down the rest. That's why those trailers went up down along the Finch. That's why Lucky Luther lived down there. His house was bulldozed a couple of years ago and his family relocated."

I said, "I seen Lucky's trailer. He seems to like it out here." But Daddy didn't say anything else. He just concentrated on the road.

I looked out the window as we crossed the Finch on a narrow one-lane bridge, leaving signs of the new highway behind us. The sun was just dipping below the tree line shooting orange sparks off the water that burned the edges of the leaves, setting them on fire. I don't know what got into me at that moment, made me confess, but I did. I guess I figured it was summer and what I was about to say had little weight to it now that school was out. I said, "Palmer and me seen the finches come back one day when we cut school. They swooped out of nowhere and filled the trees out in the Finch like they knew exactly where they were going."

Daddy took his eyes off the road to look at me. "When did you cut school?"

I said, "Back some time ago, when Palmer needed to visit RC."

Daddy said, "You ride your bike out to the cemetery?"

"Yes sir."

"How many times I tell you not to go out on that road? A truck come along that narrow piece of shit and hit you and never know it? You could be laying in a ditch for weeks before somebody would find you."

Then I said, "Well, that didn't happen, did it? We didn't see one thing the whole time we were on that narrow piece of shit." Daddy reached over and started to hit me in the face, but stopped short as I ducked, when the truck started to labor up the next hill and he had to fight the stick again to give the truck more gear. From the corner of my eye, something flashed out of the gully and before Daddy could do anything about it, he ran over a dog.

Neither one of us saw the mutt dart out from the side of the road trying to chase the tires. It misjudged the angle of its attack and ended up underneath the flatbed, tumbling over and over yelping like it was on fire. From where we stopped we could see the dog in the road squirming, biting at its ass.

I screamed, "You killed a dog, Daddy! You killed a dog!"

Daddy said, "Shut up," and then he got me good, caught me twice hard across the face. He jerked the door open, hopped out of the cab and reached under the seat to take out a .45 pistol. "Goddamit. When does it ever stop? Now you stay in the truck, don't move."

The dog lay breathing shallow quick breaths watching Daddy moving toward it. It shook hard, foamed at the mouth, and pissed all over itself, tried to get up but couldn't, its back legs already dead. Daddy kneeled down on his haunches to take a good look at the damage done by the truck. The dog seemed resigned to the fact that it was going to die, so it lay there with its neck stretched out, bowed up to look at Daddy waiting for what he would do next.

He stood up slowly, looked around to see if there was a

house nearby, an owner who would want to know what was about to happen. But there was nothing in sight, not a driveway or a side road where someone might live, so Daddy put the dog out of its misery. He got the gun real close, his right arm extended outward to its head. There was a flash of searing light, an explosion of gunpowder. The body jerked once before flopping silent in the heat.

He came back to stand for a minute in the open door of the flatbed, to put the gun away. I looked back over at the dead dog in the road, its belly already distended. My face stung where I had been popped good and I sat pinned against my door as far from Daddy's reach as I could get just in case he wanted to do more damage.

He looked at me then shaking his head, "Look, I got too mad a minute ago. I shouldn't have hit you like that, but you better not let me catch you doing any of that shit again. You hear me?"

I said, "Yes sir."

"Hell, I'm not sure I'd have hit that damn dog if you—" but then he stopped, didn't go any further with that. He lit another cigarette, drew deeply to fill his lungs then looked up in the sky to follow something with his swollen eyes. "You know, I seen those birds once myself, a long time ago. Scared the shit out of me when they flew in."

I said, "I never seen anything like that, there must have been a million flying around us. Palmer thought it was a sign of something good to come, but now I don't know. Now I'm not so sure anymore."

Daddy said, "They use to come in here so thick that they'd fly into chimneys and clog up vent pipes with their nests. Hell, I had one fly down a heat vent once and get caught up in the blower fan of a furnace. Years ago the sheriff department shot them out of the sky when they swarmed, thought they were killing old black catbirds, but when they started falling they realized it was finches. They weren't black at all. They were blue, a beautiful deep blue in the feathering. They stopped when they saw what they had done and everybody had to put screens over their vents and chimneys. That finch is a beautiful bird when you look at it up close. Thing is, you got to get up close to see it or else you'll make a mistake and think it's just an old catbird."

He looked back to the dog, flies already finding the blood that soaked its short brown mat. He pulled hard to get everything he could out of the burning tobacco before he flicked the spent butt into the gully alongside the road. Daddy looked tired all beaten up like that, and I wondered then if he had seen the birds the day Rodney Small was hanged.

He let the smoke leak from his mouth and nose while he felt around his pockets, reached inside the one riding his left hip and pulled out a crumpled laundry ticket. He circled his address and phone number, wrote out in a hand that looked more chewed up and spit out than it did the written word: *I hit your dog when he chased my tire, shot him to stop the suffering, sorry about that. Raybert Williams.* He walked back over to the dead dog, rolled its body softly onto the side of the road out of harm's way of trucks and cars that would be careless in speed and direction. There, he tied the laundry ticket to a leather strap around its neck, gave the carcass a pat on the rump then walked slowly back to the cab.

Daddy climbed in and said, "Guess he'll be all right there, goddamit." Then he started the engine, the truck shuddering into gear as it crept off the shoulder and back onto the road.

We stayed quiet after that, and I sat there imagining the finches and how they might have arrived just as Rodney

Small's neck snapped to scare the living shit out of Daddy. Or maybe it was right after the photograph was snapped, the sounds not too different really, each capturing something forever framed and in focus. Maybe Palmer was right. Maybe it was Rodney Small doing it to us, doing it to Daddy, too, the birds showing up like that. Nothing was making any sense to me and so I sat watching the land pass, watching the sky for that inkblot of birds that might have something to do with everything that was going on in my life.

Just beyond a short curve, the grade gave way, and we coasted until I could see the entrance to Coggin Philpot's concrete company. The turn off was onto an unpaved road that wound through a grove of trees before opening up into a flat graveled lot filled with concrete molds for cemetery vaults.

A tower for mixing concrete rose along the far end of the lot. All around us sat the finished products as if they had been spit out at the bottom of the tower. The lot was full and seemed cooler for being along the low-lying ground.

Daddy pulled hard on the emergency brake and then got out of the truck. He checked first for signs of the dog he had killed and when he found the truck clean, sat down on a vault to light up. He pinched the unfiltered end between his lips and drew in deeply, his injured face drawn and grim. We sat for a moment letting the cool air seep into our skin and I started thinking he was going to give me more shit about cutting school, but he just kept quiet, kept looking down the small service road that led out to the Finch. "Don't you worry about the dog back there. It was going to die anyway; we just helped it along. You understand that?"

I said, "Yes sir."

Daddy said, "Well good, that's good because I got some

real bad news boy, and I don't know how to tell you except to just let you hear it for yourself. You know your momma's pretty sick?"

I said, "She lost the baby. I already know about that."

Daddy looked at me then, "Yeah, that's right. You were there when it happened. But I'll tell you what, Raybert. Your momma wasn't even eight weeks along so I doubt that baby even looked real. I'm not so sure I'd say it died, more like it just stopped in the bud, never really got going. But that ain't what I got to tell you either. I wish that it was. I wish I could tell you what you already knew and we could be finished. That baby wasn't part of your life. Its dying had nothing to do with you, so I wish I was here to tell you about the baby, but that ain't it. There's more." Then Daddy took another strong stroke off his cigarette. He picked at the bits of tobacco left on his tongue, worked them to the tip before he spit.

After that, he told me about the boy he could not save from the swollen Finch, how my friend Lucky Luther was not going to be staying in any church housing this time, that he had died in the deadly waters before Daddy had a chance to do anything but fish his body out.

He didn't just tell me Lucky was dead. He told it to me as story, the way he always talked to me when there was something important to say. Daddy spoke in great detail about a rescue that had quickly become the body recovery that he had assisted in. He spoke evenly, calm and straight-up, like I was his equal rather than his boy. Daddy confessed to me, wanted forgiveness that I could not give him, so I sat motionless as he told me his story about bringing Lucky Luther out of the Finch.

Daddy said that when the phone rang, he didn't want to

answer it. He knew Bo Wilkins would be on the other end since the Finch was running mean. Bo said, "We need you out here, Ray. We got to find that boy. The Finch is going down."

But it was the last thing Daddy wanted to do, go out looking for some dead boy with the way Momma was feeling. He said, "Who you got going?"

"Not many. Walker, Reed, Mac, so far."

"Sounds like a crowd to me."

"We need you, Ray. There's a lot of creek to cover and it's getting late."

"I told him if the boy was out there, he was dead, but all Bo said was we had to try. Newspaper already called him that morning wanting to know if they should run the obituary. They'd run them before without asking, but I guess they wanted to be sure, wanted to be sensitive about this and not print a mistake, especially since it was a small boy we were going to get." Daddy looked right at me then. "The Finch can be a real asshole when it wants, it can suck you under and spit you out dead before God or anybody else can see what's gone wrong. There's no mistake about that."

I said, "Did the Finch get Lucky that way?"

Daddy said, "I believe so. It did exactly that." His eyes shifted then. He looked out beyond the gate that ran down to the access road leading to where the trailers had sat before the flood. He said, "Everybody was ready to go when I pulled up. We gathered over there in front of the gate; old Mac, he was huge, black as coal in his orange rain gear, already loaded down with ropes and a shovel. I was hoping he would be my partner. If there was going to be any trouble, I knew that good old nigger could save us all.

"Tom Walker surprised me, though. He's the preacher at

Tabernacle Baptist. When I saw him there I said, 'Doing some extra duty here, preacher?' But Tom kind of scolded me for that. I don't know why. I was just trying to be friendly, maybe carry on a bit to make a bad situation a little better, but all he said was, 'It's all God's duty, Ray. We do what we have to.' Then he walked on off.

"Reed Thomas came up and said, 'Amen to that,' then he shook my hand.

"Reed's small and wiry, but tough as nails. Works on the dock over at Ellenton Mills and that's a rough bunch down there. He lost a boy to the Finch about five years ago, so he's always the first to show when someone needs to be found. I thought I might partner up with him. He'd be all right, too, but instead, they put me with Charlie Bundt."

Daddy spit in the gravel and then pulled at the stubble on his unshaven face. "Charlie I don't like. He owns the auction company that's been after me for years to sell off the dry cleaning plant. I just didn't feel safe with Charlie. It's a feeling that nobody would've understood, and I would've looked like a fool trying to explain it, so I just stayed quiet. Figured Bo knew what he was doing and that it would all work out anyway.

"We pretty much knew where the boy was gonna be. Sheriff Lollis said that Lucky had been swinging from one bank to the other on a rope that was tied off a limb when he slipped, missed his footing and fell headfirst into water that boiled up around him. He came up once, the water slapping at his face, then *swoosh* he was gone. One of Lucky's brothers was there when it happened, saw him bob up in the water and then go under. From what the boy told him, Sheriff Lollis figured we'd find him in one of the caves when we went looking.

"Bo was on his haunches drawing out the plan in the dirt when he said, 'Listen up, boys. One thing. Don't go doing nothing more than you have to. We're not trying to save Lucky, only find him. If he gets away, if the Finch is too much, don't overdo it. We'll get him. We always do. It just would be nice to get him today if we can.'

"Old Reed said, 'Amen to that,' and then we all stood up and headed out toward the Finch.

"The access road was mostly underwater, but we took it in as far as we could. The trailer park sat back in about a quarter mile, facing the Finch across a gully, the caves a hundred yards farther down. We had to walk out along the fields on the other side of the tree line to get anywhere near the caves. The Finch was still mean, the water running red and fast. I didn't like the looks of any of it, but there was nothing to do but just keep moving.

"Everybody on our side was carrying a fifty-pound weight for the net and a ten-foot grappling rod. Mac carried his and shouldered the huge net, too. When we got to the caves, the water swirled and foamed and sucked inward, a whirlpool about ten feet across. Mac looked back at me, dripping with sweat and said, 'What ya think?'

"I told him that I thought Lucky was in there. Then he looked at the water boiling up along the bank, six feet higher than its normal depth and said, 'Then let's be gettin' this net across.' Everybody moved, kept their mouths shut and did what they'd been told.

"Downstream about fifty yards, we all tied our weights down, two hundred pounds on the net's bottom. Mac tossed a rope across and Bo pulled against the current, the snags every now and then, till the net was taut on the other side. When the weights settled, the Finch was crossed, the net anchored and picking up anything that tried to flow through. We tied off then and made our way back to the caves."

Daddy stopped right there and looked off in the distance. I could tell he was seeing the place all over again, thinking about what had happened out there in those terrible waters. Daddy said, "You know, there are old Indian mounds along the Finch. They say that spirits use the caves to have pow-wows with the dead. They say people are dying, being sucked up into the whirlpools because the spirits are angry. I wonder about that sometimes, about spirits and curses. Maybe those birds you saw are some kind of unsettled spirits coming back to have a look around, and when they see things they don't like—" but Daddy stopped, shook his head at all of that.

I said, "Maybe it ain't the birds doing it. Maybe Lucky was playing with that turkey, doing something he shouldn't have been doing, like old Perty Spears."

Daddy tossed his cigarette into one of the cemetery vaults in front of him. "Hell, I don't know about all that. I don't know if you can go to church and still believe in those kinds of things. I just don't know."

He looked over at me like he was waiting for an answer, but I didn't know anything about Indian mounds or ghosts inside caves. Daddy knew of things that I had never heard before, and I could tell they weighed him down, made his life more difficult than it already was. I thought then about Rodney Small and Indian caves and curses, wondered if somehow Daddy had gotten himself all tangled up with spirits haunting the Finch and ended up cursed, Rodney Small's death a way to punish him for his sins, and out there somewhere Daddy's turkey waiting for a chance to take him down.

When he asked me what I was thinking, what was on

my mind, I lied. I told him I was thinking about Lucky being underwater like that and what it must have felt like to drown. Daddy said, "He didn't feel nothing. He just swallowed water and that was that. They say once you start to drown, it's the easiest thing to do. It's real peaceful. You just let go, don't feel nothing at all." He stopped to light another cigarette and then kept on going.

"Bo shouted orders and everyone got into position, Mac at the net, Reed halfway between. The grappling hooks were ready to snare the boy when he came to the surface, and it was going to be my responsibility to get Lucky up.

"Charlie was behind me while I was tied off a rope, leaning over the whirlpool to poke at the cave. My life was in Charlie's hands. If he let go, I'd be right there with Lucky and they'd be fishing me out, too."

"I said to Charlie, 'Don't let that line slip.'

"Charlie said, 'I gotcha. Don't worry.'

"I poked the hole with the end of my grappling rod. The ten-foot got pretty far up past the suction. And I could feel a body. It was small. It was old Lucky.

"He bumped against the rod so I knew he wasn't snagged on anything. I said, 'He's here. It's the boy,' and everyone moved closer to the water's edge.

"Bo shouted at me, 'Can you get at him?'

"I said, 'Yeah, give me a second.' I worked at slipping the hook in trying to get a good grip so I could pull Lucky's body through the suction.

"Charlie had me reeled out almost even to the water by then, my feet trying to hold on to the roots that stuck out of the bank. He had the rope wrapped around a tree, then wrapped around him and was working hard, fighting against the slack. Still I kept on him, pissed him off real good, I know. Charlie finally let me have it. He said, 'I gotcha, god-damit. Now quit complaining and do what you need to do.'

"I yelled back at him and said, 'Damn easy for you to say. It's not your ass hanging out flapping in the breeze.'

"From across the creek Bo yelled at both of us. He said, 'Will you two stop pissing and whining over there? Just pull the boy out so we can finish this godforsaken job.' "

At first, Daddy smiled at what he had told me, but then he broke down and started crying. He wept hard for a moment, his body convulsing as he held a fist over his mouth, attempting to stop what was already there. Then it was over just as suddenly. Daddy said, "Goddamit," cleared his throat, gathered himself back together. He was embarrassed, I could tell, but he just looked out over the field of vaults, closed his eyes, and like he was still holding the hook, reached out into the air in front of him.

"I put myself down along the roots making sure my footing was solid, closed my eyes, imagined the boy reaching out, wanting me to pull him back into this world. I had to see it in my mind, so I could see him in that cave. I worked the hook around his body, saw it in my head as it slipped around him, felt the tug when he was caught, then I just pulled. I jerked hard one time and the boy came up free from the hole. He bobbed like a cork and then got caught in the current headed for the net.

"Reed and Walker ran the bank, kept up with the body while they looked for a chance to bring it in. But the current was too swift for either of them to hook Lucky, and so he just swam right into the net and there was Mac, already making his way out to the boy. Bo yelled at him, said, 'That's too much. Don't go out there like that.' But Mac didn't care what Bo said. He waded in nearly chest deep until the current was about to sweep him away, and then he reached out, scooped Lucky up into his arms. Mac brought the boy in with his bare hands, cradled like a baby.

"When Mac had Lucky, Charlie pulled me back to safety and I said, 'You're a good man, Charlie Bundt.' It was a joke, but he wouldn't have none of it.

"Charlie said, 'You're a pain in my ass, Ray,' and then walked past me to help pull the body from the water.

"By the time we got the body bag up to the truck, it was getting dark. Tom Walker led us in a prayer, and that made me want to tell Charlie I was wrong to doubt him. Charlie Bundt ain't worth much in my book, but he did hold that rope. He held on tight, set back and weighed me down. I wanted to say I was sorry, but then figured it was probably better just left unsaid. After the prayer, we all shook hands, figured we did what we could do.

"Sheriff Lollis came over then and said, 'This is shaping up to be a bad one. The mother wouldn't even come to identify the body. Said she still had four others to worry about. It's a shame the way people are down here. I guess you can't blame them for being so soured, the way they get treated by the county. Still, I'd throw the book at her if she didn't have those other kids. It's a no-win situation, a goddamn no-win situation.'

"He asked me to identify the body since his momma wouldn't, and I told Sheriff Lollis that I was sure it was Lucky. He was so dead, Raybert; there was nothing we could do. He was just dead."

I said, "What did he look like? Could you tell it was him?"

Daddy shook his head. "Well, he was down for a good while, but the water was running cold. He was all bloated and his eyes glassed over with a stare going nowhere. He was just dead, that's all I can tell you, son. I've seen that look before, once a long time ago—" but Daddy stopped short of saying any more.

He finished off his cigarette, tossing it into the vault with the other. I thought about Lucky and how he could never control himself, always peeing all over the place when he got excited. I wondered then if he peed when he died, if he just thought, *Shit I'm here in the water, might as well let her rip.* That's what I was thinking about when Daddy said, "Let's go," and we left Coggin Philpot's lot, the story finished, Daddy's task complete.

We headed back to town in a different direction, away from the dog Daddy had killed earlier. The night was cool as we rode with all windows down, the air rushing in between us, loud and separating so we would not have to talk to each other. There was really nothing left to say.

*T*hough he never told me how or why he had been so badly beaten the day we rode out to Coggin Philpot's, I came to believe that it was somehow connected to Lucky Luther's drowning. In my twelve-year-old mind, I was even disappointed that the drowning had not been more sensational, that in his struggle to survive, Lucky Luther had been responsible for Daddy's ear and all his cuts and bruises. I wanted him to tell me a tale, let Lucky live in his story in a way that would make his appearance more understandable to me. I wanted Daddy to tell me Lucky had raised himself from the waters of the Finch able to grab a hold, hands thrashing about with an almost supernatural will to survive against his inevitable drowning. As he drove me back to town, I thought about Rodney Small and would have just as easily found total believability in a story where Daddy held Lucky's head under while the boy gasped for air only to breath in the silt-filled water of the rising Finch. I could imagine with great detail his small clawed hands grabbing at his face, Lucky's head momentarily exploding free from the water while gnashing teeth found my daddy's soft fleshy ear, a last piece of evidence to prove him a killer of children, black or white making little difference, an equal opportunity murderer.

Neither of these stories surfaced beyond the edges of my imagination as we drove quietly into town. Still, when Daddy pulled the Buick onto Robbins Street, something seemed different to me. The place felt smaller under a moonless sky. Shadows filled in, shrinking the land and houses that sat close in on each other. A distant security lamp at the end of the alley pooled its beam below the pole reaching out only a few feet before giving up to inklike darkness. I looked down the narrow gravel road and then back to my house that sat bathed in streetlight. The lamp's pale beam suddenly began to stutter and then abruptly sucked off, a loud *pop* high up the pole bringing silence to trees and bushes that hid cicadas and tree frogs. There in the harsh silence, the house stood in darkness, abandoned of life on the inside and out.

Its silhouetted form felt like death, and I imagined Lucky and the baby that would have been my brother or sister staring out at me, trapped inside rooms that no longer felt as much like home as they had just hours before. I squinted, sharply searching out beyond each corner for the glowing eyes of the turkey my daddy had revealed to me that night in the snow. Its appearance I hoped would be proof that these deaths were intended and inevitable. I said, "Daddy, I can tell somebody's died just by looking at this house."

Daddy stopped and kneeled down on the front porch searching for the door key. "It don't make no difference. It's just a house." He stood up and looked at me, then smiled and walked over to sit down on the steps. He pulled out his cigarettes, lit the tobacco until the tip flamed. "You're a sensitive boy, Raybert. Did you know that?"

I said, "I guess so."

"You've been like that since you were born."

I said, "Yes sir."

"Did you know your momma delivered you hard?"

"Yes sir."

"Took her years to have you good and clean, and when you finally did come out, you were born with one eye blue and one eye green."

"The green eye went away when I was two."

He looked at me then like I had said something important. "That's right son, you were two, you remember that happening, don't you, when you were only two?"

I said, "Yes sir, I remember," but I really didn't. I knew only because Momma had told me a hundred times if she told me once about her miscarriages and her struggle to have a baby, and when it finally took, how she had suffered in delivery. When I finally came out the nurses and doctors had marveled over my different colored eyes before they even looked to see if I was a boy or girl.

Daddy put his hand on one leg and pushed himself up with great effort. "The world is full of death, Raybert. There's plenty for everybody."

I said, "There's more than enough."

Daddy said, "Hell, probably ten times enough. The point is, you be careful with that sensitive shit, that'll get you into more trouble than Carter's got pills. Just look at your momma." He put the unfiltered tip of his cigarette between his lips pulling hard to get everything he could out of the burning tobacco before flicking the glowing ember into the yard where grass still struggled to grow. Daddy said, "You don't have to come in if you don't want to. I'll get your stuff."

As I waited on the street steps, I felt the wind come through me, a sudden cooling breeze that had waited for him to enter the house before sneaking up to cover me like a wet blanket and chill my bones. It swam around me and took my breath away, and for an instant, I understood how Lucky Luther must have felt as he gasped for air. I was underwater in this wind until it passed, leaving me scared and wondering what Daddy had meant when he said, *Just look at your momma.*

Daddy came out then, turned back to check locks and hide the key. When he walked down to the car, the streetlight snapped back on, soaking the darkness with harsh light and rimming his head with what looked like white fire. Daddy said, "You look like you seen a ghost."

I said, "I ain't seen nothing. The wind just got under my clothes that's all."

"Well here then, put this on." He tossed me my sweatshirt. "You got to get some sleep before you catch your death of cold."

I said, "Don't say that, Daddy. Don't talk no more about death."

But he just smiled when he got into the car. "It's a figure of speech, Raybert, and I ain't seen a figure of speech ever hurt no one."

He drove me over to Hickory Point, stayed only long enough for Aunt Iris to change the bandages on his face and ear, and then he was gone again. From the room where I lay,

I heard Aunt Iris cry when Daddy drove away. I heard Uncle Clewell say, "You can't do anything about that, Iris. It's his life."

Aunt Iris said, "But did you see his ear? He's never been hurt like that before. He's gonna be deformed."

They sat up talking quietly, their conversation too low for me to hear, and so I fell asleep with the image of my daddy's face deformed with cuts and tears as frightening as the monsters I watched on *Shock Theater*. Later, I had a dream.

It seemed to take place all in the same night like I had not gone to sleep at all but instead had followed Daddy outside and then somehow lost him in the darkness there. I raised a hand to my face but couldn't see fingers wiggling only inches away. I said, "It's dark," and a voice answered back, "Yes, it is." Suddenly there was a rope in front of me tied around a large tree limb and knotted at the end in a hangman's noose. It swayed to and fro as if someone had just let go. I saw myself in the air with water below, the surface like glass. It came fast, seconds split in half, until I plunged beneath the surface, the sediment rising around me. Then I began to sink.

I realized that I needed to swim or I was going to drown. But the harder I tried, flailing my arms in the darkness, the farther I floated away from the surface. When the murky water sucked up into my nose and mouth, I tasted the silt, and then let go. It was just like Daddy had said, easy, the torrent gone as I floated beside Lucky Luther.

Nothing was wrong with him. He looked just like he had the last time I saw him. We both smiled and held each other's hand. There were no bubbles. The silt and algae disappeared and I knew then there was no other place in the world I wanted to be except with this boy. But as soon as I gave up, something interrupted and would not let me stay. I was set free to rise up through the churning waters.

I resisted, reaching out to grab Lucky again, but he drifted deeper and deeper, our grasp gone forever. The darkened waters returned and with them stinging pain in my throat and nostrils. I felt a great push as if Lucky had given me one big kick toward the surface and then I exploded out of the water, Daddy's arms wrapping around my body to yank me from the flooding Finch Creek. He pulled me to shore, as I believed he had hoped he would pull Lucky, safe and alive.

I coughed and spit up silt, rubbed my eyes to remove the murky sediment so I could see his face. It was perfect, not a cut or scratch to be found. I felt at that moment Daddy had always been a good man. I wanted to be as close to him as I could, tell him I was sorry for believing he murdered Rodney Small, like Dr. Kimball and the one-armed man, a badly mistaken identity.

I wanted him to know how much I loved him, words I could never say because they were words he never used with me, *sensitive shit*, as Daddy had said, to be avoided at all costs. In my dream, I reached out with flailing arms to find him, grab hold and never let go, but my grasp came up empty, and like Lucky Luther, he was quickly gone.

I woke up cold in a bed still covered with winter spreads realizing that mixed in with the aroma of bacon and fresh coffee was the musty scent of urine. I put my hand below the covers and for the first time in all of this realized I had wet the bed. It was odd. I was twelve years old, almost thirteen, floating in pee, taking over where Lucky Luther left off, the real thing unlike Palmer's foolishness with a glass of water. Aunt Iris came in and found me, soiled and saddened, embarrassed. I said, "Lucky Luther is dead and gone."

Aunt Iris said, "I know, Raybert, and I am so sorry about that."

"I had a dream and then, look what I did."

Aunt Iris sat down beside me on the soiled sheets and held me tightly in her arms, "It don't matter what you did as long as you're all right. Are you all right now?"

"I don't know. I think so."

"Let's get you up and out of these wet things. Why don't you go take a bath and I'll put these sheets in the wash."

I crawled out of bed and started walking slowly across the room, my pajamas sticking to skin where urine had run down my legs. At the door, I turned around and said, "Daddy killed a dog on top of all that."

Aunt Iris looked up from the bed surprised. "Did he do it on purpose?"

I said, "He put it out of its misery after it run out in front of the truck."

Aunt Iris said, "Then your daddy did something good. I'm sure it was the last thing he wanted to do with Lucky on his mind."

"He hit me, too, slapped me twice."

Aunt Iris's face fell hard then as she reached over the bed to loosen the fitted sheet. "Well, I'm sure he—"

"Daddy said he was sorry for that, too, he apologized before he told me about Lucky."

A large wet spot darkened the mattress as Aunt Iris gathered the linens, balling the soiled sheets up in her arms, evidence enough to convict me. "Well, then, looks like he did two good things today, sort of. Now you go on and take a bath."

I said, "Do you think Lucky's in heaven by now? Is that the way it happens?"

Aunt Iris said, "Lucky's name has always been on that roll, Raybert. He's an angel in heaven right now. You don't have to worry about that anymore. You don't have to worry about anything."

I turned away from the door and went to the bathroom then, but I did not believe what she said about not having to worry anymore. I had my doubts about that.

After I cleaned up, I ate breakfast sitting with Uncle Clewell. I kept thinking about Lucky up in heaven and how he had probably seen RC already. I wondered if they looked the same, spirits out of body. How would they know each other if they couldn't see their faces? I figured Lucky wouldn't wet in his pants anymore. He wouldn't need to do that in heaven. At least that was a good thing.

Uncle Clewell watched me closely, his glasses floating at the tip of his nose, eyes narrowed as if he were trying to decide if he should say something. He kept his paper raised before him but never took his eyes off me until my plate was clean and Aunt Iris returned from washing out the mattress with Pine-Sol cleaner. Once she was there, Uncle Clewell pushed himself up from the table and left without a word. I heard him go through a door leading to the garage and then watched him drive away in his Cadillac, the DeVille filling the windows as it drove past the house and down the driveway. I said, "Is Uncle Clewell mad at me?"

Aunt Iris said, "No, of course not. He's just concerned."

"Is he coming back?"

"Of course he is. You don't have to worry about him. He goes to the dealership every Saturday morning. It's what he always does. He'll be back."

I said, "I'm sorry about the sheets, hope I don't ever do that again."

"I doubt you will."

I said, "Lucky used to wet his pants all the time. He'd wet them if you looked at him funny."

Aunt Iris said, "Well, we won't look funny at you then, if that's all it takes." She glanced over her shoulder and smiled, her face tired, the skin gathering in pools below her eyes. "You're a special boy, Raybert. Don't worry about this anymore. It's just hard right now, and you've gotten too old to not see it when it's there. You shouldn't have to worry about these things at your age."

I said, "Sometimes I think Momma's gonna die."

Aunt Iris stopped washing the coffee pot and turned, leaning against the counter. She said, "No Raybert, your momma won't die over this. She's going to be all right. I wouldn't say that to you if it wasn't true; you believe that don't you?"

"Yes ma'am, I guess so."

"Well you better because it's the gospel. She just needs lots of rest right now and the doctor thinks she's best resting in the hospital. You don't need to be worrying. We'll get your mother soon enough and then go back to the house, but for now, just be happy. I want you to be happy."

"Can I stay with you and Uncle Clewell?"

She turned back to the sink then, wiping down counter tops and putting the last glasses in the dish rack. I was waiting for her to turn around and say, *Why Raybert, you can stay forever. Uncle Clewell always wanted a son.* But instead she said, "Your momma and daddy love you dearly, Raybert. You're their moment of perfection. Evelyn used those very words, moment of perfection, just the other day to talk about you. Your daddy is trying hard, probably too hard to be good all the time. I just don't know if he has enough in him to be who he wants to be. They're trying to find their way on a difficult path, so you have to be patient. I know how hard that can be, but you have to try."

Though I told her I would, I still preferred Aunt Iris's house to my own. I pretended the room I slept in was always mine. The view out across the front yard was full of blooming magnolia and gardenias; a hammock was roped across two large oaks that I could swing in every evening if I wanted. The room had two beds and still plenty of room to walk around both! And there were two dressers that were empty, just waiting for my clothing.

Aunt Iris and Uncle Clewell had tried to have children years before. They had set this room up, decorated it for two boys with wagon wheel headboards and needlepoint pictures of Roy Rogers and Dale Evans that Aunt Iris had crafted while waiting for twins to be born. She had carried them for nearly seven months until she had complications. Somehow her body rejected the babies by slowly attacking each until one and then the other died inside her womb. I heard Momma say once shortly after she became pregnant with the baby, "Iris had two growing and her body just killed them both. How horrible. I wonder how she feels about me having another?"

Daddy, who really didn't want to talk about such things, said, "She don't feel anything but joy for you, and I wouldn't go reminding her of all that. It was a long time ago."

Momma said, "Death is never long ago. It just sits there out of sight until—" and then she stopped. I thought about Rodney Small after that, how his death was still out there floating around, out of sight, but never put to rest. I wondered if he would ever die completely away, as long as he was there in that picture to think about. I knew looking around my room in Hickory Point that Aunt Iris understood death.

Her time spent with Momma would be good, especially since she was so fragile and all.

Around noon I turned on the television in the den to watch *American Bandstand*, teenagers dancing to music I found exotic and new. Wilson Pickett was dancing and gyrating in his sequined tuxedo and patent leather shoes, his black hair wavy and slicked back. I stood up and tried to dance to the music, my stuttering steps and awkward body behaving foolishly, but I was having fun.

I remembered hearing this voice floating out through windows when Edgar Doyle drove into Sparkstown for his six-pack, and I wondered what he would think about it if he were here to see this show. "Spook music" is what he would call it. He would probably take his pistol and shoot out the television screen and then say *Spooks is spooks*. But I didn't have to worry about Edgar while I was with Uncle Clewell and Aunt Iris, and so I moved my feet trying to copy Wilson Pickett's dance steps as he lip-synched "Funky Broadway." I danced in the den with Dick Clark and his *American Bandstand*. I was concentrating on my feet trying to make sure they would not get tangled up at the ankles in such a way that I would lose control and tumble to the floor when a news bulletin flashed across the screen with tragic news from Los Angeles. Robert Kennedy had been assassinated at the Ambassador Hotel.

Aunt Iris came into the room and said, "Oh my God. Not again," then went out to call Uncle Clewell at the dealership. There were reporters at the hospital saying there was still a glimmer of hope that he might make it yet, but you could see it in their faces, that same blank look from five years earlier, like wild animals frozen in oncoming lights, Bobby Kennedy was dying and there wasn't anything that could be done.

They showed schematics and drawings of how Sirhan Sirhan had slipped through security, sidestepped big old Rosey Grier to find a spot to wait and then plunged through the crowd yelling, "Kennedy, you son of a bitch!" Shots were fired, people injured, and Kennedy mortally wounded.

The film report showed a young busboy holding his head, Kennedy lying prostrate on the floor of the Ambassador Hotel food service pantry. We sat and watched the events unfurl, Walter Cronkite, his familiar sad and forlorn monotone back on the air to report the death of another Kennedy while Aunt Iris cried trying to understand how someone could do it again. When the phone rang, she thought it was Clewell returning her call, but instead it was the hospital calling to say Momma was in big trouble.

The nurses did not know of her history with Robert Kennedy, that at one time she had been obsessed with his campaign for the presidency. She had been watching some late morning gardening show, the television only on as background noise as she drifted in and out of sleep. She was about to doze off again when the first bulletin came through her television set to jolt her awake.

When she saw Bobby Kennedy lying on the floor, his blood pouring out into the Ambassador Hotel, she later said that she could feel her own life draining out of her body. She imagined Bobby's eyes looking right at her, a voice coming through amid all the screaming and yelling that said, "You were right. I should have come to dinner." When they finally came on the air to announce that Kennedy had died, Momma thought they were telling her she was dying, too. She looked below the covers where her Kotex pad had come loose to soil her sheets and knew she was bleeding to death, Kennedy's wounds somehow piercing her body as well.

She tried to grab a spent syringe out of her butt when they gave her a sedative, threw it at a nurse and then had to be restrained until they could pump her body full of enough drugs to knock her out. They moved her into a psychiatric ward the day Sirhan Sirhan was moved to the Los Angeles County jail to await trial for Bobby Kennedy's murder. In the ward were six rooms along a dark corridor, an annex to the regular hospital building, where she received daily medications that were supposed to regulate her mood swings.

Palmer cried when I told him about the miscarriage and my dream and how I had wet the bed. When I told him about what Momma had seen on the television, he said, "It was just a matter of time before Kennedy got it. Nobody likes those guys. I'm surprised he lasted as long as he did. He never had a chance. But I can't believe your momma's in the psycho ward over this and Inez is walking around town. That ain't right if you ask me." Then he promised to never let me out of his sight again.

Each day I rode with Aunt Iris to the Hickory Point Hospital where I waited in the lobby while she visited Momma. I was never allowed to see her because of where she was being kept. I watched the television or read *Highlights* magazine, drew get-well cards that Aunt Iris would present to her as proof she was still loved and not forgotten. In the afternoons during the next few weeks, we drove over to check on the house, bring in the mail, and look for Daddy. Whether by intention or just timing, he was never at home when we came by, though there were always signs he had been there. He left plates in the sink for someone else to clean, and lived out of the boxes until Aunt Iris moved his clothes back into his room. One day we came by and found the water in the shower running, towels wet on the floor, but Daddy was nowhere to be found. Aunt Iris said, "That's your daddy for sure. He's run off so much on your Momma, I could just spit."

I said, "Did Daddy kill the baby?"

Aunt Iris looked at me hard then, said, "You don't think like that."

I said, "Well, was it because of Bobby Kennedy?"

"No. Nothing like that happened at all. Your momma's just very sick, Raybert, and your daddy can't be here when he's needed. I don't understand him. Nobody does. There ain't a thing in the world we can do about it but pray. Pray for your daddy, Raybert."

In the afternoons, she would drop me off at the City Pool where I swam with Palmer, Tommy Patterson, and Billy Parker. We played pool tag, assassinated one another and fell off the high board turning somersaults as we died. Later we sunned our backs and talked about Lucky Luther's drowning. We each dove as deep as we could, blowing out all the air until our bodies were deadweight and our lungs felt like they would collapse. We were trying to feel Lucky drowning, to get as close to death as possible before exploding back to the surface full of sound and light and breath-quenching air.

The last time I dove, I sank to the bottom and lay there looking up toward a surface where brilliant explosions of sunlight hit the water and seemed to sizzle. When I closed my eyes, I could hear Lucky just beneath me, calling out to swim upward and save my life. I was under a long time, but as in my dream, I felt an unwanted push from behind, a gentle kick that sent me floating away from his voice, toward the illumination, toward my life going on.

XIII

*I*n all the sadness that came with the storms that summer, I had completely forgotten about Evel Knievel's jump in the Houston Astrodome. I had not ridden my bike much or been out to our makeshift jump since the day I froze at the top of the run. I wasn't even sure if the jump had survived the torrential rains that washed Daddy's yard away and then continued until Lucky lost his life in the swollen Finch.

While I lived in Hickory Point, I pretended that Uncle Clewell and Aunt Iris were my parents. When I said my prayers at night, I prayed silently putting them first, praying for my aunt and uncle before I prayed for Momma and Daddy. I asked God to bless Ray and Evelyn, calling them by their first names, thinking it would somehow separate me more. I looked for signs that He had heard my prayers, a falling picture frame or a slamming door would have done just fine, but He gave me something bigger than that; He gave me Evel Knievel.

I had to believe the jump was a sign from God because of the way it was revealed. Uncle Clewell had no idea how obsessed we had all been about the stunt or how we had built the ramp down in the dead end by the high school before the storms hit and changed everything. He had seen the jump listed in the *TV Guide* earlier in the week and then decided to go see Inez. He drove there by himself to ask if Palmer could spend the night and then work at the dealership on Saturday helping to wash Cadillacs, give them a spit shine as Uncle Clewell liked to call it, and make some money to boot. Edgar said, "As long as he makes money, I don't care what he does." And neither did Inez. She told Uncle Clewell she was more than happy to get rid of him for that night.

Uncle Clewell shook his head when he told us about the visit later. "Can you imagine saying you want to get rid of your own child? And I don't think it was a joke, either. She didn't look like she was joking one bit." It was my uncle who did all this for me and Palmer, not Daddy and certainly not Momma, who remained in the psychiatric ward, and for all I knew at the time was restrained and drugged so she would not attack any more nurses.

When Uncle Clewell brought Palmer over, he let him trigger the garage door a block away from the house so that by the time they turned into the driveway, the door was fully open. I went out to greet them when I heard the door start up, its motor grinding hard to pull the hinged panels off the ground. I had to squint to keep my eyes from burning in the brightness that reflected off bleached concrete when Uncle Clewell's DeVille swung into the drive. It was good light, hot and irrepressible, and quickly my eyes adjusted as Palmer and Uncle Clewell walked into the cool shade of the garage.

Palmer's moonlike face still glowed in the shadow, his smile bowing up from ear to ear. He ran over to wrap his arms around my neck and said, "I missed you."

I said, "Shut up, Palmer," and pushed him away. He paid little mind to my rejection as he ran through the utility room ahead of Uncle Clewell to hug Aunt Iris and thank her for taking such good care of me. Palmer said, "We can't let anything happen to him from here on out."

Aunt Iris smiled and said, "Well, we're glad you're here, too, Palmer. We'll just take care of both of you."

I took Palmer up a small stairway leading from the kitchen into curving halls, passing through enough nooks and small passageways to spin his head until he was hopelessly lost as we arrived in front of the door to my room. I showed him the bed he would be sleeping in, let him put his clothes in a drawer of the chest and then opened the closet door, a walk-in that was nearly empty except for the few clothes I had brought over from Ellenton and the boxes Aunt Iris stored on shelving above the hangers.

Palmer walked in and held his hands out straight from his body like he was taking measurements, moving slowly in a circle to get the feel of the large empty space. He felt the carpet and flicked the light on and off a couple of times, closing the door when he did just to see how dark the closet would get. I said, "We won't need to sleep in here."

"Yeah, but it's nice to know about it, just in case."

He walked across the room to the windows and looked down onto the yard where boxwood shrubbery ran thick and full along the edge of the house. He was barely tall enough to see out and so stood on tiptoes to gaze across a yard that could have easily swallowed up his own house and its small plot of land. Palmer said, "That would be a long jump down there, wouldn't it?"

I said, "Yeah, but there ain't no reason to jump, Palmer. Not while we're here."

He seemed distracted by the unfamiliar geography around him, the rambling stairway and hall that had brought him up to a bedroom twice the size of either of ours in Ellenton. The distance this house placed between him and the ground severely limited his ability to move quickly at a moment's notice, something he always felt was necessary at his own house. Palmer's eyes darted around as he gazed out the window lifting his nose into the air, sniffing like a dog in search of something more familiar. It suddenly dawned on me that he had never been in a house outside his own neighborhood, and so had no clue how someone could live like this. I said, "It's just a house, Palmer."

He said, "I know what a house is," but his words came out weak and distant and made me feel he wasn't so sure. He stayed fixed to the windows taking in as much as he could, walking over to the other side of the room to view the plot of ground below where Aunt Iris was bent over in the late afternoon sun working her garden, weeding tomato plants, okra, and green beans.

I said, "Come on, I got something else to show you," but when I touched him on the shoulder, Palmer's body jumped. For a moment, I wasn't even sure he recognized me. He seemed smaller standing there, arms at his sides, tennis shoes untied. He fiddled with the frayed edge of his cutoffs, wrapping the loose threads around his fingers while he continued surveying the room. Finally I hit him in the head and said, "Palmer, wake up."

That seemed to help, his eyes blinking clear again. "I've never seen a house like this before. Your closet is almost as big as my room."

"It's not my closet."

"Close enough. Are you going to live here now?"

"I don't know. I don't think so."

We walked to the end of the hall to a small dormer that was a door leading us outside to a balcony. Though Aunt Iris had asked me not to go out there, Palmer looked so scared standing in the room that I wanted him to see an escape, so if he ever felt the need to run, he could find open air and a magnolia tree for a way down.

Once we stepped outside, his eyes brightened and he seemed more at ease. Palmer gauged the distance he would have to jump to make a sturdy enough limb of the magnolia. He crawled close to the edge and looked over into the back-yard where Aunt Iris had planted beds of wildflowers around bird feeders and ceramic statues of angels with outstretched arms, then he moved back over and slid up next to me. Our shoulders touched as we scrunched close against the wall so Aunt Iris would not see us. Palmer said, "You got to sell a lot of Cadillacs to live like this."

"Uncle Clewell says he's the only dealership between here and there."

"Well, I could get used to this, if I wanted to."

I said, "I already have."

Palmer smiled and seemed happy again. We stayed on the roof until Aunt Iris called us downstairs where she had prepared TV dinners on TV trays while Uncle Clewell searched the *TV Guide* for the channel that would carry the jump in what commercials had called the "eighth wonder of the world."

That evening, the scene in the Astrodome was like a carnival with red, white, and blue bunting draped evenly down the length of the twenty Greyhound buses. Uncle Clewell had a console color television, the picture as big as life, like we were really there watching through a window inside the Astrodome. All the color made the jump seem bigger, more impossible, and Palmer shook his head saying, "I don't see this happening."

Uncle Clewell said, "Vegas is saying he won't make it by three to one odds, and Vegas loves Evel Knievel."

Before Evel's jump, other daredevils and stuntmen took center stage to perform their own life threatening acts for the capacity crowd. Jimmy "Boom Boom" McMahon was a human stick of dynamite, the "Boom Boom" important because he not only blew himself up once, he did it twice on-camera from four different angles, including slow-mo. Locked in a double-sided wooden box, the dynamite blew off the sides twice *Boom! Boom!* and Jim McKay said, "If I hadn't seen it, I wouldn't believe it." Boom Boom McMahon walked away from the destruction weak-kneed and assisted under each arm, but he waved to the crowd as a roar went up that I'm not sure he could actually hear.

There were others, a human cannonball shot from a large red, white, and blue cannon, the trajectory cutting across the line of Greyhounds to remind us of what was still to come. The man exploded into the air, turned a somersault and landed neatly into a net on the other side. He rolled down to the bottom, flipped himself out of the netting onto the ground and then ran around waving at the crowd, his body still smoking from the explosive blast.

The Priddy Brothers jumped ramps in a battle of "Superhero" cars. They drove junk heaps that were decorated to look like cars cartoon heroes drove on the pages of our favorite magazines. From opposite ends of the Astrodome floor, each brother accelerated toward the ramps, one driving the Green Hornet's Black Beauty while the other was in the Batmobile. A collision took place in midair, the capacity crowd standing on their feet as we did in Uncle Clewell's den as the cars clipped each other and came crashing down on top of a pile of flattened wrecks. Dressed as Batman and the Green Hornet, the brothers jumped out of the cars, chased each other around the junk heap, faked karate punches and dashed off into the darkness of the Astrodome tunnel.

Between each stunt, the television was full of commercials stretching out an hour-long show into a two and a half hour spectacular. Even Evel got into the act as he sat down in front of a television in a Relax-A-Vision recliner. He watched all his past disasters, his body flipping over and over as he crumpled into retaining walls or landed in piles of stacked tires or cardboard boxes. A close up of him mouthing the words *Ouch* from the reclined chair made us all laugh again.

A young woman in a miniskirt dried her hair as she listened to music coming out of her hairdryer—"Swing with Hi-Fi while you dry. It's Groovy!" Somebody opened a bottle of Fresca and the TV screen became a blizzard. Aunt Iris brought in snacks from the kitchen after dinner: Twinkies and Instant Ovaltine, Cokes and popcorn after that.

Finally, Dynamite Dan blew himself up in a Ford Fairlane, but we were tired of human bombs going off, so nobody paid much attention. Palmer said, "RC told me once, if you can't buy a car, buy a Ford." We laughed out loud and the preliminaries were over. Evel Knievel's jump was all that remained.

The daredevil came out of a tunnel and started making passes down the length of the jump. He would accelerate, then let off just in time to stop dead at the end of the ramp, the point where, when he did it for real, he would go airborne. Each time he stopped, the crowd chanted, "Evel! Evel! Evel!" The crowd seemed to feed off the practice runs, and Evel seemed to feed off the screaming crowd.

Several times he hopped off the bike to walk the length of the jump, his small frame even smaller as the Greyhound buses dwarfed him. He talked to his crew, hands gesturing fast, pointing to the ramp and then back into the tunnel where he would take off. Adjustments were made, and then Knievel got back on popping wheelies and standing on the seat while he accelerated along the entire length of the Astrodome floor.

The crowd went wild with every gesture as he flirted with the jump, teased it, always with his cape flapping nervously behind him. When he seemed to feel good about the jump, Evel made one final pass along the line of buses waving to the crowd before disappearing into the tunnel where Jim McKay waited with one last question, "How do you feel, Champ?"

Evel's face was nervous, his eyes blinking too fast. Still he looked into the camera and said, "Jim, what I'm about to do is nothing like what our boys over in Vietnam are doing, so since all the armed forces can see me over there tonight, the first time something like this has ever been done, I'm dedicating this jump to them. I'm gonna make it because I have to. I got my mojo working, and it's time to get it on." He swallowed hard, pushing the microphone and camera out of his way, then flipped his visor down sealing his face from the rest of the world.

I said, "I guess Ronnie Doyle's watching this tonight, if he's not out in some jungle."

Palmer said, "He should be over here watching with Erlene Hobbs and that baby bouncing on his lap."

Uncle Clewell seemed to agree. When he got up to adjust the roto-tenna again, he patted Palmer on the shoulder and said, "Watch out Sport, let me get Evel tuned in real good."

From behind the motorcycle, the camera caught Evel gunning his engine, the opening to the Astrodome a hundred feet from where he straddled his Harley, the ramp some fifty yards past that. He waited as I had at the beginning of my run, and I imagined I understood his hesitation in letting loose and flying up the ramp and into history. I had been there, I thought. I had been Evel Knievel up to that moment of indecision.

Palmer leaned over on the couch, nudged me in the side and whispered, "Think his pecker's in a cup?"

I said, "It better be," and then pushed him away.

Whatever had stayed in me that afternoon, would not let me push the pedal downward, seemed to pass through Evel instantly as his feet left the ground, the motorcycle jerking forward to accelerate for speed. He wound out each gear, a coordinated dance of rhythm and acceleration as Knievel rocketed toward the point of no return. Just as he hit the ramp, Jim McKay said, "That's it, he's got to go now." And I heard Palmer whisper to himself, "Got to go now," his eyes scanning the screen, locked on the figure flashing past the world.

And then it seemed that time stopped as Evel left the ground surrounded by exploding fireworks and a million flashbulbs all going off at once. He rode high in the saddle, hands grasped tightly to the handlebars, feet firmly holding the motorcycle in perfect flight. He looked like he might soar forever, like he could circle the Astrodome time and time again, the cheering crowd holding him aloft, the Harley indifferent to gravity. The speed, the perfect conditions of the Astrodome air, the trajectory taken off the ramp were without flaw. He crossed those twenty buses set one next to the other, a two-hundred-foot leap in living color, like he had done it a thousand times before. When he landed firmly in place, upright and safe on the ground, the jump suddenly seemed simple. It seemed, well, just a little too easy.

We watched the replay, the slow-mo, the camera that was embedded in the middle of the jump to catch Evel as he flew across "the DMZ," a label Evel himself had given the center of the buses in honor of those who were fighting in Vietnam. We saw the angle of impact when he landed, and we saw him fly toward us as he entered the other side of the tunnel to decelerate. Still, he had to lay the bike down as he hit piles of cardboard boxes and netting to break his fall. We were as much a part of the jump as *Wide World of Sports* could let us be, and while Evel Knievel was in the air, I felt the sensation, free and floating up there with him.

Uncle Clewell let us watch the replays and listen to comments Evel made, his thanks to the soldiers, his belief in God, the United States of America, and Harley Davidson. When we turned off the television, the world was suddenly a good place to live in because Evel Knievel had tempted fate and won. He took that leap out of pure faith that he would fly high and land safely, even after many crashes and broken bones. Uncle Clewell said, "Remember what you saw tonight. He didn't have to do that. He didn't have to get back on and ride after his last crash, but he did. He got back on that hog and rode it."

Palmer and I went upstairs, our hearts still pumping hard from the jump and all we had seen that night. We got ready for bed, refusing to let sleep take over, and talked about going back down to the jump by the high school, using Evel Knievel's preparations as our own. Palmer promised to make the jump, too, if I would, and when I agreed, Palmer asked, "Who's going first?"

I said, "We'll flip for it."

Palmer said, "Deal, but we got to do more than promise." He opened the door to the bedroom and waited for the house to fall quiet. Once Uncle Clewell and Aunt Iris were in bed, he said, "Come on," and led me back out onto the balcony where only a moonless night could reveal his next plan. Palmer stuck his face so close to me I could feel his breath when he spoke. "You said you promise to make the jump; promise again."

"I promise."

Then Palmer pulled out a small pocketknife he had stolen off Edgar. I had told him not to take those kinds of things, but he just said, "Edgar doesn't need to be around sharp objects." He smiled then and stuffed the knife into his pocket like it was his own. That night on the roof, Palmer said, "Give me your hand." He took a finger and sliced it ever so slightly, nothing more than a paper cut, but deep enough to draw blood. He cut himself in the same fashion and then we rubbed our fingers together. We became brothers there on the roof. He put my finger in his mouth and I put Palmer's in mine; the sharp metallic taste of blood shocking my tongue disappeared when I swallowed. Palmer said, "I don't know why I never thought of this before. This is as good as it gets, Kemo sabe."

We were now connected through Evel Knievel and our mixed blood, shared cells that would multiply until the bond scattered throughout our bodies. We were blood brothers, as close as we could get to the real thing. I said, "Let's stay like this forever."

Palmer said, "Groovy," like the girl who had sung along with her hairdryer before Evel's jump. He stood up then, leaning over quickly to kiss me on each cheek. Palmer said, "That's the way they do it in France. I saw it on one of those proper manners films in gym class. It's okay for guys to do it."

I said, "I wouldn't make a habit out of that," then hit him hard on his arm before he could do it again.

In the room, Palmer's mood changed, as he stood in his underwear uncertain about sleep. He looked at the closet and then back to the twin bed where Aunt Iris had already turned down his sheets.

I said, "What's the problem?"

"Can we push the beds together?"

"What for?"

"It would make it easier to sleep."

"Not for me; now go to bed, Palmer."

He said, "What if I wake up?"

I said, "I'll be right next to you." But that didn't seem to be enough. Only after I said, "Shut up, Palmer, and get in bed," did he bury himself beneath his covers.

"Leave a light on or crack the door. I don't know where I am."

I said, "You're with me."

But Palmer shook his head, "Not unless we move the beds together."

Later, I got up to go pee, and on the way back decided to crack the door so a glow from the hallway light would soften the dark and give shape to my room. I said, "Now don't be such a pussy next time," as I walked back across, but Palmer was already quiet, his breathing deep and hard. He had fallen asleep, safely tucked away for the night. I got into bed, wondering what would happen next—if we could be as lucky as Evel Knievel had been that night jumping two hundred feet in the air to land safely on the other side. In my mind, Evel remained suspended, bright and illuminated, like the television screen itself. The sight of him soaring over all those Greyhounds gave me great hope, Evel Knievel in the perfect air of the Astrodome. It was my sign.

I closed my eyes and let Palmer's deep easy breathing rock me to sleep. *Now I lay me down to sleep.* Everything would be all right. *I pray the Lord my soul to keep.* And everything would work out. *If I should die before I wake . . .* Thank you God for Evel Knievel. *I pray the Lord my soul to take.* And thank you for Palmer Conroy. Amen.

CHAPTER
XIV

*M*y stay with Aunt Iris and Uncle Clewell lasted a little over a month, beginning with Momma's miscarriage and continuing through the assassination and burial of Robert Kennedy. It came to an end shortly after Evel Knievel's jump in the Astrodome. In my mind a lifetime had passed in the weeks Momma remained in the psychiatric ward. In that time, Momma was diagnosed as having manic depression. When I saw Palmer and told him about her newly discovered condition, he was shocked. "Your mother ain't crazy. That sounds like Inez to me. She's the real maniac."

Aunt Iris warned us that when Momma did finally come home, it would have to be different than before she lost the baby. We would all have to look out for her, Aunt Iris said, be careful, and make sure she stayed on her medicine. Palmer became excited when he was included in this. He said, "We can work in shifts, around the clock, twenty-fours a day. Always thought I'd make a good nurse." All these new rules worried me as I packed my belongings and prepared to go home. But what worried me the most was *why* she was coming home now.

At night, I would hear Aunt Iris talking about Daddy, saying he was crazy to bring her home, that she needed to stay and get well. She was afraid he was taking her out because of money, but Uncle Clewell told her to stay out of it, that money concerns were not something they could interfere with, and she couldn't be nosey about that, even if she was Daddy's sister.

Aunt Iris said, "But who takes care of her? Maybe I should have a say in this."

Uncle Clewell said, "That don't matter. Stop taking care of her then, but don't be nosey about Ray's money."

I didn't know very much about Daddy and Aunt Iris when they were younger, before they moved to Ellenton. Daddy never said nothing, but Aunt Iris would tell me about growing up in Pawnee, Oklahoma, how the land was flat as a piece of plywood and the wind blew all the time. She told me about tornado alley and how three had come over their house in one night but waited to touch down on the other side of the road. Their neighbors had been hit hard, roofs torn away, pets missing, but Iris and Daddy were spared any damage at all. She said it was weird how storms like that would pick and choose where they wanted to cause tragedy to occur, sparing some and destroying others.

Aunt Iris told me about my grandmother, how sweet and caring she was. How she worried about my daddy after he quit school to work in the oil fields. Aunt Iris said, "That's when he started drinking, when he was sixteen, and hanging out with those roustabouts and roughnecks who worked the derricks." When the war came, Daddy enlisted and was gone almost overnight. Aunt Iris said, "Momma was so happy when he went to war. Best thing that could have happened to your daddy was getting into a B-25. It got him out of Pawnee, got him out to see there was something more to the world. And I guess in some ways, even with the war going on, it saved his life. He never got sent over. The war was finished before he could go."

When I asked about my granddaddy, Aunt Iris just said, "Ain't nothing good to tell you about him, except he died as we all expected him to. He died and we buried him and then Momma died of influenza the next winter. They never saw anything good, Raybert, just war and depression. They were just used up quick, and then they were gone."

She told me that with the war on and nothing to keep her in Pawnee, she left to come to Ellenton and work in the mill. There was an article in *Life* magazine about parachutes and how all women would have to stop wearing nylon stockings because the nylon was going into making the canopies. There was a picture of Ellenton and the mill on the front page, a soldier landing on the lawn with a parachute the mill had made the nylon for. Aunt Iris said, "I just had to be a part of that. The South looked nice to me and you know, it didn't look like the wind was blowing, so I packed my bags and came looking for work. Wouldn't you know it, I found your uncle instead."

She said that after the war Daddy didn't know what to do with himself. He went out to Pawnee for a while, but there was nothing for him there, so he came to Ellenton. Aunt Iris said that after he married Momma it was almost like he picked up where he left off in Pawnee and his life got heavier instead of lighter. He took after his daddy more than he did his momma and got involved with bad men, made it harder on himself than he needed to.

I imagined she was talking about Rodney Small when she said that because then she said, "He keeps going out and getting himself in all those fights like he's trying to pay something back. I wish I knew what it was. He's been trying to better himself for a long time now, but with your momma sick and the way he's always getting beat up, I just don't know if he has enough left in him. He's so much like Daddy that sometimes I think the old man has come back to life to get one of us and he's chosen Ray, and he won't give up until he gets him."

Though nothing Daddy did made any sense to Aunt Iris, he could argue on one point: he had no insurance for Momma to stay at the hospital any longer. It was just one more thing he was no good at, and so when he got the first bill, he tried to understand. He said, "This was because she lost the baby." When he got the second, he said, "How can she go from bad to worse?"

Aunt Iris said, "Is there anything we can do to help?" But Daddy never said how they might ease the burden.

When the third bill came, Daddy said, "Enough is enough," and went down and arranged for Momma to leave. He said, "She can sit in her own room all day, if she feels puny. That won't cost us anything."

Aunt Iris said, "Who's going to look after her then?"

Daddy said, "I can do that. I can take care of her."

Aunt Iris said, "Ray, you can't even be in the same room with her when she's sick. You can hardly take care of yourself, much less Evelyn," and then they didn't talk again until it was time to go get Momma.

Daddy left fast on foot looking like he was running from something, and that made me worry about his reasons for bringing momma home, especially since my life had evened out while I lived with Uncle Clewell and Aunt Iris. They gave me a baseball glove and bat and I joined a Little League team playing centerfield for Yarborough Seed and Feed. Palmer joined, too, and played shortstop, a perfect position for a boy who was just a bit more than four feet tall.

I was not very good, and the position I was given was the telltale sign. No kid ever hit the ball into centerfield unless it was by accident. Most hits were ground balls, "worm burners" as Palmer called them, which stayed in the infield where the more coordinated kids played the positions.

Palmer surprised me by how fast he became an efficient infielder. Because he was small and fast, his body was able to get in front of a ball quickly, knock it down and glove it for fast throws to second or first. He could turn a quick double play or throw a kid out trying to take home plate on his own. When he batted, he always got on base, but not because he could hit the ball. Palmer was so small, wild young pitchers had trouble throwing him a strike.

When he crouched down in his batting stance, Palmer was even smaller, so most pitches thrown at him were head high or in the dirt for balls. He walked nearly every time he batted, and so he was used as the lead off hitter, almost always guaranteed to get on base and then score as the heart of the lineup got bloop infield singles and lucky extra base hits into right or left field. He oiled his glove at night and worked on stretching out his hat since even the largest size was too small for Palmer's large moonlike head.

In center, I was left alone for the most part. Every now and then a ball would trickle between the legs of the second baseman or a batter would barely connect and loop one at me. I would have to run up on a dying ball that I could never catch, chase it down and hurl it back toward the infield. I was never very accurate with my throws and usually my aim was at whoever was waving his arms the hardest. I could not remember the different strategies, how to hold a runner on base or when to throw the ball home or to a cutoff man so a run could not score. Mostly I stood in center and watched the action before me, a lone fan in imaginary bleachers cheering when Palmer would make a diving catch or tag a runner he and Tommy Patterson trapped in a rundown. I was no good at baseball, but at least my summer was more normal than it had ever been before. I had not seen Momma since Uncle Clewell carried her out to his car the day of the miscarriage, and now Daddy wanted her home and I was headed to the hospital to pick up someone far different from the person who had left me a month ago.

The small psychiatric ward where Momma stayed for most of the month was connected to the hospital by a covered walk, leading to a door you could only enter after being buzzed inside. The hallway was dark and cool, lit only by small ventlike sconces embedded low along the wall. I remember a great silence surrounding us, the air cold, antiseptic, and sweet like rubbing alcohol. As I walked beside Aunt Iris I wondered how anyone could get well living in such a dark place. There was no movement in the hall, no patients walking in bathrobes or nurses or doctors moving between rooms. It was almost like everyone had known we were there but didn't want anyone else to see us take Momma away.

Outside the room, Aunt Iris stopped me and said, "Your mother is a little nervous about seeing you, so be careful and don't mention any Kennedy. That's all gone now. Just show her how much you love her. Promise?"

"Yes ma'am."

Aunt Iris gave me a kiss on the forehead then pulled a

Kleenex from her purse to wipe away the lipstick. She placed her hand on the back of my shoulder pushing against me ever so slightly, nudging me forward as she knocked on the door and then opened it to reveal not only Momma but my daddy as well. Both of them were waiting in the room, sunlight exploding through open blinds to fill the air with clear bright light, Momma in a wheelchair and Daddy standing behind, anxious to push her home.

My first reaction was to look at Aunt Iris and say, "Can't she walk anymore?"

A soft laugh feathered its way through the room and Daddy said, "She's okay, son. They wheel everybody out of this place. Ain't no big thing."

It was strange to hear his voice after I had not seen him for so long. Daddy looked good, his scabs healing and his ear, though slightly misshapen, fully skinned. He was dressed in a suit, but didn't wear a tie. The collar was unbuttoned and pulled out to lie awkwardly on top of the lapels of his jacket. He was nervous, rocking back and forth on his heels, fidgeting with the handgrips on the wheelchair like he really wanted to get the show on the road, get things moving. He said, "Well aren't you gonna give your momma a hug?"

I walked over to the wheelchair, afraid to touch her, remembering what Aunt Iris had said about being careful when she finally came home. She was beautiful and seemed fully recovered, not frail and breakable, as I had been warned. She wore a sundress and tennis shoes, bracelets on her wrist. She looked young, her face glowing in the light that filled the room. Her hair was pulled back so I could see her whole face and though her skin was very white, she was not pale; Momma looked well and very much alive. Her teeth still made her mouth seem awkward and uncomfortable, but she smiled anyway as she held out her arms. "I won't break, Sweetheart. You can give me a hug."

I leaned down and was gathered up, Momma's grasp firm and reassuring. She smelled sweet and clean, her hair tickling my nose. I stayed close with my head tucked into her neck until she began to cry. She stroked my hair with her hand and whispered, "I missed you so much, Sweetheart. I missed you so much."

Daddy leaned down and whispered, "We can do this later, let's get out of here," and Momma quietly released me, reaching into her lap for a Kleenex. Her eyes kept looking me over, head to toe, her voice weepy when she said, "You look so big, so grown-up. I think you've grown this summer, don't you?" She turned around in the wheelchair to Aunt Iris. "Iris, hasn't he grown? Hasn't he just grown up?"

Aunt Iris walked over, put a hand on my shoulder to gently pull me away. "He's growing like a weed."

Momma let me carry the vase of flowers Aunt Iris had made sure was changed daily while she was in the hospital, freshly cut summer blooms of irises and lilies smelling sweet and full in my hands as Daddy wheeled Momma out into the hot summer sun. We met Dr. Redmond at the front of the hospital. He smiled, leaned down to talk quietly to Momma for a moment and then asked if Daddy would walk with him up the sidewalk.

We stood in the hot sun while Dr. Redmond talked to Daddy, his hands gesturing out in front of him. He looked back to where we stood, smiled once and waved, then walked on dragging Daddy along beside him. They stopped at the door and I could tell Daddy wanted to get away. He lit a cigarette, scissored it between his first two fingers, then poked at Dr. Redmond's chest stopping him in mid-sentence. The doctor's mouth dropped open, his hands on his hips while Daddy talked. Aunt Iris said, "What is he doing now?"

Uncle Clewell said, "Not much, if I know Ray."

Momma sat in the wheelchair looking at me, her lips pinched into a tight little smile while she rubbed my back waiting for Daddy to finish. When he did return, he grabbed Momma's chair and pushed her right past Uncle Clewell, nearly running over Aunt Iris's foot on his way to the car. Momma said, "What did Dr. Redmond want?"

"Nothing more than to wish you bon voyage and best of luck with everything."

Aunt Iris looked at Uncle Clewell and said, "I'm not just gonna stand here and let him ruin this." She stomped off toward Daddy before Uncle Clewell could stop her, grabbed him by the arm and said, "Ray, you have done some bad things in your life, but this takes first place in stupidity."

Daddy said, "Get off it, Iris."

"I'm not getting off anything, Ray Williams."

He grabbed his sister's arm and marched her away from Momma while she sat in the chair waiting for someone to open the car door.

Uncle Clewell said, "Let's get your momma out of the sun while they talk over there."

I said, "Is Daddy in trouble?"

"It's his middle name, no doubt about it."

While we helped Momma into the DeVille, I heard Aunt Iris say, "This is wrong, what you're doing to her. She needs to be inside where people can help her."

Daddy said, "That ain't for you to say."

"Then who, Ray? Who needs to say it? It isn't you, that's for sure."

Daddy looked over to Clewell, spread his arms out like he was giving up. "What the fuck, Clewell?"

Uncle Clewell closed Momma's door and said, "She's your sister, Ray. I can't tell her what to do."

Daddy put his arms on his waist, bounced up and down like he was ready to jog off, to get the hell away from Aunt Iris. I thought then he might just give up and wheel Momma back inside, but instead he jabbed a finger in his sister's face and said, "I done made up my mind about this. It's done, so get off it. Get the fuck off it."

Uncle Clewell walked over and put his hand on Aunt Iris's shoulder, but she just jerked away, her face beet red, like she might be getting ready to have a sunstroke. He looked real pitiful at Daddy, said, "Goddamit, Ray, you beat all, you know that? You just beat all." He came back over to the DeVille and closed Aunt Iris's door. We all waited to see what Daddy would do, standing where Clewell had left him, pissed off in the hot sun. Aunt Iris worried out loud that he might just take off from right there, leave Momma alone again and out of the hospital for us to take care of. She said, "You watch what he does now. Just watch. He's not coming back over here. Not for anything." It's what we all expected him to do, to take off and not even look over his shoulder at the mess he was leaving. I think he surprised us all when instead of running, he calmed himself down and walked over to get in the backseat with Momma and me.

Nobody said much to him after that, but I could tell Aunt Iris was madder than a hornet. She sat in the front seat and for a long time didn't even look into the back when somebody talked to her. Momma acted like nothing had happened, or else she just avoided the whole mess. When everyone was in the car, she said, "It's a beautiful day for a drive.

The light reminds me of early fall. Let's go somewhere fun. Let's pretend its somewhere in September and we're on a secret vacation." Then she whispered in my ear, "No one needs to know where we're going, nobody in the world except us."

I liked that, a secret vacation, like the permanent one Palmer and I had planned that no one else knew about. It was fun to imagine such a place, and so I looked out the window pretending the landscape was new and unknown. I played along with Momma and told her we were disappearing, headed to a secret place only we knew about while Uncle Clewell took us all out to eat at the K&W over in Winston-Salem.

At first, Momma enjoyed the cafeteria, ate fried chicken for the first time since before she had the miscarriage and said, "That's heaven on earth right there." Then she had Daddy go get her another drumstick just so she could take it home with her. While she ate, Momma's will to keep our little game going broke down, and she suddenly burst into tears sobbing openly at the table about the lost baby and her long hospital stay. She seemed so upset that I believed Momma would be sad the rest of her life until just as suddenly, she stopped crying and laughed out loud.

She told some story that no one could really follow, then she wept again. Aunt Iris was worn with worry, but Daddy acted like nothing was wrong. He laughed when Momma laughed and then seemed to just sit there when she cried, waiting for the storm to pass. Before we left for home, Uncle Clewell stopped in Old Salem for some Russian tea and Moravian cookies, but my parents never knew we were there. They had fallen asleep against each other—already exhausted from the short time together.

Aunt Iris went home with Uncle Clewell after dropping

us off. She looked at Daddy and said, "Evelyn's your problem, Ray. I've had it up to here. Let's see what you can do." Daddy just followed Momma inside still half asleep, his back to his sister when he said, "See ya later, alligator."

The days that followed seemed to prove Aunt Iris right. At first Daddy played like he wanted to take care of her, but then he began to lose interest. He came home less and less until he wasn't there much at all.

Momma showed few signs of her illness, at least signs that I could see. My birthday was so close I was completely distracted. While she busied herself with house chores, planted her own garden of midsummer vegetables and tomatoes, I followed the advice Uncle Clewell had given me the day Momma lost her baby and I told *her* what I wanted for my present. I didn't tell my daddy. I asked Momma for a GI Joe, something I had wanted all summer long.

I followed Momma to the clothesline and back inside where she ironed everything rather than taking it to the dry cleaners. I told her about Billy Parker's GI Joe. I said, "Billy Parker's is fully equipped and ready to engage the enemy in battle."

Momma said, "Sounds exciting, if you like war." She ironed underwear and T-shirts, Daddy's handkerchiefs, bed sheets and pillowcases. Because Daddy came home less and less during that time, I would sit up late with Momma and work on my GI Joe. I said, "Billy Parker told me you could buy an F-4 Phantom jet so Air Joe could fly neighborhood combat missions."

Momma said, "Does it really fly, like around the yard or something?"

I said, "No, not really. It's a toy, but he said his daddy

told him air power was superior to anything on the ground, that it had changed the face of war forever."

Momma's mouth turned up along soft creases, "I always wondered how that happened." Then she pulled out clothes she had already ironed just to iron them again, waiting to see if Daddy would come home.

On those occasions when he did come through the door, he was tired and exhausted, barely touching the plate of food Momma always left wrapped in tinfoil and warming in the oven. He would tell me to go to bed and then disappear with Momma into their bedroom, AM static once again melting through the walls. I listened closely, holding my breath so I could hear if Momma ever mentioned my GI Joe.

Sometimes she would cry when Daddy yelled at her. "You shouldn't be so hard on me, you need to take your medicine. It's what they want you to do." Later, he would tell her she was beautiful and that all her hard work was paying off. Momma laughed when he talked sweet like that and then Daddy laughed, too. He'd say, "Be a good girl and come here," and then the wall between our two rooms would tremble and shake until I thought the plaster might fall.

Palmer came by as much as he could, but since the weekend that Evel jumped in the Astrodome, Edgar had insisted that the boy start making money. We had washed cars at Uncle Clewell's dealership the day after, and Palmer had taken home ten dollars that Edgar made him hand over as soon as he walked inside the door. Edgar called it room and board money. Palmer said, "I told him it was RC's house, not his, but that wasn't too smart."

I wouldn't see him for days, but when he did come by, he

was always depressed because he wanted to be there with Momma. Palmer said, "Is she sticking to her medicine? Make sure she takes it, whatever you do. I wish I could be there. You need help with this!" Instead, he spent most of his days at the YMCA cleaning chewing gum off floors, setting pins and oiling the bowling lanes, taking up the slack left after Ronnie Doyle went to war.

When Momma's mood was good, she cooked eggs and bacon, squeezed fresh orange juice and served Aunt Iris's homemade blackberry preserves with buttered toast three times a day. She made sure I got to all my baseball games and even convinced Uncle Clewell to come over on Sunday afternoons to teach me how to shag fly balls in the alley beside our house. When I reminded her about the GI Joe doll, whispered in her ear or slipped her a scribbled note that read *Have you asked him yet?* Momma would just smile and say, "Ask him what?"

I never told Daddy what I wanted, so I guess he decided on his own that thirteen was old enough to be given something real. Maybe he was trying to make up for everything he had done in the past—Rodney Small, his constant disappearing acts. For whatever reasons he had, Daddy decided on his own to get me a Daisy BB gun. On my birthday, he brought the rifle home, wrapped in plain brown paper and laid across his shoulder, surprising me and Momma when he showed up at the front door.

I can't tell you what my emotions were when he gave me the rifle. I can't remember how I first reacted because I had no feeling for the present Daddy gave me that day. I remember Momma's gasp though, and then her words, "Why did you buy the boy a gun?" Daddy didn't answer her. He just huffed and acted like she had said nothing. He bundled up the papers and tossed them into the empty fireplace. He looked at me then and said, "What do you think?"

It didn't take long for me to come around. Awed by the smell of oiled metal and shiny new plastic butt and pump action, I touched and held the rifle, shouldered it and sighted down the barrel. Daddy showed me how to aim for distance and accuracy. "Lick the sight before you look down it, gives you a clean shot that way."

We moved outside into the backyard where he had set up beer cans and some dead pieces of wood to aim at and kill. In a world flattened by dull sunlight, I shot the gun with newfound skill, Daddy easily adjusting my aim with a soft nudge of the rifle at my shoulder or a single word to encourage me to squeeze the trigger slow and steady. We stayed in the yard throughout the afternoon before going in to sit side by side at the kitchen table and eat melted ice cream and cake. There he emptied the BBs into a small plastic cuff-link box he had found for me to use as an ammunition case. He showed me how to clean the gun, oil the spring mechanism and polish the metal barrel. Together we placed the rifle in the gun rack, locked it and hung the key on a hook nailed in the wall. I sat alone looking at the polished blue barrel glistening as Daddy and Momma argued in the kitchen.

After Momma had cut the cake and put ice cream in bowls, she retreated to her room to watch patiently from the window while Daddy taught me how to shoot the rifle. Sometime late in the afternoon, she must have convinced herself that the gun was a bad idea because she came out into the kitchen and turned on Daddy like he was the enemy. She said, "My God, he's only thirteen years old."

Daddy said, "By the time I was thirteen, I'd already killed my first deer."

Momma said, "He doesn't need to do that. He's got nothing to prove. Besides, he didn't need a gun. He wanted something else." But when Daddy asked what I had wanted, she couldn't remember. All she could say was, "He needs something better than you."

Daddy turned an about-face and left the house after that, slamming the screen door behind him. Momma disappeared into her bedroom and did not come out until suppertime to warm up cold eggs and grits. She left the few dishes on the table and told me to go to bed though it was still early with plenty of light left in the sky. Through the walls, I heard her call Aunt Iris and promise that she would stay put. Momma promised over and over to be good, but once she hung up the phone, she moved quickly around the house, gathering her purse and keys like she was about to miss an appointment, some sort of date to be kept. She slammed the door on her way out and drove off in the Buick. I did not see her again until sometime early the next morning after Aunt Iris had fixed me breakfast.

During the next few days, Momma's illness seemed to grow. Aunt Iris gave in more and more. She told Uncle Clewell, "He might let her rot on the vine, but I just can't stand by and let it happen, not when it's right here in front of me."

While Aunt Iris was preoccupied with Momma's health, I began sneaking the gun from the locked rack when no one was around. I'd head off into the woods on the other end of the alley, shooting at anything that moved, playing army while I became my own GI Joe. The BB gun's magazine could hold thirty shots and I could pump them through in less than a minute. I was getting muscles in my left pump arm. I could keep both eyes open and hit with deadly aim.

No Coke bottles were left in my neighborhood. Discarded beer cans lay riddled with holes, BBs rolling around like death rattles inside their aluminum carcasses. I shot out the streetlight in front of my house and chased away three stray dogs, sent them yelping with tails tucked under their rumps after shooting at them from my bedroom window—GI Joe, the deadly sniper. By the end of the week, the gun stayed propped beside my bed, loaded, cocked, and ready to kill.

Once when I was home alone, I shot myself. I meant to remove the magazine to clear a jammed BB. When I went to unscrew the end of the barrel, *Pow!* right in the palm of my hand. It stung like shit, Jesus H. Christ! Fuck! A blood blister formed dark blue and deep, but that was it. No broken bones or skin, just a blister as big as a dime in the middle of my hand. The fact that I survived, the BB only blistering my palm, gave me a sense of control over the rifle and even more so over my life. It made me feel invincible.

The next day, I showed Palmer the rifle for the first time, and he said, "Holy shit, Kemo sabe. Where did that come from?" I told him it was from Daddy for my birthday and then he tried to kiss me as an apology for not being there to give me something. I said, "I'm a sharpshooter now. Don't start that shit again," and then we rode our bikes behind Nichols Market where he stole twenty-four empty bottles and a wooden crate as my present. Palmer set the crate on a stump behind my house while I loaded twenty-four BBs into the magazine. Palmer said, "Show me what you got," and so I busted off each bottleneck with only one shot. When the gun was empty, there were twenty-four jagged-edged bottles where before smooth green glass had swirled.

Palmer said, "Let me see that thing." He held the gun

out from his crotch like it was his dick, said, "Hi yo Silver, away!" He raised it up to his shoulder, drew a long bead, cocked his eye. "Could this thing kill something?"

I said, "This thing's a killing machine," then grabbed the rifle out of his hand. I stood in front of a dogwood tree where a small bird flitted among the branches. I said, "Watch this," and then loaded one BB into my gun. I sighted down the barrel carefully following the bird until it stopped on a small branch, hidden behind a leaf. Palmer said, "Don't you see what you're aiming at?" But I wasn't listening anymore.

Perhaps it was the euphoria of twenty-four BBs, twenty-four bottle tops or the fact that a gun can bring insensitivity to the idea of life itself. Perhaps it was killing something just to make a point or showing off for Palmer, ignoring his warning when he said, "No need to sink that low." Whatever the reason, I shot and killed the bird while it rested there on the tree limb. It fell to the ground unafraid, dead weight, nothing. Palmer looked shocked, all the color leaving his face. He acted like I had just shot him, breaking an invisible bond, crossing over to become Edgar Doyle, or worse yet, my own father.

He said, "Why did you do that? Didn't you hear me yelling? Are you deaf?"

"You asked if I could kill something."

Palmer said, "It was just a question."

We ran over to look in the dirt below the tree. There on the ground, one wing outreaching and crushed, lay a small bird, a blue finch that I had killed in the same way I had shot the tops of the bottles—with one squeeze of the trigger.

Palmer said, "It's a finch, you killed one of the finches."

I said, "I didn't think—"

Palmer said, "Well that's obvious. I saw it and tried to warn you, but you couldn't wait, could you?"

"I thought—"

"No, you didn't, Raybert. That's the last thing you were doing."

I said, "Is it dead?"

Palmer said, "Not only is it dead, it's dead because of you." He looked at me then with eyes sunken so deep into his skull I could not look at him for fear I might fall into the deep black holes and be lost forever. Without warning, Palmer lost control of his voice and in that same shrill, ear-piercing tone he used the day President Kennedy was shot, he screamed, "WHAT DOES THAT MAKE YOU NOW? GOD?" Without waiting for the answer I did not have, he turned and walked out to my front yard and then down the hill toward his house.

I watched as he walked home, his birthmark pulsing again, glowing red hot on the crown of his head. Its impression was blinding, like that late afternoon in November five years earlier when Palmer Conroy showed up in my life for the first time. It burned into my eyes to remain even as he disappeared inside his house. I moved the small finch with the toe of my tennis shoe, rolled it over to discover the dark red spot against its blue feathers where the BB had found its mark. I didn't know what to do standing there alone with a dead bird at my feet. I tried to touch it, tried to pick it up but could not lower myself to the ground. I was frozen once again, unable to finish what I had foolishly started.

I looked for Palmer, felt the blood that had made us al-most brothers drain out of my body until I was completely empty, his birthmark burning against the skin of my eye-lids whenever I squeezed them shut. I turned and ran home, carrying the BB gun back into the empty house. Inside, I locked the rifle in the rack and then went to my room to lie down, wrapped in the sweet familiar certainty of my own geography, waiting.

That evening, I hit the only home run of my life as a baseball player and no one I cared about was there to see it. Palmer never showed for the game, and Momma no longer came to watch me play. She just wanted me to go to Legion Field early, said she had things to do. She drove fast and reckless the few blocks, whipping into the parking lot and almost running over the dozen parents who sat in lounge chairs watching the games. She told me to catch a ride home, but when I said, "Who with?" Momma just looked at me, her eyes distant and blank like she was waiting for the wheels inside her brain to catch up so she could speak. Finally she seemed to focus just enough to know she had to go. "Anyone with a car will do. I haven't got time to come back. Play good," and then she spun away, her speed making heads turn as she disappeared in a cloud of red dust.

Through most of the game I was useless. I stood in the outfield and prayed that nothing would come my way each time a batter swung at the ball. I swore I would never play again after that game. I worried about Palmer and how he had left me so abruptly after I killed the finch, his birthmark still blurring my vision, making my game even worse than it already was. I kept rubbing my eyes looking beyond the outfield fence trying to focus, trying to find Palmer out there walking on the other side searching for lost fly balls. My own act of murder kept my mind off the game, kept me so preoccupied that Tommy Patterson had to whistle at me to come into the dugout when it was our time to bat.

Somewhere in the later innings, I hit it, the ball slipping from the pitcher's hand, a mistaken throw that slowed down, dropped just the slightest as I lifted the bat from my shoulder, closed my eyes and swung. When I finally looked, the ball was high in the air—going, going, gone—the outfielder stopping at the fence, his glove tossed high in the air in a last effort to knock it down. I looked at the umpire and said, "Is that a home run?"

The man behind the mask just blinked at me, wiped a bead of sweat from his eyes and said, "Run the bases, son," and so I did. As I circled first, I felt numb. There was nothing there, no sense of excitement or joy. Afterward, I couldn't even remember hitting the ball or crossing home plate. It was as if I had stood outside myself and watched the whole thing happen, detached, unable to claim something that was good. I could only think about the finch that was still lying on the ground behind my house, the scarlet imprint in its deep blue crest growing outward to become the birthmark glowing against Palmer's skull. I heard his words over and over, what he had said before turning his back on me, *What does that make you now?* It was a question that made me dizzy while I circled the bases alone.

After the game, I waited in the parking lot until the lights were turned off on the field and I knew nobody was coming. I started running, the wind picking up, pushing against my back, thunder rolling in the sky above me. I ran across parking lots, cut through alleys uptown trying to out-race the storm. The narrow streets behind storefronts were filled with discarded boxes and trash bins overflowing their tops. I ran through dark puddles, splashing my ankles and soiling my uniform with mud as words hurriedly spray-painted on the brick buildings caught my eye. *Eat me* and *cocksucker* dripped down the walls scaring me into running faster.

By the time I turned onto Robbins Street, a sheet of water fell from the sky, its runoff flooding the gutters until it spilled out into Third Street. I stood in the middle of the road, kept an eye on Palmer's house and let the water cool my sweaty skin. My house was empty, the windows dark, nobody waiting for me to come home, so I decided to run down the hill letting the rain sting my face, thinking it would help my cause if Palmer saw me wet and whipped by the storm.

I crept through the gate, saw a light on in the trailer, the crawl space door closed and locked. I needed to tell Palmer I was sorry for what I had done. I wanted his forgiveness, so I walked over and knocked on the trailer door. When nothing happened, I knocked again, tried the doorknob and said, "Palmer, it's me, Raybert, let me in." The trailer was locked, but I heard someone moving things around inside, scurrying, whispering. When the door finally did open, Cindy Conroy stuck her head out and said, "Palmer ain't here. He's working the Y tonight, they got leagues."

I said, "He missed the ballgame and I was worried. . . ."

Cindy looked flustered, her hair wild around her face, her eyes red and glassy. She wore jeans cut off high up her legs and was braless in a tank top, her nipples hard and pointy against the fabric when she leaned out of the trailer. She was smoking a cigarette, looking out beyond me like she was scanning the backyard for others who might see her. She said, "You got to go, Raybert, Palmer ain't here." And then she cracked the door just enough so I could see Edgar Doyle sitting shirtless on the cushions, his head back and eyes closed. There was a nearly empty bottle of liquor sitting on the table, Edgar's .38 beside it, the chrome gun heavy and dangerous in the dull light. Edgar looked like he was passed out or drunk, but I wasn't going to wait to find out.

Cindy said, "Go, you little shit," and then she closed the trailer door, locking it behind her.

I ran around the corner and stood in the wet shadows of bushes wildly overgrown and watched the trailer thinking of Cindy and how she had looked, her arms gathered in front of her, bare feet tucked inward pigeon-toed. She looked different from the night she ran to Johnny Troutman, rougher somehow and scared when she closed the trailer door and locked the rest of the world out. I stood there trying to understand what I had just seen. I stood in a silence so dead, I did not know if I would ever be able to hear anything again. Then lightning crackled through the sky above my head, and I got so scared I could feel my knees begin to buckle. I knew if I didn't run then, I would fall down right there and never get up.

I found myself in full flight running up Robbins Street, into the alley and under my window where I hoisted myself up into my room. I stood in the dark for what seemed like forever watching Palmer's house through a storm that showed no signs of letting up. It was a desolate scene at the bottom of our street, and even from that good distance, I did not feel safe. Palmer's house looked unsettled, the shingles warped and separated, ready to fly off and disintegrate into nothing at any moment.

That night in my room, I could feel all our chances to escape slipping away. It was an empty feeling, like watching that baseball fly across the fence, its responsibility for flight mine, though I felt outside it all, lost and untethered, a feeling as deadly and lethal as Edgar Doyle's silver-plated .38, loaded, cocked, and placed right smack between my eyes.

*F*rom then on, Edgar Doyle kept close tabs on Palmer and his sister, never letting either stray too far from his sight. Each day I watched as the carport door would open, the glass pushing outward to flash ambient light across its smooth surface like the winking eye of a lighthouse. Palmer and Cindy appeared on the steps, Edgar Doyle right beside them like he was their real father. He stood at the edge of the carport keeping close watch as Palmer mounted his bike for the ride to the Y. Cindy would sit on the carport steps, chain-smoking cigarettes, the trailer waving ominously in the heat behind them.

I only got to see these glimpses from my window as I watched Palmer leave the house each day to pedal up Third Street in the rising heat. Cindy stayed outside after he disappeared. She watched Edgar as he bent down on his knees to go through his boxes. He tossed stuff out like he didn't care about it anymore, like whatever he searched for was worth throwing everything else out. I wondered if it was my daddy

Edgar Doyle was looking for or maybe evidence of Momma sneaking out to meet him, his fine piece of snatch. It was hard not to think such things.

Aunt Iris continued having a difficult time. Momma had found her crazy clothes out in the garage and began accusing everyone of plotting against her. She screamed and threatened that if Iris ever tried to hide the clothes again, she would skin her alive and boil her in oil.

Aunt Iris said, "You need to take your medicine, Evelyn. It will help you not think like that." But Momma was done with anything she had to put in her mouth and swallow, and though we did not know it at the time, she had already flushed her prescription down the toilet, cursing each pill as it plopped in the bowl.

She surprised everyone by coming into the kitchen one afternoon wearing the crazy clothes, ready to go to her doctor's appointment all on her own. Aunt Iris said, "You look like Betty Boop in that ridiculous stuff."

Momma just posed, pushing her hips out and spreading her arms to show off her body. She said, "Nothing's wrong with this sexy thing."

She told Aunt Iris that she would drive herself across town and had jingled the keys in front of her. "My mind's made up, so get out of the way, sister." She spun the car out of the garage and drove carelessly up the street while Aunt Iris called the doctor to tell him she was coming by herself, that he had better look out for her.

Later she would tell Aunt Iris that everything had been fine as long as she was outside and moving, fresh air filling her lungs. Inside, the waiting room was so stuffy and hot, she couldn't breathe. The plastic vinyl seat started sticking to skin exposed by the Liz Taylor outfit, pulling at her thighs until she thought she'd go crazy. She flipped through magazines and complained out loud about the elevator music that was making her sick to her stomach.

When she tried to smoke a cigarette in the waiting room, one of the nurses spoke to her through the glass window asking that she step outside if she needed to do that. Momma said that it was all the shit going on around her that made it impossible. "It was too goddamn hot and depressing. Einstein himself would have gone crazy sitting in that room."

She said the women behind the glass kept laughing and talking about her, that she recognized one she went to high school with, a bitch even back then. They made phone calls and glanced into the waiting room looking straight at her, laughing out loud. When she'd had enough, Momma stood up to walk outside for a cigarette, but instead something had snapped and she made a sharp turn, flip-flapping her way to the glass partition.

Momma said, "It was like I knew I was walking up there, but I was outside my own body cheering a cheer. *Ra Ra Re, Kick 'em in the knee! Ra Ra Rass, Kick 'em in the ass!* I walked right up to those girls, stuck my middle finger into the window, waved it like a flag on the Fourth of July, mostly at whatever-the-hell-her-name-was 'cause she was the bitch in high heels."

The next thing she remembered was walking out into heat so unforgiving it made her stomach tighten and cramp, the vomit on its way up into her throat before she could get to the car. The doctor's office called Aunt Iris and she rushed uptown to help with the search. Momma's car was still in the parking lot but sat empty, vomit on the ground in front of the door. They found her soon enough crumpled behind the building after someone inside reported the phone lines had suddenly gone dead. She was sitting against the back wall, tightly gripping a fistful of telephone wires.

Dr. Redmond told Aunt Iris that Momma needed to be back in the hospital, but she said, "Ray won't do that." Then she crossed her heart and swore that she would keep her on the medication.

Dr. Redmond said, "You can try, but I doubt it'll work. Evelyn is awful dangerous to herself."

From that moment on, she had Dr. Redmond call in Momma's prescriptions to the Rexall and then went there herself to pick them up. She organized the pills, set them out for Momma to take with a glass of water each morning. She slept in the room with her sharing a bed since Daddy was still missing. Uncle Clewell quietly paid for the rewiring of the telephones, and with all of Aunt Iris's care, Momma wavered, but she held her own and seemed to get better.

One afternoon in early August, the paper arrived with the picture of a full moon hanging below a headline, ECLIPSE TONIGHT, RONNIE DOYLE DEAD: A HERO. The odd placement of words and photograph seemed to confuse Momma as she tried to make some kind of jumbled sense out of what was in front of her. Momma was reading the article for a second time when she tossed the paper down onto the kitchen table and said, "All this will bring him home. You just watch," then got up and walked outside to sit on the porch swing and wait.

Aunt Iris followed the details on the back page where they continued in the obituaries. "It doesn't say how the boy died, just that he was a hero." She looked out toward the porch where Momma sat motionless in the swing, then spoke low like she was talking to herself when she said, "This can't be good. This can't be good at all."

By suppertime, everyone on Robbins Street had heard the news and knew of Ronnie Doyle's fate. We had just finished eating dinner on the front porch, tomato sandwiches and cantaloupe, homemade sweet pickles and cold potato salad. Aunt Iris cleared the TV trays and was serving us each a second glass of iced tea when Bernie Potter came outside, walked across the street and stood in our front yard looking toward the bottom of the hill. Momma said, "Now what in the hell does she want standing in our yard like that?"

Aunt Iris said, "Evelyn, watch your tongue."

Momma said, "I ain't watching nothing. It's my property."

If Bernie heard Momma, she paid her no mind, just stood there by the curb on Daddy's dying grass and said, "Isn't it just awful, that poor boy?"

Aunt Iris said, "Do you know any more about what happened?"

Bernie said, "No, just what I read tonight. He died in some place called Pleiku, wherever that is."

I said, "It's in Vietnam," but then felt silly, my face burning red hot when Bernie smiled and said, "Thank you, Raybert," and then repeated my words to Aunt Iris in her singsongy voice. Then she said, "It's just awful to die in a war like that, even if he was a hero." She stood there for a long minute with her arms crossed, looking back down the street. "Well, let me know if you see anything," and then she turned to go.

A flat light seeped beneath the canvas awning, skirting our front porch while Momma watched Bernie cross the street. Momma said, "What a sneaky b-i-t-c-h," spelling it out like she was trying to make it mean more than it ever could. Her hair fell in strings around her cheeks, floated in disarray from failed attempts to pin it back with bobby pins. She stroked her neck, rubbing beads of sweat smooth against her skin while her eyes stayed fixed on some distant point that I think Aunt Iris recognized but was helpless to do anything about.

Aunt Iris said, "Evelyn, did you take your pills today? You need to be consistent if you want to stay well." But Momma just lifted herself off the swing like she wasn't interested in what Aunt Iris had to say. She said, "Ray'll be here soon, and he'll be hungry. Then he'll want to do something about all this." She left the porch, moving through the house to the kitchen where she started making Daddy a sandwich.

At the bottom of the street Palmer's house remained as deserted and empty as any other day, the curtains pulled tight, the house itself standing weakly in a yard that always needed the grass cut. It was in stark contrast to when RC died. The block had been lined with cars and people coming to the house to pay their respect while toting along casseroles and cooked hams to feed the grieving family. Now there was nothing except the noise of the bugman spraying the neighborhood trees a block over on Vance Street.

Aunt Iris and I were watching Palmer's house for signs of life when I turned and saw the Cadillac appear at the top of the hill. It swallowed the road as it took a sharp angle in toward the curb. Inside, Uncle Clewell was not alone. A shadowy figure rode beside him, and as the car came to a stop in front of our house, I could see what Momma had already known. Daddy *was* coming home riding shotgun in the DeVille.

When the car came to a stop, he opened his door and

stepped out, all spic and span, clean-shaven and wearing that same suit he had worn when he wheeled Momma from the hospital. Although he had been a deserter since my birthday, Daddy still had strength in his step and he came to the porch with his head held high, his eyes focused and forward-looking. I slouched in the swing dressed in my Grubb's Feed and Seed uniform and could not look at his face, afraid I would somehow reveal my sudden disappointment that he had come back home.

Daddy slid onto the porch like a piece of melting ice. He said hello to Aunt Iris, leaned over and kissed her cheek. He smelled of Vitalis and English Leather, a colliding mix of hair oil and cologne wafting across the porch as he straightened back up and glanced over at me. He said, "Well looky here, Roger Maris, how you doing slugger?" He tussled my hair with his scratched-up hand and then magically palmed a baseball card of the outfielder, tossing it into my lap.

On the back of his picture were Maris's stats: 61 in 1961 to pass the Babe, 851 RBI's and over 1,300 hits in twelve seasons, a Hall of Famer still waiting for the call. I flipped the card over to look at his picture. Roger held a bat on his shoulder like he didn't care if he ever hit another homerun, like he couldn't have cared less about the record.

Daddy tried to smile though it was difficult. Up close I could see his face was cut and bruised, his lip badly split again, and I thought one of his teeth was missing near the front. Aunt Iris said, "Are you back to stay now?"

Daddy looked at her like she was just crazy. He said, "I never left, Iris. Been here all the time." He tried to smile again, but it didn't work any better than the first try.

Uncle Clewell said, "He wanted to go see Ronnie Doyle."

Daddy looked through the screen door. "There's the viewing tonight. Thought that would be the right thing to do knowing Edgar and all." He stretched his neck out farther to look inside the house. "How's Evelyn?"

"She's holding her own, so for right now, she's all right. You got to keep her on it, Ray. You can't just assume—"

"I got you, Iris." Then Daddy looked at me like he was telling his sister to shut up.

I said, "She takes her medicine twice a day. Aunt Iris puts it out on the table for her. She's taking real good care of Momma."

Daddy acted like he didn't much care to hear that come from my mouth. He said, "Well thank you, Dr. Kildare. Didn't know you were an expert on such things."

Momma came out onto the porch then and stood beside me, her hand touching my shoulder. She was looking at Daddy like nothing at all was wrong, like he hadn't been gone for weeks. Daddy just smiled when he saw her.

Momma said, "Ronnie Doyle died in the war."

Daddy said, "That's the news all right. Thought I better go visiting. You feeling up to a drive?"

Momma said, "I think I should go with you, if that's what you mean. But you ought to eat first. Your dinner's sitting on the table." Then she looked at me and said, "Clewell can take you to your game tonight."

I glanced down at Maris's face and could see something that had been oblivious to the photographer's eye, a disappointment in what had happened in his career, his eyes dark and sad. I thought of the homerun and the fact that still no one I cared about knew I had hit it and probably never would. Then it struck me that my face could have been put on that baseball card, the darkness of my own eyes going unnoticed and irreconcilable. I said, "I'll just strike out. I don't want to go."

Daddy looked back at me when I said that. "You don't get better unless you play."

I said, "I know that."

"Then what's the problem?"

"There ain't no problem."

Daddy's eyes sliced toward the door. "Then go get your glove."

The roar of the bugman at the bottom of the hill distracted me, the oily white cloud billowing, coming toward us to suffocate any chance that I could win this argument. Daddy was making a point, and though he needed only to come back home to stake his claim as my father, I felt that familiar sick feeling in my stomach for who he was and what I still believed he stood for.

I got up, but instead of going toward the door, I jumped for my bike that leaned against the front steps. Daddy tried to catch me, but my quick step caught him off guard and he missed terribly when he tried to lip his cigarette and then get close enough to grab me off the bike. He flicked the half-spent cigarette into the yard, whistling through his teeth for me to stop, but the roar of the bugman ate up the shrill noise. I ignored his command, diving then into the wall of white where my eyes burned and the sweetness of the bug poison irritated my throat.

The cloud dissolved into an oily blue hue as I leaned full speed into the corner at the bottom of the hill. I pedaled the short distance to Park Street where the fog cleared except for the faint smell of diesel, and there where Third Street cut across, I saw Palmer stealing a stop sign.

He had stopped on his way home from the Y, shinnied up the pole in the poisonous cloud and was wrenching off the top bolt, the bottom already loose and dangling. Now he was racing, the bugman's spray no longer hiding his theft. I skidded to a stop below the pole leaving a thick black arc of tire rubber and watched Palmer work the bolt. He sweated, his T-shirt wet against his back. The rust from the pole flaked onto his cutoff jeans while his small stumpy legs gripped tightly, metal cutting deep indentations into his snow-white skin.

The sign broke free and fell to the ground slicing into the dirt at the bottom of the pole. He shinnied down the rusty shaft so quickly that he scraped huge raspberries on the inside of both his thighs. Palmer said, "Shit God almighty!" then rubbed spit into the palms of his hands to gently touch the wounds with cool saliva.

The sign was almost as big as Palmer, but he still picked it up and flew it over into the tall grass of a vacant lot. "Don't tell nobody I done that."

I said, "Okay."

There was an awkward silence while we stood facing each other. It had been a long time since we were together. Palmer said, "Ronnie Doyle's dead. He got killed in Vietnam."

I said, "I heard. Daddy came home to go see him."

"That don't surprise me. He and Edgar are cut from the same mold. Hell, Edgar probably took that picture of old Rod, said, 'Smile, you're on *Candid Camera*!' "

I said, "I don't doubt that."

"I'm suppose to be at home, but I don't want to go. Edgar is being a real asshole right now."

I said, "That ain't nothing new."

Palmer laughed then and the moment of awkwardness

was broken. He leaned over to give me a hug. The motion of his small body reaching made me want to move, push him away, but I didn't. I let Palmer Conroy hold on, his head pressed against my chest, the birthmark glowing red hot in the dying light.

I said, "I shouldn't have killed that bird. I'm really sorry about that."

Palmer said, "It's in your blood. You can't do nothing about it. Just don't do it again or you might not be able to stop." Then he let go, and I felt a sudden need to tell the rest of it, to confess what I had seen that night in his backyard. I said, "I was at the trailer the other night."

Palmer said, "When?"

"After I killed the finch."

He got real nervous then, like it was the first time he had heard such things out in public, the secret no longer a secret. "I guess he had the pig in there?"

I said, "Yeah."

"Well, I can't stop what he does with her. No way."

I said, "Forget it Palmer. He had the gun with him. Scared the shit out of me."

Palmer said, "Everybody is saying Ronnie Doyle is a hero, but he didn't even kill anybody over there. Ronnie died taking a shit against a tree."

"What?"

"He walked off a road, pulled his pants down and then just when he was about to drop it, a sniper shot him through the neck. *Kablamb!* Edgar got the letter from his sergeant, but he's telling everybody a different story. He's telling a lie."

I stood there for a moment trying to think about the Ronnie Doyle I knew, this creature of fast cars and parade queens leaning against a tree in some jungle with his pants dropped to his ankles, and just when the getting was good, just as he was about to drop an anchor, *Pow!* Lights out for good. I said, "Man, what a way to go."

Palmer nodded. "No hand and eye coordination needed there, I guess. Edgar's pissed at the world. Now he says he's gonna sell the Catalina. I heard him tell Inez he was putting a For Sale sign on it after the funeral; said he was going to drive Ronnie's BelAir from now on. Ain't that some kind of shit."

"So, what are you going to do?"

He waited a moment looking around to make sure no one else would hear what he was about to say next. "Well, I've been thinking about all that. I got something I want you to see. Come on, let's get the hell out of here." And so we rode our bikes side by side through the last dying wisps of the bugman's spray, two delinquents on the run pumping pedals all the way out to Finch Creek.

Deep along the back edge of the woods where Rodney Small had hung, one lone picnic table sat overgrown and forgotten. The trail leading down to it was nothing more than a path of vine and poison oak, wide enough for a boy's foot or bike tires to navigate. Palmer sat down on the top of the table, lit up, then tossed me the pack of menthols. The coolness with which the smoke went down gave me confidence. I felt as though I was Palmer's accomplice, that I had been there when he decided to shinny up that pole to steal the stop sign. I imagined encouraging him to take it by offering the double dare he could not refuse. It was something I could hold on to, and I felt safe in the woods, waiting for Palmer Conroy to show me the goods.

I sat down on the table and inhaled deeply, the glow of the cigarette cherry red and burning upward toward my fingers. Palmer walked over to a large dead tree that had been hollowed out near the bottom of its trunk, knelt down and reached so far up into the hole that I imagined his arm eaten off, devoured by the very thing he was reaching to get. When it came back out, he held a mayonnaise jar with a paper bag rolled up tight inside sealing off the contents from the rest of the world. Palmer said, "I bet these are worth twenty-five to life."

Under the green canopy that hid us, he unscrewed the lid and pulled out the paper bag. Then he showed me more pictures, Polaroids of his sister Cindy, naked in the trailer. There were poses revealing every God-given inch of her body. Pointy breasts with dark round nipples, long slender legs spread in one photograph, another with them pulled up under her so she held her breasts up like she was aiming both at a target. She had beautiful blond hair that fell past her shoulders in tight curls. Some pictures had her breasts playing peekaboo with her hair. In others she held the long curls up with slender arms stretching her torso toward the ceiling of the trailer, red panties pulled down to her knees, light downy hair sprouting between her legs.

I had seen Cindy sunbathing in her bikini and I had imagined her with Johnny Troutman that night he peeled out in his Barracuda, but now I saw her in a way I never could have imagined.

Palmer said, "Edgar Doyle took these." Then he shuffled the pictures like a deck of cards. "They thought I was gone, but I come back out from the crawl space and sat under the window after Cindy went inside. Edgar took these pictures long after Inez was snoring away in the bedroom. He was telling her to 'Take it off baby.' He said, 'You're nothing but a dirty little girl, so show me what ya got.' "

I said, "She did what she was told."

Palmer said, "The pig can follow directions, that's for sure. She wants to be Miss America or something."

I said, "She's got my vote."

Palmer arranged the Polaroids like he was sizing them up, getting things in order. "While Edgar's burying Ronnie in the ground, I'm gonna bury him. I'm putting these where Inez will see what her lover boy's been up to."

I took one last look at Cindy's nude body, poses she seemed to enjoy making, though on the night I had seen her in the trailer there was real fear in her eyes. I said, "Edgar sure likes taking pictures, don't he?"

Palmer said, "Between Rodney Small and my sister, he's a real Norman Rockwell. But he can't find these and it's driving him crazy. He's been turning the house upside down looking for them." He stuffed the bag of evidence into his pants and snubbed out his cigarette. He said, "That's my plan, but you got to be ready to go because we won't have much time."

"What for?"

"I ain't waiting no more. I think we should leave for the beach as soon as I take care of Edgar." He jumped off the table and walked over to his bike. "I've almost got all the stuff we need, but we got to leave before Edgar sells RC's car, so get a bag packed."

He rode up the path, the bike teetering against the hill until he turned onto flatter ground, stopped and looked back at me, his silhouette small against a white sky. Palmer said, "You promise you'll be there?"

I said, "Yeah, but when are we going?"

"Soon, so be ready. Just promise me you'll be ready. You're going to have to help me drive since I can't reach the pedals."

I said, "I promise."

Palmer smiled, and then raised his arm to throw a salute. "Atomic batteries to power, turbines to speed. See you later Kemo sabe." Then he turned and disappeared.

I stood for a moment looking around at what was left of my world, the summer thick and full but quickly coming to an end. I didn't want to go home and face Daddy's belt. I thought it would be better to stay, to find a place to lie down and wait for the eclipse, when the earth choked off the light from the sun and turned the lunar surface so dark that Palmer and I could easily escape without being seen.

I had forgotten to say anything to Palmer about the full moon eclipse, and though at the time I thought little more about it, later I wondered, if I had mentioned something that night, if Palmer and I would have stayed together and watched the moon darken before trying to escape, would things have turned out differently? Would the eclipse have even mattered to us, maybe changed the way our summer was about to end?

CHAPTER
XVI

*I*n the middle of that moonlit night, I was awakened by a kiss. The soft touch of warm damp skin to my cheek eased me awake and I opened my eyes to find Momma, illuminated and floating above me. She was smoking and I could smell Daddy's Jim Beam on her breath. Momma stayed close, her mouth lowered until I thought she might kiss me again. Instead she passed cool fingers over my face, touching my mouth to keep me quiet. "Shuuu. Don't be afraid, it's me."

I said, "Hey Momma."

Momma said, "Are you all right? Are your wounds healed?"

I had left the woods shortly after Palmer, knowing full well who would be waiting to punish me for the way I had disobeyed his command to stay put. I had expected Daddy's belt and wasn't disappointed. He stood me on the porch, made me lower my uniform pants in front of the whole neighborhood as he made his point to not sass him again. Daddy said, "You're a smart little man, ain't you?"

I said, "No sir."

He raised his eyes at that, said, "Well now, it seems just a while ago you were smarter than you are now. Where did you go to get dumb again?"

I said, "Nowhere."

He sat there looking at me with my pants at my ankles. I could see through the living room windows where Momma stood, her hands over her face while Aunt Iris tried to coax her back into the kitchen. Uncle Clewell sat on the davenport smoking a cigarette, reading about Ronnie Doyle. Daddy said, "Ain't nobody in there gonna help you out here. It's just you and me. Understand that?"

I said, "Yes sir."

Then he stung my legs with a belt doubled over in his hand striking me three times against the back of my thighs until welts rose across burning skin. He waited to see tears well up and then hit me hard three more times, the leather strap whistling as it broke across the hot night air.

When Daddy had finished, it felt like a hundred hornets had left their stingers deep beneath my skin. My thighs burned, and if I moved or flexed a muscle, it felt like he was hitting me all over again, even after the belt had been re-looped through his pants.

Daddy said, "Now get your britches up before somebody walks by here and sees you half-naked." He left me on the porch to sort myself out while he went inside to finish his dinner and get ready for Ronnie Doyle's visitation.

While Momma waited, I felt below the covers for damage the belt had caused, but the sting was gone, the welts no longer swollen on my legs. I told her I was okay, that the whipping no longer hurt, and she smiled and said, "Good. Then you need to wake up, darling. I need a copilot tonight."

I said, "Where we going?"

Her face flushed deep red like what I had just asked set her on fire. "It's your daddy. He's at it again."

I sat up and rubbed sleep from my eyes. "I thought he was looking at Ronnie Doyle?"

Momma laughed at that. "He saw him all right."

Momma had found what was left of her crazy clothes. The blouse was different, a white tank top now, and I could see her shadowed breasts stretching empty and slack, free from the pushup bra that made her something more. She still wore the skirt and the flip-flapping shoes, though the rhinestones were falling off, the shooting star on her right foot nothing more than a clutter of colored stones. She was disheveled, the sexy look roughed up around the edges, and so instead of getting up, I sat there and asked, "Where's Aunt Iris? Does she know you're up?" but that just brought Momma in close again.

She took me by the arm, jerked me enough to shake loose any sleep that was left. "This has nothing to do with her. It's about your father. He's drinking with niggers and sleeping with whores. Now get dressed. I need a copilot and that's your job."

I crawled out of bed and put on my shorts, a T-shirt, and tennis shoes. Earlier my parents had been steadied by the death of Ronnie Doyle. Now something had gone terribly wrong; Momma was dressed up no differently than those she sought. I thought about her medication, trying to re-member if she had taken it that day or any day before. I could see Momma sitting at the kitchen table, Aunt Iris putting the pills before her, but it was impossible to remem-ber Momma actually taking the medication. That image of her head tilted back while she drank a glassful of water was nowhere to be found.

I looked out my window to see the Catalina still covered in Palmer's carport. He had seemed so ready standing there in the woods straddling his bike that I thought he might have shown up by now. Below my bed, I had a small bag of things packed that I would take with me. It was tucked away, ready for when Palmer drove up beside my window and said, "Hi yo Silver, away!" Momma was chasing her tail bad when she came into my room to get me. I didn't want to go with her and risk missing Palmer, but if I didn't, she'd go alone and I might not ever see *her* again. There was no choice that was good in any of this, so I just tied my tennis shoes and followed her outside.

When I stepped off our back porch, I looked into the ink-black sky. A shadowy darkness sliced along the edge of the moon, the eclipse just beginning. I met Momma in the garage where she waited in the Buick. We sat in the heat and dead air, her hands locked on the steering wheel with the intent to go somewhere as soon as something in her head clicked and gave her direction. When her eyes cleared, she opened her door to slide a foot outside the car and said, "Help me push." We slowly guided the Buick out of the garage and into the alley until it faced the street. Momma said, "Buckle up for safety," and then she turned over the ignition, gunning the engine quickly before Aunt Iris could wake up and come stop her from hunting Daddy.

We headed out Highway 52 in the fading light of the moon, past service stations, the Donut Dinette and the all night Kwik-Pik. These places seemed magical to me, parking lots bathed in neon and fluorescent light, people mingling, sitting on the hoods of their cars, smoking cigarettes and drinking beer while they watched the sky above them. They lived in a world I could only imagine, a world I dreamed of running away to with Palmer Conroy as soon as he was ready to go.

Momma seemed more at ease traveling and I imagined us on a road trip to the beach, nighttime driving, if we could have just kept going, kept pushing to the coast. I could have told Momma about Palmer and our plans for living at Myrtle Beach, suggested that we go by and pick him up on our way out of town, but she was after Daddy, and I knew that there was nothing I could say or do that would stop her. I remained silent as we rode on the backside of Ellenton. Where we went, no streetlights followed, only shadowed houses with curbless red dirt yards. We moved slowly as if she wanted to sneak up and surprise him and those who she was so certain gave him cover.

She had become suspicious of Daddy while they were at the funeral home, had seen the way he looked at the boy in the casket, and then talked to that woman with the small child. Some bitch, Momma said, who bounced her baby boy on a knee and looked at Daddy like he owed her something. She told me this as we drove, how she knew Daddy was fucking that girl, the eyes of the baby like his, droopy and soft. Momma said, "He'd have put his dick in her right there if I would've let him. But there was no way in hell he was going to do that to me in front of God and that dead boy."

She went up to the casket and put her hand on the boy's cheek, the skin tight and cold, stone-cold, Momma said. "It felt like rock in midwinter, that boy was no more than a piece of stone." When Daddy came to stand beside her, to view the body of Ronnie Doyle, Momma pulled him close and through her growing rage, said, "You can't fuck everything you see in front of you. That bitch over there keeps looking like there's something going on. If you fucked her, that's one thing. If the baby's yours, you won't get out of here alive."

Momma said she got dizzy then. "I had him by the balls. He was so full of shit he couldn't even talk straight. He looked over to Edgar and then we left, and when I got out into the car, I had to stick my head between my legs to breathe."

I said, "That girl was Erlene Hobbs, Momma, and that baby was Ronnie Doyle's. Everybody knows that." But she didn't hear a word I said.

She kept her eyes straight ahead concentrating on the road running out before her. "Raybert, your daddy is such a pitiful human being, just pitiful." Then she accelerated the car and I didn't try again. There was no reason to say anything more.

We continued searching for the man who had brought her home that evening and then disappeared to let her chase her tail. Each time she failed to find any trace of him, the ease with which she drove would begin to twist and turn into unforgiving conspiracies. Momma said, "They know I'm coming. They're helping him do this to me. I swear to God, I wouldn't spit on them if they were on fire."

Back in town the houses of friends and neighbors became part of Momma's suspicions and Bernie Potter became the bull's-eye at which she aimed the car. She drove into her neighbor's yard stopping only inches away from the azalea beds, and then went to bang on the screen door before she barged right past Mr. Potter to confront Bernie face-to-face. She accused her of fornication, betrayal. Momma said it was Sodom and Gomorrah and everyone involved would turn into a pillar of salt if she had anything to do with it. Bernie took it all quietly, listening to Momma rant and then trying to console her.

Mr. Potter came out to the Buick while Momma stood inside the door screaming at Bernie. He was a small, thick man, tanned around the neck and arms, balding, a paunch sticking out that pushed his undershirt beyond his belt. He leaned into the window looking around as if he was thinking about buying the car. I said, "Is my daddy here?"

"No Raybert, we were asleep. It's past midnight. We were asleep."

"Where's Momma?"

Mr. Potter took a deep breath and glanced back at the house. "She's screaming at Bernie about your Daddy. Do you know where he is?"

I said, "No sir. He went to look at Ronnie Doyle tonight, that's all I know."

"To look at him?"

"Yes sir, at the funeral home."

"Oh, you mean the viewing. He went to view Ronnie Doyle's body."

"Yes sir, he went there tonight."

"Did your momma go with him?"

"Yes sir. But they got into some kind of a fight and he brought her home, then he left."

"And you haven't seen him since?"

"No sir. But Momma thinks he's doing something bad, something about Ronnie Doyle's baby being his. I think she's confused about things. I was supposed to have a baby brother or sister, but Momma had a miscarriage."

Mr. Potter raised his eyes at me, then he said, "I heard about that, and I'm real sorry Evelyn lost the baby. It was a shame, really was. Things like that shouldn't happen, but they do all the time, no reason that you can find to explain. They just happen."

I said, "Well, I think she's confused about that. I think she's just upset being out of the hospital and all."

Mr. Potter looked down to the ground outside the car door and then spit into the grass. "Your Momma's as good a woman as they come when she's right, Raybert, but she can get as crazy as an old coot sometimes, just downright crazy."

I glanced back up at the moon, the shadow of the earth halfway across, its remaining light murky and dulled. Mr. Potter said, "I can't let her keep yelling at Bernie, no matter what's going on in that head of hers." He turned then to go back inside, his steps heavy in the darkness. He disappeared through the door and the shouting stopped. In a moment he reemerged with Momma, dragging her by the arm. She no longer yelled, but she was not very cooperative in leaving either.

Mr. Potter opened the driver's side door and shoved her inside. When he pushed her down, her head popped the top of the car like an egg cracking on the side of a pan. The impact stunned her for a moment and Momma sat dazed while Mr. Potter talked to her in a voice that was quiet but stern. "Now Evelyn, the boy says you were with Ray this evening, so you got no cause to be here. We haven't seen him, so do yourself a favor and go across the street and wait. Don't come back over here tonight, do you understand?"

Momma sat there, her jaw tightening, the muscles clenching like a fist. She never looked at Mr. Potter, just stared straight ahead as if she was already back on the road headed for her next stop. Momma said, "Wayne Potter, don't think I don't know what you're doing. You keep Bernie away from my goddamn husband or I'll splatter you both to kingdom come."

Mr. Potter looked over at me, his eyes sad and tired. He said, "Don't let her come back, boy. Make her go home." Just then Momma saw Aunt Iris come out on the porch to find us sitting in Bernie's front yard. Before she could get down the steps, the Buick lunged forward nearly running over Mr. Potter's bare feet, tread marks ripping across soft fescue to cut deep gashes into the lawn.

We left, bouncing the car into the street, almost hitting Aunt Iris who moved a split second before she would have been run down. She jumped up onto the curb yelling at Momma to stop as we swerved down Robbins Street toward Palmer's house. The dying moon had changed everything with its shadow, the fading geography of my street completely altered as Momma took the curve in front of Palmer's house.

Like that night we witnessed Evel Knievel jump in the Astrodome, the first moments along Third Street slowed to a crawl. There in the shadows created by an eclipsing moon, I saw alongside Palmer's house a carport so abandoned and empty that I knew immediately everything was over. The tarp was tossed away, crumpled in the front yard, and Palmer Conroy was gone. What I viewed as we passed made me feel utterly alone, and I believed then that I would never escape a world that had no plan for me. I could not see any significance to my life now that I had failed to be there for Palmer, as I had promised.

We drove for what seemed like hours and found nothing, Momma steadfastly refusing to go by the dry cleaning plant where I knew Daddy would be waiting. Each time I suggested it, she would say, "Save your breath, Raybert. I wouldn't go over there if Jesus himself was saving souls at the counter." In her short-circuiting mind, we remained in pursuit, looking through every dead-end corner of Ellenton while my eyes helplessly scanned the roads in search of the Catalina.

It was shortly after the eclipse was full, the night at its darkest moment that we ran out of gas. The car sputtered and coughed, lurched forward in an attempt to keep going before it died in the parking lot of the Legion baseball field. The sudden turn of events, the loss of motion, the bleak darkness that engulfed us seemed to take Momma by surprise. She sat in silence looking out over the deserted diamond, sighed and took her hands from the steering wheel. "Well. I never saw this coming."

We sat in the darkened car listening to the engine pop and tick as it began to settle down for the night. I wondered where Palmer might be, how far down the road he could have traveled by now driving a car whose pedals he could not reach.

Out on the field an old stray dog was jumping high into the night air snapping at candle moths that strayed from a security light dimly illuminating stands behind the backstop. It chased its tail, gnawed at its ass, and hiked its leg along a fence line holding the advertisements of local businesses. The mutt exhausted itself in play before collapsing along the warning track to breathe heavy and fall asleep on the cool red clay.

I said to Momma, "Can I have a dog?"

Momma looked at me like I was crazy.

I said, "I'd keep it fed. It could sleep in my room with me."

Momma said, "Dogs have fleas."

"I'd keep it clean. I'd even pick off the ticks."

Momma acted like she was ignoring me then, like she

hadn't heard a word I said. "You should have gone to your ball game. You have to learn stay out of trouble."

"I ain't any good at it. I hate baseball."

"You're too young to hate anything, Raybert. I should have taught you better."

"I hate Daddy for what he does to you."

Momma turned then and slapped me in the face for saying such a thing, but just as quickly grabbed ahold and hugged me hard, her skin sweet and damp in the late night air. Momma said, "I didn't mean to do that, Sweetheart. God knows it's not what I meant to do."

I was crying, my face streaked and sticky from the tears, when I said, "Then why do you let him do it?"

Momma said, "Do what?"

"Everything, everything he does."

Momma looked at me and shook her head. "Sweetheart, your daddy doesn't do anything to me. I do it to myself." She looked into the sky for the first time that night and saw the moon completely covered by the shadow of the earth, its glowing rim the only sign that some terrible calamity had not extinguished it completely. "Raybert, if things were different you could have a dog, but with the way things are, well, I'm sorry . . ." Her voice trailed off almost inaudibly into a whisper.

She opened the door to the Buick; the click of the latch alerted the stray of our presence. It rose quickly, tail tucked between its legs, and scurried off the clay track, its bark an unconvincing threat as it moved into the shadows of the visitors' dugout. With Momma's door open, a great distance seemed to grow between us. It scared me to feel such emptiness because I knew I still needed her, that I would never stop loving her, and even if she was sick, I would always want her to stay. In that brief moment I felt if I stopped talking, Momma was going to leave and I might never see her again, and so I broke another promise I had made to Palmer, and told her that he had stolen the Catalina.

Momma said, "I thought Palmer Conroy was your guardian angel, but now it just seems he's headed for trouble. He reminds me of your daddy. You ought to stay away from boys like that, I guess, but I know you can't."

I said, "Well, he's gone now. He's headed down to Myrtle Beach for the rest of his life."

Momma said, "Well, he picked a nice spot to run away to."

I said, "His feet can't reach the pedals so I don't know how he's going to do it. I was supposed to go with him."

Momma raised her eyes at that. "Then what are you doing here?"

I didn't have an answer I could tell her. I could have said *I came with you because you're a crazy old coot and you made me miss the chance,* but I didn't want to hurt Momma any more than she was already hurting, so I just said, "I went for a ride with you instead."

She looked away then, her eyes steeled and full of tears. "Well, we didn't get very far did we, and I doubt Palmer will, either."

We sat in silence watching the dog find its courage to come out of the dugout. The stray lifted its head to sniff at the empty air, rolled around on the infield like it was scratching its back. It got up on all fours then, circled three times to wind itself up into a furry ball before settling back down.

I said, "Aunt Iris just wants you to take your pills, that's all. It'll make you feel better."

Momma smiled at that. "Would it make you feel better, Raybert, if I took my pills? Would that help?"

I said, "Yes ma'am. Aunt Iris would feel better, too, and maybe Daddy."

Momma said, "Your daddy's got so much more to worry about than whether I'm taking my little old pills. . . ." Her voice trailed off again, almost inaudibly into a whisper, and then she said, "I've got to go."

I said, "Maybe Daddy's at home. We could call him to come get us."

Momma said, "We got the car, honey. And it's out of gas."

I said, "We could walk home then, it ain't that far."

"*Isn't* that far, Raybert. I know I taught you better than that. You got to let them know I taught you something. You understand?"

"Yes ma'am."

Momma said, "Good because I've got to go now."

I said, "Can I come?"

"No, you got to stay here where you belong. I've got to go pee over there in those trees. Will you be all right alone?"

"Yes ma'am."

Momma said, "Good, all right then."

She looked into the sky, once more shading her eyes to stare at the shadowed moon and then turned and walked out across the parking lot, her Liz Taylor shoes flip-flapping in the silent night. She hummed a melody in a voice I had never heard before, sweet and lovely. I watched her move, glide almost, across the gravel. Her body, skin tanned by the darkness, absorbed what little light there was as she disappeared ghostlike in and out of the shadows. The dog out on the ball field lay undisturbed as she passed, like Momma was already a natural part of the night, carried perfectly on the moonless air. She walked up to a line of trees that grew some yards past the outfield fence, and just as she turned, the moon cracked through the other side and doused her top in shimmering light. Illuminated, Momma waved in a long arcing motion that had much greater permanence than a wave used when walking off just to pee, then she dipped beneath the limbs and was gone.

I stayed in the car to see what would happen next, but Momma was gone for good, and I knew it, even though I waited, hoping she would reappear. When the moon was full again—the land lit up for the final few hours of night—I got out of the Buick, locked all the doors, and walked home.

Sometime before dawn, Daddy's voice woke me up, brought me out of my room when I heard him ask, "Will this work, what we're doing?"

Dr. Redmond was there leaning over him holding some papers out for Daddy's hand. He said, "If we don't, something terrible will happen to Evelyn."

Daddy said, "Something terrible already has happened; let me have those papers." Then he hunched his body over the kitchen table, his hands shaking as he scribbled his name on the lines pointed out to him with the doctor's steady finger.

They had found her shortly after I came home and told Aunt Iris what had happened. A sheriff's deputy spotted her walking alongside a road, striped down to nothing but her panties. Dr. Redmond came to our house and they put Momma in bed until Daddy could be found so he could sign the papers. I stayed in my room watching Palmer Conroy's house hoping I would see some life around its edges, Palmer driving back by to pick me up for our escape to Myrtle Beach. But he never appeared, and before Uncle Clewell could find Daddy and bring him home, I fell asleep across my bed.

Now bleary-eyed and in my underwear, I watched from the doorway as Daddy committed Momma to the state hospital in Raleigh. He still wore the suit he had on when he and Momma left for Ronnie Doyle's viewing, though now it was ruined, torn, and blood-stained. He looked up at me and said, "Get dressed. Your momma's going away for a long time and you need to say good-bye."

When Daddy finished scribbling his name on the papers, Dr. Redmond had Momma carried out to the ambulance. Unlike when she miscarried, there were no good-byes. Momma was sleeping deeply from her ordeal and the Thorazine Dr. Redmond gave her to keep her quiet and unaware of what was going on. Her hair was wild and explosive, pushed to one side revealing scalp in a bald spot on the back of her head. She was pale and drawn in her face, eyebrows dark against ashen skin. Momma's mouth was all shriveled up and caved in where her teeth had been removed for her own safety. She looked as crazy as she was, old and tired, and I hardly recognized her when they brought her out to the ambulance.

Daddy and I rode with Uncle Clewell in the DeVille following Momma to the train depot. We could see Momma in front as Dr. Redmond and Aunt Iris huddled over her. Daddy said, "See that. Your momma's in good hands now, good hands."

The streets were still dark, dogs barking alongside sleeping houses as we passed by. Ferrell's Barbecue already had smoke pouring from its stacks, drifting the hickory air through our open windows. Daddy said, "I could sure eat a chopped sandwich right now, hush puppies and sweet tea." He looked at me and then at Clewell, smiled like he was wishing the restaurant was where we all were headed rather than the train depot.

I said, "It's too early, ain't it?"

Daddy said, "What do you think, Clewell? We could stop and knock on the door and see if they could give us some to go." Uncle Clewell smiled, but of course he kept driving, kept accelerating to stay close to the ambulance that carried Momma.

At the depot, the Southern Crescent sat idling after it had been flagged for a passenger. The great diesel engine glistened in yellow light flooding the tracks. It heaved and hissed from beneath its wheels while men scurried around the cars checking connections and brake lines. A conductor met us on the platform, and then Daddy and I watched as Dr. Redmond and Uncle Clewell carefully maneuvered Momma toward the train, up the narrow steps and into a sleeper car.

For a brief moment, we watched as the lights came on in a window and Momma's wilted body was laid on a bed inside. Daddy said, "There she is," like he was pointing to a shooting star, so quick, if you blinked, its spectacular blaze would be missed. Daddy said, "They stopped this whole train just so your momma could get on board. How about that?"

The light went out in the window and in another moment Uncle Clewell appeared at the back of the car moving down the small set of steps to rejoin us. Dr. Redmond and Aunt Iris would attend to Momma until the train rolled into Raleigh where hospital nurses waited with an ambulance to take her away. We stood on the platform and watched as the train eased out of the terminal, shadowed figures in the windows of passing coach and sleeper cars. I felt every eye was on us, judging Momma and Daddy and the failed life that was rolling away in front of them as the train passed out of the station and rounded the far curve of track. Like a snake slithering away in the dark underbrush, the train disappeared, taking with it everything I had known as my family, leaving me nothing, even though I stood beside Daddy, his hand resting across my shoulders.

Later when Uncle Clewell dropped us off back home, I could hear Daddy, alone in his bedroom tuning his radio in a futile attempt to find his jazz on a station that had gone off the air hours ago. He let the static play to fill the empty room and before I fell to sleep, I heard him snoring deep and hard.

In the morning, he stood in the alley below my window smoking a cigarette, picking the tobacco off his tongue. He stood there for a long time surveying his grass, apologizing to Wayne Potter as he worked to repair the ruts Momma had made in his yard. He seemed to be sizing things up, looking back to the house and then to the street, almost as if he were looking for something that would tell him what to do next.

When Aunt Iris called to say Momma was holding her own, that she had been committed to the state hospital, he hung up the phone and walked back outside to breathe. There he stubbed his cigarette into the gravel with his shoe and then walked away. He had stayed long enough for a call that told him Momma's hospital stay would cost him nothing and then he disappeared from my life forever.

*T*he day Ronnie Doyle was to be buried with full military honors, RC's Catalina appeared alongside the curb of Palmer's house with a For Sale sign in the front windshield. The sudden reappearance of the car was not all that surprising when I saw it from the window of my room, the last day I would be in the house on Robbins Street. Momma had been right in her crazy mind to say Palmer would not get far. I had heard the rumors about his trip to Myrtle Beach, that he never actually made it out of town, but instead had recklessly driven into an alley behind Robertson's Radio. Later Sheriff Lollis said that he couldn't understand how he had done it, driving the car while he used a baseball bat to push on the accelerator and to pump the brakes to slow the Catalina down in the alley behind Robertson's Radio.

He had broken into the store with RC's key, which he had kept hidden on a string in the crawl space under his room. Palmer was caught stealing things that were on his list for Myrtle Beach: *a hi-fi stereo needle, a guitar, the Rascals record,* "Beautiful Morning."

A sheriff's deputy had seen him while on his rounds checking locks and peering through plate glass windows of uptown stores. He had watched as a small shadow moved through Robertson's Radio looking in record bins and pulling instruments off the wall. Sheriff Lollis said, "How he drove that big old car, I ain't got a clue. Thank God though we caught him when we did. He could've done real damage if he'd got away after that."

At home, the rest of his plan fell apart when Inez Conroy found the pictures and a note Palmer had left that said, *You better ask Edgar what he does out in RC's trailer. Ask the pig about it, too.* While in her rage, Inez found the trapdoor and then discovered all the other things beneath the house that Palmer had stolen. She ratted him out to the police, gave them more evidence of his delinquency, and when she went to the station to tell them to throw away the key, Palmer said, "You must of done something bad in another life to have all this happen to you in this one. I'm glad you don't want me anymore." Then he was taken away and placed in temporary care by social services.

Aunt Iris said, "After all that, she still gave over her own flesh and blood. Maybe it's better for Palmer, that sweet little boy. Maybe he will be better off living somewhere else." I wanted to believe that what Aunt Iris said was true for me as well as Palmer Conroy. I was getting ready to move in with Uncle Clewell and Aunt Iris, and so I hoped wherever Palmer Conroy was going, he would be loved and cherished, as he should be.

There were always rumors about him after that. A few weeks after I had moved, Aunt Iris said that she heard Palmer was only a short distance away from Hickory Point living in a home for troubled youth. She went by at Thanksgiving with socks and a sweater I couldn't wear anymore, but they had no record of his ever being there. One weekend, I saw Billy Parker at Belk's buying a Boy Scout belt and troop patch. He had sworn Palmer was getting his Eagle badge in church on Sunday, but I knew if he was getting any badge at all, he was stealing it. He would steal merit badges and service stars, pinning them to his T-shirts like he had earned every last one of them. When I asked him once why he just didn't join a troop, Palmer said, "I can't be no tenderfoot. That would be ridiculous."

Around Christmas, Momma came to visit me at Aunt Iris's. We watched Elvis's *Comeback Concert* on television. He sang all the songs that made Momma happy, and she even sang along when he played "Viva Las Vegas." Before a commercial break, Elvis leaned over and let a young girl kiss his cheek. When the camera zoomed in, it looked like Palmer Conroy was sitting right there behind her. Momma said, "My goodness, there's Palmer sitting right in front of Elvis." But when the commercial break was over, the seat was in shadows too deep to know if we had really seen him or just imagined it all.

Palmer Conroy remained in my mind much like the Ellenton turkey Daddy had spun around our heads the night he trudged home in the snow, and like that old bird, the sightings were plenty, but none was ever confirmed. The truth be told, I don't know whatever happened to the boy because I never saw him again. I don't know if he lived to be old and happy or whether his adult life remained as tortured as his youth.

The day after Momma was committed, Uncle Clewell took me to Ronnie Doyle's funeral hoping we would see Palmer and I would at least get to say good-bye. Edgar Doyle sat alone under a tent with Erlene Hobbs who lightly rocked her baby. Her face was pale, eyes out of focus like she didn't understand what she was doing there in a cemetery holding a baby, its father dead and waiting to go into the ground. Only a handful of mourners and a military color guard showed up. His mother, Edgar's ex-wife, was too broken down with grief to come to the gravesite of her only son. Uncle Clewell said, "I can't even imagine how hard that would be to bury your own child." Then he put his arm around my shoulder as a soldier blew taps and they lowered Ronnie into the grave.

On the way back home, the roads became a confused clutter of fire engines and sheriffs' cars. Behind Palmer's house, RC's trailer was fully ablaze, intentionally set after Inez had cleared out the carport of Edgar's possessions, placed his boxes inside the trailer, dowsed everything in kerosene then disappeared with Cindy after striking the match. Firemen scurried around the burning frame trying to contain the hot fire, to keep it from spreading to a house that just as easily should have burned to the ground.

Aunt Iris said, "What a shame, what an awful shame the way all this has turned out. I wish we could turn it all back, start over again, and do everything differently. I wish we could have seen this coming. The signs were there; we just missed them all."

Momma was never out of the hospital for very long. Her visits to Aunt Iris and Uncle Clewell's were always short, but loving and sweet. She was the mother I adored, leaving behind the crazy clothes and behavior that had convicted her to an institutionalized life. My daddy became a shadowed figure I would see from time to time on the streets of Ellenton while Uncle Clewell and I rode to the old house to check the locks and then try to find him to see if he was safe, if he needed anything. Mostly Daddy ignored us, but sometimes he would stop, walk over to the car and talk awhile. He always tried to smile, even when he was badly beaten. He told me to listen to Uncle Clewell, that he was my daddy now, though Uncle Clewell objected to such a notion. He asked about Evelyn, said that she was still his girl, but that he knew everything was better off the way it was. That was as much as he ever offered in those brief conversations. He would slip away, disappearing before Uncle Clewell could ever get a good read on him or find out where he was living or what kind of trouble was hurting his life.

Each time we saw Daddy, his body was further bent and ravaged by his brawls, until for a long period of time, we could not find him at all. That next spring, the news came that he had died alone, found on the ground behind the dry cleaning plant that had been offered up at auction a few months earlier.

The day I was told of his passing, I went into my room and dug deep into a drawer until I pulled Rodney Small's picture from beneath a pile of clothes. I had long ago stopped looking at it, though its image still haunted me whenever I thought about Daddy. With his passing, I felt the connection so strong that I had to see it one more time, that poor boy who died unjustly so many years ago. In my hand, the picture seemed less alive than ever before, bent and torn, the faces more faded. It seemed less significant now that Daddy was gone.

I cupped it gently in my hand and walked out into Aunt Iris's garden. There the bright light brought Rodney Small's fate into sharper focus, my daddy forever connected in life, and now in death. I gazed upon the faces one last time, still unsure how it had all happened, how he had allowed himself to be a part of such a terrible act, then knelt down into the dirt and lit it afire. The picture burned until nothing was left but wispy ash that then blew apart, disappearing into the freshly turned earth of Aunt Iris's wildflower garden.

I never understood just what my daddy had done to Rodney Small. I never asked for an explanation; his place in the picture was proof enough that he had been there and participated in the terrible murder of an innocent black boy. But what I have come away with in the years since is a belief that everything he did to himself—the awful beatings, his disappearance from my life after Momma was gone—had something to do with the picture that was now ash committed to the earth. Rodney Small and my father, once and for all resting in peace.

After the picture was gone, I got on my bike and rode back to the hill that I had pedaled so often I could close my eyes and know when I needed to turn by the change of smell in the air at the bottom. Palmer's house was deserted, the yard wild and overgrown, Inez and Cindy long gone. The shades were pulled, the carcass of the trailer still in the backyard as a reminder of what that summer had brought to this street and those who lived on it.

When I passed by, I had to wonder where Palmer might be, the rumors of the rest of his life just beginning to take shape and grow. Palmer Conroy was gone, but the memories of a boy who put me in my place that day I had killed for the simple act of watching something die, remained alive and well in my head, his words ringing loud and clear, shouted at the top of his lungs, *WHAT DOES THAT MAKE YOU NOW?*

It was almost as if someone stood behind a closed curtain and orchestrated what came next. Above Robbins Street the sky broke into a shimmering flutter of birds, the finches returning again to nest along the creek. It was time for this to happen, nearly one year to the day Palmer and I had cut school and ended up along Finch Creek looking for the tree from which Rodney Small had swung. They came from out of nowhere diving down around me swooping and singing again, darting across Palmer's house then rising straight up into the air following some ancient need to come home, to be back among the familiar. They filled the sky, the sun a trembling eye behind their mass of wings, then dove again in a magnificent pattern of chaos showering me with a breeze warm and reassuring. I watched them swarm unafraid of their close flight around me until they found their direction and then disappeared beyond Palmer's house headed toward the creek bed and the trees and bush that awaited them.

When the finches were gone, the sky washed clean and still, I found I was pedaling away as fast as I could go, heading toward the dead end where the ramp had stood a summer ago. Until that moment I had all but forgotten the promise made to Palmer that we would jump like Evel Knievel, take that leap of faith and fly out across the dead-end street. I had no idea what was left of our jump, but that was where I was headed, my bike navigating easily the familiar landscape before me.

When I arrived, the frame was in disrepair, the long year having pushed the ramp onto its side. All the junk Tommy Patterson and Billy Parker had piled up in front was gone, just the frame and plywood remained. I stood looking at the broken wood, the swarm of the finches hot in my head. I moved, slowly at first, but then with a directness and quickening speed that surprised me as I pulled the frame upright and made repairs. I hammered the plywood back into the two-by-fours with rocks I found along a ditch at the end of the street, and when I was done, the ramp was standing on its own, wobbling and uncertain of its place, but standing just the same.

I moved back a block to where I imagined the chalked line had been drawn when we readied the ramp. From there I eyed the distance to the bottom, taking aim, my foot rising to the pedal, ready to push off, this time to push through the thoughts of disaster and impending doom, to find Evel Knievel's mojo and get it on.

I wore no protective gear, thought nothing of how this might change my life as I had before; I just pressed down onto the pedal and found it moved easily. I accelerated, pumping the bike as fast as I could make it go, the ramp coming quickly as I looked to the top and then beyond at the uncertain air and where it might take me. I remembered Jim McKay's last words as I hit the ramp. *Got to go now* was on the end of my tongue when I shot straight out into the flat afternoon light, rising, rising, rising. I was crazy gone wild to hang out in the air like that, my escape off a wobbly ramp just the beginning, a distance too great to measure in one leap, suspended, looking forward to where the finches were rising now to color the sky an immaculate blue, pure and full in flight, and Palmer Conroy somewhere cheering me on, waiting for me to land. *Hi yo Silver, away!*

ACKNOWLEDGMENTS

Recently this past spring, I was in New York City to work
with my editor, Maureen O'Neal, on the final draft of *When
the Finch Rises*. It was a Tuesday evening in late May after a
long day of revisions and then dinner with my agent. The
unique visit to Manhattan to edit the manuscript in the Ballantine offices had occurred because of the need to hurry the
book up. It was decided *When the Finch Rises* would be a
drop-in title for fall 2003 when Ballantine made the offer in
late April, and Maureen had graciously invited me to visit
New York, where we could put our heads together and get
the book done. Stella Connell, my agent, had just treated
me to a wonderful dinner and then laid out three copies of a
contract for me to sign that would seal the deal, even though
I had already turned the manuscript over to Maureen just
hours before. When the ink had dried, Stella gave me a con-
gratulatory hug and said good night, and I had a nice quiet
walk up Fifth Avenue toward East 26th, the Empire State
Building rising in front of me, illuminated in cascading red,
white, and blue lights. It was then that I realized what I was
about to do, publish a book that had been years in the making, my book about two young boys who were now as real to

me as anyone in my life. Palmer Conroy and Raybert Williams were getting their day and I was happy for them.

As I strolled along Fifth Avenue, I thought about momentum, the momentum that it took to get this book off the ground, to find the characters and then the story that would be told. It was momentum that began so subtly, a wish perhaps to become a writer, years ago when I lived in L.A. It began with Ginger McDonald helping me believe in the possibility of writing. I have no idea where she is today, but if she were here beside me, I would say thank you. This book is finished because of her subtle push, her thoughtful encouragement that got me on my way. Jim Clark and the creative writing faculty at the University of North Carolina at Greensboro helped me keep that momentum rolling. There I was nurtured and given the chance to write full-time. Fred Chappell's kind but stern guidance pushed me and the momentum built. Teaching at Georgia Perimeter College in Atlanta afforded me a comfortable place to become a writer, and I have to thank Lawrence Hetrick for believing enough in my stories to be the first to publish me in the college's literary magazine, *The Chattahoochee Review*. Pam Parker is a friend and colleague, probably my first "fan," who has supported me from the first story on. The visits to her classes, her praise of my work in story form, uplifted me always and made me believe I would one day finish the boys' tale and see it in print. Jacquelyn Belcher, the president of Georgia Perimeter College, allowed me to go on sabbatical to finish the book. Her support is immeasurable. Without her belief in the arts at GPC and the need to support the endeavors of her faculty, the momentum would have stopped and Palmer and Raybert would have been lost forever. Thank you President Belcher for not allowing that to happen. You alone were ultimately responsible for that.

Outside the college were folks like Lee Smith and Jill McCorkle. Lee's kind words and encouragement helped introduce me to the literary community and helped me see the possibility that waited once the manuscript was finished. Jill McCorkle has been my constant North Star. She has read everything and been so important in my career that words do not do her justice. What I will do in the future is give to others as she and Lee have given to me. Somehow the Golden Rule, slightly altered, applies here: *Do unto others as they have done unto you.* I will always give back. It is a lesson Jill and Lee have so graciously taught me.

The momentum was greatly increased when Stella Connell found me. She fell in love with my writing and made me believe it was good and then became my agent. In a twist of fate, she introduced me to Maureen O'Neal here in Atlanta shortly after she had read the manuscript, and I fell in love with Maureen's insight into the characters and the story. She knew what the boys needed and helped the momentum grow with her enthusiasm for the story and her keen eye for the necessary detail. Without these two ladies in my corner, Palmer and Raybert would still be looking for a home.

There are others, as always, who offered love and support, John Simmons for his many conversations regarding my struggling theology that now rests within the pages of this book; George and Jayne Cavagnaro for their encouragement and celebration at each and every turn of my career; Rob Jenkins, my department chair, whose long afternoon conversations about writing always sent me away inspired and encouraged; Bob and Nannette Gantz, who never let me believe such an endeavor was beyond me, all good lifelong friends. And, of course, to the ladies at Seawatch Inn at the Landing in Garden City Beach, South Carolina, Renata Beebe, Brandy Cagle, and Kim Saunders. Your support and understanding made my weeks at the beach quiet and productive as I struggled to get the story down on paper that first time. Thank you.

Strolling down Fifth Avenue that evening I realized the momentum had peaked, the motion forward strong enough to push the book over the edge, taken away from me and released into the public for enjoyment and review. I have confidence the boys will be okay out there alone. They have had good support all along the way, and I believe they are ready to be on their own. As I finished my walk to the hotel, I thought about the boys and wondered what Palmer and Raybert would have wanted to do if they had been there beside me. I knew they would want to climb the Empire State Building, lean over, and spit off the edge. Palmer would have wanted to look for signs of King Kong's claws, and Raybert would have gazed southward toward the river and tried to imagine a skyline with the twin towers still standing. I knew then I needed to thank the boys for being there, for allowing me to tell their story, to be a passenger in the Catalina as they navigated through the light and dark of their young lives. And so I thank you most, Palmer Conroy and Raybert Williams, for the last two years. Thank you for choosing me to tell your story. Thank you for letting me live inside your lives. Hi yo Silver, away!

ABOUT THE AUTHOR

JACK RIGGS'S writing has been published in *The Crescent Review*, *The Chattahoochee Review*, *The Habersham Review*, and *Writing, Making It Real*. In 2000, he was selected as an "Emerging New Southern Voice" at the Millennial Gathering of Writers of the New South at Vanderbilt University. He has been a finalist in the *Glimmer Train* Fiction Contest and was nominated for a Pushcart Prize. The author teaches at Georgia Perimeter College in Atlanta. You may visit his Web site at www.jack-riggs.com and e-mail him at jriggs@jack-riggs.com.